Frogs and Kisses

NLA Digital, LLC
1732 Wazee Street, Suite 207
Denver, CO 80202

FROGS AND KISSES © 2016 by Shanna Swendson

Production Manager: Lori Bennett
Cover Illustration: Nina Berkson
Book Design: Angie Hodapp

ISBN 978-1-62051-256-2

Frogs and Kisses

An Enchanted Inc. Novel

Shanna Swendson

To all the fans
who never quit asking for more.

Author's Note

The first Enchanted, Inc., book was published in 2005, and although there are no precise date stamps in that book or elsewhere in the series, that's when I mentally set the book. I worked out the timeline for events in that book on a calendar for that year because when I was writing it in the fall of 2003, I figured that was the year it was most likely to end up being published. I stuck to that timeline for the rest of the books.

But that means that time passes more slowly in that universe. By the seventh book, *Kiss and Spell,* only a year had passed for the characters. Now, as I return to the series more than a decade after it began, I've decided to maintain that timeline rather than trying to jump ahead or pretend that the books are always happening now, whenever that happens to be. This book begins in the fall of 2006 and moves into early 2007. I've tried to keep technology, pop culture references, and events consistent with that time.

That's why no one has smart phones (the first iPhone wasn't released until June of 2007) or tablets. No one's talking about the new *Star Wars* movies (they're still recovering from the prequels). And there are some businesses referred to that were still operating then that no longer exist.

One

It was a crisp fall day, the sky was a crystal clear shade of blue, the remaining leaves on the trees in Central Park were a brilliant gold, and I was on a romantic Saturday-afternoon stroll with my handsome boyfriend—fiancé, actually. It was taking some getting used to that. "This is for real, isn't it?" I had to ask the question. The last time my life had been just this perfect, it had turned out to be a bizarre facsimile of a romantic movie created in the elven realms as a kind of prison.

"I'm pretty sure it's real," Owen Palmer said, giving me a smile that made my heart flutter.

"You're sure we're not off in elf land?"

"You'd know. You're back to not having a trace of magic in you, so they wouldn't be able to sustain the illusion for you. If that's where you were, it wouldn't be perfect."

"Okay, good. Just checking."

His smile transformed into a mischievous grin as he stopped and released my hand so he could pull me close with his arm around my waist. "Of course, if you want to be absolutely certain, you could try breaking the spell."

As somberly as I could manage, I said, "It's probably better to be safe. Just in case. You never know."

Owen was nearly physically incapable of keeping a straight face. Even if he didn't smile or crack up, he blushed adorably. "We really do have to remain vigilant."

Our kiss may have set off a few fireworks, but not the magic kind. Although there was a lot about him that could have come straight out of a dream, he was most definitely right there. When we both came up for air, I said, "Looks like we're still here. It must be real."

"Must be. But at least we're sure."

"And we should probably check every so often."

We resumed walking, and I couldn't resist lifting my left hand to let the sunlight glint on the sapphire in my engagement ring. "You do like it?" he asked, sounding a little uncertain.

"I love it."

"When Gloria took it out of her jewelry box to show it to me, I thought it was better suited to you than a huge diamond would have been, and I suspected you'd like having a family heirloom."

"It's perfect. Just my style."

"Speaking of style, have you come up with any ideas for a wedding?"

"I've thought about it, but nothing seems quite right. If we have it here, then my family has to travel and we're throwing my mother in among all the magical people, which we really don't want." Both of us shuddered at the thought of that. My mother is as immune to magic as I am, but not in on the secret, and she has odd ways of interpreting the strange things she sees. "If we have it back home, our friends and your family have to travel, and my mother takes over the planning." We shuddered again at the thought of the kind of wedding she'd want for us. Pink, puffy Southern belle bridesmaid dresses would be only the beginning.

"I'd say that a minister and a couple of witnesses would be the ideal solution, but I know that would hurt a lot of feelings."

"My mother would disown you before you even joined the family. But not in the fun way where you never hear from her again. You'd still have to be around her. You'd just never be allowed to forget how you wronged her. It would be a life sentence."

Maybe it was the mention of my mother, but I was starting to get that weird itching sensation on the back of my neck that told me I was being watched. Of course, we were in Central Park, with much of the rest of the population of Manhattan, out enjoying the gorgeous fall weather, and I was with a guy good-looking enough to stop traffic, so obviously *someone* was looking at me. The question was whether we were being watched specifically.

I tried turning halfway around, like I was looking at the statue we'd just passed. There were people behind us on the path, but I didn't recognize anyone.

"Do you feel like we're being watched?" I asked Owen softly.

He paused a long moment before answering, his dark blue eyes scanning our surroundings. "Maybe," he said.

The next time the path intersected another one, we

veered off in a new direction. "Is it still there?" Owen asked after a few minutes.

"Actually, I think it's worse." Or maybe it was just that thinking about it made me hyperalert and it was all in my head. Given the way my life had gone for the past year or so, being vigilant about my surroundings was second nature. I wouldn't have been surprised if I started noticing things that weren't there.

Even worse, I was seeing things that *were* there, things most of the people in the park probably couldn't see. Magical creatures tended to love nature and draw power from it, and Central Park was the best location for that in the city. As a result, the place was teeming with people with wings and pointy ears. There were small ones in the grass and underbrush, and tall ones walking around us. Ordinary people probably didn't see the small ones and saw the large ones as normal human beings.

But if I wasn't imagining things, there were more magical creatures than usual out today. "Are you seeing more fairies than you'd expect?" I asked Owen softly.

"I don't know. I don't usually conduct a census. There are always a lot of fairies in the park."

Even though nothing had happened to us, I felt like a gray pall had fallen on our beautiful day in the park. We turned at the next path intersection, and for a moment, I lost that sense of pursuit. "Maybe they were just going the same way we were for a while," I said hopefully.

"You can hardly blame us for being paranoid," Owen said, draping his arm around my shoulders. "Not too long ago, we were kidnapped by elves, and before that, we had just about every magical creature in Manhattan chasing us."

"Yeah, and then there were all those people working for Ivor Ramsay and Phelan Idris. At least I'm not seeing any of those skeleton creatures or harpies. These seem like ordinary fairies and sprites," I said.

We reached another intersection in the walking path. To one side, there seemed to be a lot more fairies. To the other, the way was a little less populated with things that looked magical. Without having to consult each other, we turned to the less magical area. I didn't know exactly what Owen's reasoning was, but it was easier for me to detect specific sources of magic when there were fewer of them.

Sure enough, that overall tingle that made me aware of magic soon eased. I found myself breathing more easily, and there was less tension in Owen's arm around me. We were in my favorite part of the park, along the lake and near the picturesque Bow Bridge. This really did feel like the setting for a romantic movie, probably because it had been used in so many of them. "Maybe we should test our reality again," I said to Owen. "You know, just in case."

"Hmm, do you hear jazz standards or pop songs in your head?"

"There doesn't seem to be a soundtrack at all."

"Then I'm pretty sure we're not acting out a movie again." We stopped at the apex of the bridge's arch and moved closer to the railing so we weren't blocking the way for others. "But we should probably test it to be sure." His lips had barely touched mine—with no accompanying background music to emphasize the surging emotion—when I couldn't help but twitch. "What is it?" he asked.

"I'm feeling it again. Someone's watching us."

"We're making out in the middle of a bridge. That tends to draw attention."

"No, I feel magic."

He stood very still for a moment, and then the twinkle in his eyes faded. "You're right. I feel it, too." He released his hold on me and took my hand. Together, we hurried off the bridge.

But when we left the bridge, we soon found ourselves in the Ramble. It was easy to get lost in there, though I supposed it was also easy to lose someone in there. I didn't know if the magical creatures who lived there would still help us when we weren't carrying an enchanted brooch, but once we were out of public sight, Owen could draw on his power to defend us, if it came to that.

When we rounded a corner and found ourselves face-to-face with a familiar woman, I immediately moved to stand in front of Owen, blocking him from her as well as I could.

"It was my ancestor who frogged Philip Vandermeer, not me, so you can relax," Sylvia Meredith said. I didn't think that made things much better. She may have been only the descendant of the person who'd stolen my friend Philip's family business a century ago after turning him into a frog, but she'd been using that business to fund the bad guys we'd defeated recently.

"You herded us here!" I accused.

"Some friends helped, but you made it awfully easy."

"What do you want?" Owen asked, stepping out from behind me.

"I need to talk to you."

"To me in particular, to us, or maybe to the people I work for?"

"Both of you. And MSI in general. And your boss, if you can get him."

"What do you want to talk about?" I asked.

"Some things you need to know."

"I'm not sure there's anything we want to hear from you," I said.

"You're going to want to hear this. Have you heard of the Collegium?"

Owen frowned slightly. "I thought it was just a story. Maybe it was real once, but it hasn't been around in ages."

"That's what you think. We've been more quiet and subtle in recent years, but that's about to change."

"You're with the Collegium?" Owen said, raising a skeptical eyebrow.

"What's the Collegium?" I asked.

She said to Owen, "Do you want to explain it, or do you want me to?"

"The stories say they were a cabal of sorts, a coalition of certain magical families, though no one was sure which families were really involved," Owen said. "Supposedly, they had some legitimate businesses in the magical world, but their primary function was to destroy or take over any competition, and they then used their position to gain power elsewhere."

"Like a magical mafia?" I said. "Only instead of giving people concrete shoes, you turn them into frogs."

"We very rarely resort to that these days," Sylvia said.

"Now, before I tell you anything else, I need your promise of protection."

"Protection from what?" Owen asked.

"From the Collegium, of course. You don't talk about them to outsiders and stay off a lily pad for long."

"Then why are you talking to us, if it puts you in danger?"

"Because I'm *already* in danger. I'm considered high-risk. I was the scapegoat for what happened with Ivor Ramsay, and they're probably going to get rid of me to avoid connecting that affair to the Collegium. So I thought my only chance was to trade the information I have for whatever protection you can offer me. And believe me, what I've got is worth it."

"What have you got?" Owen asked.

"Nice try, handsome, but you'll have to guarantee protection for me. You talk it over with your boss, and then I'll talk."

"How will we let you know?"

"Don't worry, I'll be able to find you."

"Do you have a deadline?" I asked, but there was no reply. A dense mist suddenly arose, so that I could no longer see Sylvia—or anything else more than about two feet away in any direction.

"Can you see anything?" Owen asked.

"It's a real fog, not an illusion," I replied. We didn't dare move, given the steep hills and rocky ground in that area. Owen waved a hand and murmured a spell, and the fog gradually dissipated, but by the time we could see our surroundings again, Sylvia was gone.

"Okay, that was weird," I said.

"For us?" Owen said with a wry smile. "Very low on the weird scale, but I'll agree that it's somewhat odd."

"There's a magical mafia? How did I not know about this?"

"I don't know much more than that, and I'm still not convinced it's real."

"Philip was turned into a frog so his business could be stolen," I pointed out.

"A hundred years ago."

"And the family that did that was still running it until earlier this year."

He nodded. "Good point. But that doesn't mean it was a vast cabal. It could have been just the one family of crooks. We should probably talk to Philip about this, and then we can bring it to Merlin to see what he has to say."

Yes, Merlin is my boss. And yes, it's *that* Merlin. I work for a company called Magic, Spells, and Illusions, Inc. They do pretty much what it says on the label, but they also function as a kind of de facto authority in the magical world, since the magical Council that's supposed to run things isn't all that effective. "Sounds like a plan to me. Now, shall we get back to our perfect fall day?"

I let Owen report the incident to Merlin, since he knew more about the Collegium. I was a little surprised when I got word that Merlin had agreed to Sylvia's terms, since she'd so recently been an enemy. Supposedly, she'd been blackmailed into helping with Ramsay's scheme, and the takeover of Philip's company had happened long before she was born, but I still wasn't sure I trusted her. Now we had to wait for her to contact us again.

I was on the subway after work one evening the following week, crammed in with the other commuters, when I felt someone bump against me. That was hardly unusual, but then the person who'd bumped me whispered, "Well?"

I turned to see Sylvia, a shawl pulled over her head. "You're on," I said. "You can come by at any time."

"I'm not going there. No meeting in public, either."

"Then where?" I tried to think of a location for a secret meeting that wasn't public and that wasn't our office. "My place?" I suggested. "It's warded, and lots of people enter through the building's front door, so it won't be too obvious."

"Yes, that will work."

I gave her the address and added, "How about at seven?" By then, Nita, my one roommate who wasn't in on the magical secret, would have left for work on the night shift at a hotel registration desk, so it would be safe to talk freely. I just hoped the place wasn't too messy for unexpected company.

"Make sure you aren't followed," she said.

"I live there," I pointed out. "They wouldn't have to follow me to know that's where I'll end up."

She got off the subway a stop before I did. I had a few errands to run before I went home, so I called Owen as soon as I was out of the station to let him know about the arrangements. Next, I called home to see if anyone was there and gave my roommate Gemma, who answered the phone, a heads-up that company was on the way. Then I picked up some dry cleaning and got a box of cookies for refreshments, since I wouldn't have time to bake.

When I got up the stairs to my floor, Sylvia was

standing in the hallway. She must have gone straight there. "It's about time," she snapped.

"We still have forty-five minutes," I said as I unlocked the door.

Gemma greeted us when we entered. Her boyfriend, Philip, was also there. Gemma must have rushed to get ready after my warning, because there was no laundry lying about, and there were only a few dirty dishes in the sink, so the apartment was reasonably presentable for company. "Please, have a seat," Gemma said to Sylvia, gesturing toward the sofa. "Can I get you anything?"

"A stiff drink would be good." Then Sylvia shook her head. "No, probably better not. I need to keep my wits."

Philip stood on the opposite side of the room from Sylvia, his arms crossed over his chest and his normally pleasant face set into a fierce glare. Sylvia sat in the chair nearest the window, constantly glancing over her shoulder and then back to the front door, as though worried that at any moment someone would come bursting in.

She nearly jumped out of her skin when the intercom from the front door sounded. It was Owen, and I buzzed him in. Her paranoia made me think of something. "How's the boss going to get in?" I asked Owen when he entered. "You and Philip are here all the time, but it's going to look weird if the boss comes to my apartment. That is, if anyone is watching."

"I think that's under control," Owen said, grinning. I followed his gaze to see a flying carpet hovering outside the window, Merlin seated cross-legged on it as if he were sitting comfortably on his living room floor.

I went to open the window, and after pausing to give

the tiny driver instructions, Merlin swiveled on the carpet and slid off, stepping through the window into the room. The carpet zipped away. He took off his overcoat, and Gemma hurried to take it from him.

"Good, we're all here," Sylvia said. She drained the glass of water Gemma had given her like it was the stiff drink she'd asked for, gripped her knees, and braced herself before speaking. "And believe me, you need to hear this. You're sure you'll get me to safety?"

Merlin nodded. "You have my word that we will do what we can to keep you safe. What do you have to tell us?"

She took a long, slow, deep breath and let it out in a big whoosh. "Well, to start with, Ivor Ramsay was Collegium. Magic, Spells, and Illusions, Incorporated, was pretty much a Collegium outfit for the longest time, and we still have a lot of people there. His idea to bring you back so he could defeat you and solidify his power was his own, and it didn't sit well with the higher-ups. That's why I'm in trouble, since I backed him, but I didn't know it wasn't sanctioned."

"I don't suppose you could provide me with a list of suspect staff," Merlin said.

"I never had that kind of information, just that we had people there."

Philip, who'd been silently scowling at Sylvia all that time, crossed the room to stand in front of her and glare down at her. "There's got to be more than that. Otherwise, I don't see why we shouldn't just let them have you."

"Boy, you hold a grudge, don't you?"

"If you'd spent a century eating flies, you might bear some resentment."

"Well, no, that's not all. MSI is a big part of their plans. Without the company, they're not the major player in the magical world. With you in charge, they don't have MSI in their pocket. You need to be on the lookout."

"For what?" I asked as I tried to remember every mafia movie I'd ever seen. "Are they going to drive us out of business? Burn us down? Scare our employees out of working? If they want to replace the boss, they have to have someone else to take his place, so do they have someone already working there, ready to move up? I can't see how they'd be able to come from outside and take over without us noticing."

"This isn't some mobster movie," she said with a scathing tone, and I couldn't help but wince guiltily. "But I don't know exactly what they have planned. They may not have planned anything yet. I do know that the heads are meeting, a lot. This is bigger than any of you realize, and you've foiled some schemes that have been decades in the making. They won't want to lose again. Now, is that worth my safety?"

I wasn't so sure that a bunch of vague warnings was enough, but Merlin nodded. "Yes, we will keep you safe. If you leave with me, I can take you to a secure location now."

Sylvia stood. "I'll leave with you because your carpet lets me get out of here without any followers noticing me, but I'm going to wait before I disappear. If I lie low and play it cool, they'll be less suspicious that I've been up to anything, and I can keep my job longer. I need a little time to move money into secret accounts to set up my new life, since I doubt you'll be willing to fund me at the level I'd like. You can drop me off somewhere."

"If you insist." Merlin got out his cell phone and pushed a button. A moment later, the carpet flew up to the window and hovered. Philip and Owen helped Sylvia and Merlin out, and the carpet flew away.

I sank onto the couch Merlin had vacated. "What do we do about this? These warnings are too vague to really act on."

Owen sat beside me and took my hand. "I suppose we'll start by vetting our employees to see who might be a threat. We may need your help with that, in case they're using magic to hide anything. We'll be careful about anyone we hire, and we'll need to solidify our relationships with any powerful individuals or companies we know we can trust."

"What you need is a Donnie Brasco," Gemma said.

"Who is that?" Philip asked.

"He was an FBI agent who managed to infiltrate the mob by going into deep cover. They had no idea he was FBI and told him all kinds of stuff. There was a movie about it with Johnny Depp." She paused for a moment of silent contemplation, a faint smile on her lips.

With the slightest hint of irritation, Philip said, "I'm afraid that won't be so easy. These are families that you have to be born into. A wizard couldn't just get a job with them and learn all their secrets. Unless..."

"Unless what?" I asked.

"Well, the one exception I'm aware of is that they make use of magical immunes, and although those do occasionally occur in magical families, they generally must be recruited from outside the company."

Before I had a chance to react, Owen turned to me and said, "Don't even think about it."

"I wasn't thinking about it!" I protested, and it was mostly true because I hadn't had time to start considering it. "But it would never work because I'm too well-known. By now, everyone in the magical world knows who I am and where I work. It would be like trying to infiltrate the mob while wearing an FBI jacket. Besides, I have a wedding to plan."

Owen released my hand that he was holding and slipped his arm around my shoulders, pulling me against him. After kissing the top of my head, he said, "And don't you forget it."

I got called to Merlin's office the next afternoon. Technically, my job was marketing manager of the company, but I seemed to spend most of my time dealing with crises of a very non-marketing variety. I'd used marketing to help counter a rival wizard selling evil spells, but otherwise I did stuff like finding moles within the company and defeating a variety of nefarious schemes. Getting called into the boss's office after we'd learned about a threat was a good sign that I might be about to take on a new project.

Philip was there when I arrived, wearing a visitor's badge. Sam the gargoyle, head of security, perched on the back of a chair. Rod Gwaltney, Owen's friend from childhood and the personnel director, arrived soon after I did. Minerva Felps, head of Prophets and Lost, entered in a swirl of scarves and perfume. Owen joined us a few minutes later, looking distracted.

Merlin began by briefing Rod and Minerva on what we'd learned from Sylvia. "I don't know how credible her information is," he said, "but I believe it prudent to follow up. Mr. Gwaltney, I would like you to investigate our current employees. Miss Chandler can lend her immune perspective, in case they're hiding anything. Sam and Mr. Palmer, I'd like you to make sure the building is secure and free of surveillance devices. I will be talking with other organizations."

We all nodded, accepting our assignments, and Merlin continued. "Mr. Vandermeer here can function as something of a consultant, since he has experience with the Collegium. Do you have any other suggestions?"

Philip glanced around the room before saying, "The real danger is that you don't necessarily see them coming. They approached my brother and me with an offer to buy out the company soon after we inherited it from our father. We refused it. Some of my top employees then either quit abruptly or disappeared. The offer was repeated, and the next thing I knew, I was sitting on a lily pad. I still have no idea what became of my brother. He's officially missing."

"I'm not sure that playing defense will be good enough here," I said. "We need to know what they're planning so we can counter it."

Owen closed his eyes for a second, looking like he was in pain, and shook his head. "Katie, no."

"I agree with Miss Chandler," Merlin said, surprising me. "We need to get someone on the inside of that organization."

Two

I was on the verge of at least pretending to protest an undercover assignment when Merlin went to the intercom on his desk and called for his assistant, Kim, to come in.

Kim had been one of the first people I met at the company. She was also magically immune and had been working in the Verification department when I was hired. She'd resented the fact that I'd very quickly moved up and out, and she'd taken my old job as Merlin's assistant when I was reassigned. We'd managed to cooperate on some things since then, but I still felt like she saw me as a rival to her ambitions. Now I was afraid I knew what Merlin had in mind, and as much as I knew there were good reasons why I shouldn't go undercover, it still irked me to think that she was getting the job.

"Ah, there you are," Merlin said to her. "I have an assignment for you."

She practically came to attention. "Yes, sir!"

"We need someone to infiltrate a secret magical organization. The only people they hire outside their families are magical immunes, and one who has been ousted from MSI might be considered a valuable find."

"You want me to go undercover?" Her eyes widened and her face lit up. I could see her mentally preparing new stationery and business cards for the position a successful operation would surely earn her.

"I want you to try. I'm going to dismiss you from your employment here, which will leave you angry at our organization. That should make you a tempting prospect for them. However, there is no guarantee they would take you on."

"What you'll need to do is make yourself available," Philip said. "I know of some places you can go where you might come to their attention." He smiled slightly. "That is one benefit of an organization as tradition-bound as they are. They haven't changed their ways in a century. Your first step will be to apply to work at my company. They should notice that. Then there are a few restaurants and bars you could frequent where they might approach you."

I couldn't help but start to feel some resentment at not being chosen, even though I knew I'd be a bad choice. It sounded like it would be fun. And it wouldn't be like going undercover in the real mob, so I wouldn't have to worry about being shot and having my body dumped in the river. These people turned their enemies into frogs, and that spell wouldn't work on me.

"You really wanted that undercover assignment, didn't you?" Owen said to me as we left Merlin's office after briefing Kim.

"Kinda," I admitted. "But I get why it wasn't me. If I suddenly popped up, looking for a job with them, I might as well be wearing a light-up button saying, 'Hi! I'm here to infiltrate you!' Still, it would be really cool. And better than working on updating our marketing materials."

"Maybe while Kim's on assignment, you could go back to your old job as Merlin's assistant."

The idea tempted me for a moment, but then I sighed and said, "It's probably best if I don't. I'd have to leave again when Kim came back, and then I'd have to pick up where I left off with the marketing. I really ought to try staying in one job here for more than a few months."

I may not have been going undercover, but I wasn't off the hook in our efforts to defend the company against the Collegium. I spent enough time in Rod's office that I was beginning to think maybe I should just resign my marketing job and consider what I was doing security.

At first, we just pored over paperwork. "I don't know why you need me for this," I grumbled on Friday afternoon, after several days of reading personnel files. "Company paperwork isn't going to be magically veiled or altered, is it?"

"It depends on who did it. I haven't been in this job forever, you know. The person before me may have hidden plants in plain sight. And you never know if a reference letter or transcript might have been altered."

I stared in dismay at the stacks of files that all looked meaningless to me. "I don't even know what to look for."

"If something's been magically altered or hidden, we'll consider that a red flag."

It was tedious work, both of us having to look at the same document together, him reading what he saw and me making sure that's what I saw. It reminded me of my early days at the company, when that was what I did all day. I wouldn't have been surprised if it was ridiculously easy to recruit MSI immunes, as boring as their jobs could be. In the time we'd been combing through the records of employees who'd begun work before Rod took over in personnel, we'd yet to find anything remotely fishy.

When we finally reached the bottom of the stack, I wanted to throw all the files in the air in celebration, but my joy was tempered by the fact that finding nothing meant we hadn't gained anything.

Apparently, I wasn't alone in that dismay. Rod sat there, frowning. "Something's wrong," he said. "We should have found at least one."

"Well, if the personnel director was in on it, he'd hardly have put the real info in the records at all," I said, grasping at straws. "Maybe they didn't even bother keeping two sets of books, so to speak."

"True," he said, nodding. "I guess we need to check the paperwork of the people who came in under my watch—reference letters should be a good start."

"Is there a way to find people who might have applied under the former person but were hired under you?"

"That's a good thought. Maybe the initial applications had some indication that these were people who were vouched for." He got up from his desk and went to the outer office, calling out, "Isabel, I'm going to need some more files."

While they were going through whatever filing system

they used, I stood and stretched. Rod came in with a reassuringly small stack of files. "That's it?" I asked.

"It's enough. Unless you just like reading employment files."

I forced a grin. "My, what a lovely small stack."

We returned to our seats at his desk, and he opened the first file. He didn't even have to start reading before I pointed out, "This is one of them."

"How do you know?"

"That reference letter is blank. There's just a symbol on it, something like a starburst with a rune-like letter in the middle. I bet Owen could tell us what it is."

He leaned over the page. "It looks like a regular reference letter to me."

I squinted at the symbol. It looked familiar, but I couldn't quite place it. Then for a split second, I somehow squinted hard enough to make it look small and distant. "Hey, wait," I said, frantically reaching for the pile of files we'd just gone through. I tossed aside the first three, but then there it was, on the top of the fourth employment file: that same symbol, very tiny. "See, there it is," I said.

He leaned over to look. "I don't see anything."

"Then it must be veiled, and you'd have to be in the know to unlock the spell. Maybe they've coded all the Collegium people. That reference letter must have been just in case the new personnel director was also Collegium. If he had been, the symbol would have been enough, but since it was you, you see a normal reference letter."

He pushed the stack of files toward me. "Well, since you're the one who can see the symbol, have fun with that. Do you want some coffee?"

"No thanks. I'd probably spill it on your files."

"Okay, then. I'll let you work. I'll be back in a bit."

At least this work wasn't nearly as tedious as reading every single part of every file. I just had to open each folder and check for the symbol. Soon, I had a stack on either side of me, those without symbols on the left, those with on my right. I'd barely registered the symbol before, dismissing it as perhaps a part of the form. It was a magical company, so arcane-looking signs on paperwork weren't anything to get excited about. I supposed I should have found it odd that Rod never mentioned it, but it really hadn't occurred to me that it might be meaningful.

I'd just tossed the last folder aside when Rod returned. "Find anything?" he asked.

I gestured toward the pile at my right hand. He picked up the top folder and raised an eyebrow at what he saw inside. "Really? Him? Okay, then."

"What?"

"Oh, just someone I've had to counsel several times for not performing up to expectations. I guess he thought his connections got him out of having to work."

"It's a wonder you haven't been turned into a frog."

"Or he isn't as important to his masters as he thinks, and they weren't about to blow their long game over him."

The next one made him grin. "I bet you got a kick out of this one."

"Yeah, Gregor. Who'd have guessed it?" Gregor ran the Verification department and had been my first boss at the company. He had a tendency to turn into an ogre when he got angry, and the magically immune verifiers were the only ones who could see it, so they'd literally put him in the worst possible spot—or maybe the best. "You know, if they're looking for magical immunes, he made an outstanding recruiting tool. He could identify the ones who showed promise, make their lives miserable, and then they'd jump when the Collegium made them a good offer." I leaned back in my chair, shaking my head. "That explains so much."

The list of possible Collegium-linked employees included a couple of members of the sales staff, a lot of accountants, and most of the middle management, and they were scattered through just about every department other than Research & Development. "How did they manage not to end up with any?" Rod mused out loud, shaking his head.

"Do these Collegium people sound like innovators to you?" I asked. "They seem more like parasites who feed on other people's work. I guess there was Idris, but I wonder if he was really Collegium or if he was a convenient patsy."

"Good point. If they didn't really have the skills to do R and D work, it would show up pretty quickly, and if you've got those skills, you don't need some secret society pulling strings to get you a job."

I looked at the pretty substantial pile of folders representing all the employees we suspected might be Collegium-linked. "How many people do you think have come on board since you've been here who are with the Collegium?"

He shrugged. "There's no way of knowing. I guess I could look for any relatives of past Collegium people. I find it hard to believe that it's that widespread and I'm just now hearing about it. I mean, I heard stories growing up, but it was always something that happened long ago. It was history."

"Like the way stories about fairies are always said to take place right before they vanished?"

"But they didn't vanish."

"Exactly my point." Well, it wasn't, because I'd learned not to think about people with wings as anything different from anyone else, and I never really associated our fairies with the creatures from storybooks. "Even the really old stories were set in some mythical lost time before things changed. But most people don't know that they're still here."

"And I suppose it is a secret society. If everyone knew about it, it wouldn't be so secret. They can't be that bad, though, if no one's talking about them."

"They turned Philip into a frog and stole his business, and there's no telling what they did to his brother," I reminded him. "The people who've run afoul of them can't talk, unless you can understand the nuances of 'ribbit.' But now that we know, what do we do?"

He looked at the stack of files and grimaced. "I guess we take these to the boss."

It took both of us to lug all the folders to Merlin's office. "Can't you just poof these things up there?" I asked as I nudged a wayward folder back into my stack before it could slip out.

"There's a slight risk they could be intercepted. I'm not taking any chances," Rod said.

Merlin raised his eyebrows when he saw how many files there were and heard our explanation. "So, she was telling the truth about how deeply the Collegium has infiltrated our company," he said.

"Now, what do we do?" Rod asked. "We can't fire all these people. The company would shut down."

"We would also be revealing our awareness of them," Merlin said. "No, I think it best that we merely monitor the questionable personnel and only act if they give us reason to fire or reassign them."

"We probably should find something to do with Gregor," I said. "Right now, he's probably running a recruitment scheme for them."

"Or we keep him in place and make sure we recruit the next immune who quits," Rod said. "That would be a good way to get our own double agent."

"Kim's still out there," I said, "and it's only been a few days. I think we'd be better off counting on her." And I couldn't believe I just said that. I did think she was loyal to MSI, or at least thought that was her best chance at advancement. I found it hard to believe that she hadn't been approached by the Collegium earlier because she had been one of the few really competent verifiers in the company.

"Surveillance may be tricky because they have people in Security," Rod said.

"We will have to rely upon those we know we can trust." Merlin leaned over his desk, staring at the folders. "But we don't know that any of these people mean us harm. It might merely be a case of networking. I know there are a number of employees here who came from the various magical secret societies at universities. Their fellow members recommended them."

"Yeah, well, there's secret, and then there's secret," Rod said. "All the magical people know about the societies at school because that's where you get your training. It's only a secret to the nonmagical world. This stuff takes 'secret' to a whole new level."

"And there's that threat that they want to take over," I said. I checked my watch. "Speaking of Kim, I'm supposed to casually run into her today and see if anything has happened."

I went back to my office to grab my coat and purse before heading out to a bar near the office where MSI people tended to go after work. When I entered, I tried to act surprised to see Kim. "Hey! How's it going?" I asked. "I was so sorry to hear what happened."

She gave a dramatic sigh. "It's okay, I guess. I just didn't expect it."

"Let me buy you a drink," I said. I climbed onto the stool across the table from her and flagged down a passing waitress to order drinks for both of us. "Now, tell me how you're doing," I said to Kim. "Any leads on a new job?"

"Nothing yet. Not even a nibble, but I've put in some applications."

"Something's bound to come along. It's only been a few days."

I had what I needed, but for appearance's sake, I had to sit and make small talk with Kim until we finished our drinks. That was as challenging as any assignment I'd ever taken on. We'd never been all that friendly.

She didn't have any better news at the meeting after that, or the one after that. Then it was Thanksgiving, which I spent with Owen's foster parents. The Monday after the holiday weekend, I was thinking about possible alternative plans when my assistant, a young elf woman named Perdita, stood in my office doorway and rapped lightly on the doorframe.

"Mr. Hartwell has called a meeting," she said, hopping anxiously back and forth from one foot to the other, probably because she knew what I thought about meetings. "You need to get to the conference room right away."

I couldn't help but groan out loud. "Really? Did he say what it's about?"

"Nope. Sorry. Should I have asked?"

"No, it's okay." It wasn't so much the idea of a meeting I hated. Sometimes those were necessary to work with a group. But my marketing role fell under the Sales department, and it was like working in a fraternity house. Everything was an excuse for a party. Owen had joked about the great "We Opened a New Box of Pencils!" festival, complete with commemorative T-shirts, but they had once thrown a party to celebrate new computers in the department. When someone called a meeting, I never knew if we were going to talk business or get our groove on while sipping corrosive drinks out of pineapples. If I showed up with notes and documents, I felt like a square as the conga line went past. If I showed up ready for a drink, I felt unprepared when asked to give a status report.

What I found in the conference room was the unholy spawn of a meeting and a party. There was a bowl of punch and a tray of store-bought cookies on the table in the back of the room, but a slide with a graph on it was projected on the screen at the front of the room. I slid into a seat in the back row and got out my notebook and pen.

It appeared to be the "just because we're in the

holiday season, that doesn't mean you can slack off, and here are some numbers to motivate you" meeting. Since I wasn't out making sales, it mostly didn't apply to me, so I let myself focus instead on the other people in the room.

The sales department had the highest concentration of Collegium-linked employees that we'd found, and I supposed that made sense, since selling was all about networking and connections. I wondered if they cut special deals with Collegium people at other companies. Still, I had a hard time picturing any of these people as sinister. Their organization may have done some awful stuff, but these individuals seemed to be just doing their jobs. Well, when they weren't partying.

I was so lost in thought that I blinked, startled, when I thought I heard my name. I came out of my daze to find every eye in the room fixed on me. "Oh, sorry, I was thinking about something you said earlier," I lied to cover up my daydreaming. "What did you ask me?"

"What do you have in the works for a holiday-related campaign?" Mr. Hartwell, the director of Sales, asked.

"The one I came up with three months ago, when we did our planning for the holidays," I snapped without thinking. Only after I'd spoken did I realize that maybe I could have worded that more diplomatically. "Everything was planned and approved then, and most of it has been implemented. You don't start working on your holiday campaign after Thanksgiving."

"Can you remind us what you have going on?"

I forced myself to count to ten and consider my words before responding. "The details are in reports and kits that were sent to each of you, and I don't have that in front of me, since I wasn't planning on this meeting. But we do have advertising to our target markets, new packaging that was automatically implemented the day after Thanksgiving, and holiday pricing for consumer spells. We released a new range of decorating spells last month."

Sam's standing offer to join the security team was sounding better. It was hard to prioritize selling magical Christmas-tree lights when I had to worry about tracking down a potentially dangerous secret society.

"I assume you're already planning your spring promotions," Mr. Hartwell said.

"Yes, that's in the works. I'm still getting details from R and D about what they'll have ready for release."

Fortunately, that seemed to do it for my part of the meeting, but it left me seething. I supposed he was only expecting me to do my job, but considering that my position didn't even exist a year ago and the company had done without it for centuries prior to that, I found it both amusing and annoying that every so often, when he remembered I existed, Mr. Hartwell suddenly felt the need to publicly make sure I was carrying out my duties.

I was still simmering at the end of the day when I headed to Owen's lab in R&D. I found him in his office, in his usual position, bent over an old book. "Want to get some dinner?" I asked.

He looked up as though just then noticing me. "Oh, hi, no, sorry, I want to get through this tonight. Tomorrow, maybe?"

I tried not to let my disappointment show. "Okay. See you tomorrow."

Now in an even worse mood, I decided to head for that bar where I usually met with Kim. I didn't want to bring my bad mood home, and I figured that if I went there without seeing Kim, it would look less suspicious that I went there so often.

I'd just ordered a glass of wine when a woman about my age took the stool next to me. "Rough day?" she asked.

"Not too bad. It just didn't end well. Why do people have meetings at the end of the day?"

"Don't you hate that?" She got a drink for herself, and we sat in companionable silence for a moment before she faced me, smiled, and said, "I don't suppose you'd be interested in a new job?"

Three

The only reasonable response to a total stranger offering you a job was, "What? You don't even know who I am or what I do."

She quirked an eyebrow as her lips twitched in amusement. "Well, actually, I do. I know more about you than you'd think."

I was on the point of telling her no thanks when I realized what might be happening. I knew the Collegium recruited immunes, and I knew that the room had been full of people linked to the Collegium when I'd been snippy to Mr. Hartwell. Had that made me ripe for recruitment?

Playing it cool, I said, "What do you know about me?"

She leaned closer and dropped her voice so no one around could hear. "Your name is Katie Chandler, and you're immune to magic. You work at MSI, where your unique talents are being wasted. You're doing marketing plans for salesmen, which you could do anywhere. But if you had a job that used your gifts, you'd be in miserable working conditions. You had a job that made use of everything you could do, but you got shoved out of that. They rely on you for too much without giving you credit."

"Okay, you know about me," I said, feeling a little queasy about exactly how much they did know. "What are you offering me?"

"The company I work for needs people like you. There's opportunity you wouldn't have at MSI. More money, for one thing. You wouldn't believe the perks. But I think what would mean the most to you is that you wouldn't be a second-class citizen just because you're not a wizard."

"Sounds too good to be true." I returned my attention to my wine.

"Well, there are a few catches. I can't guarantee you'd be chosen. You're the sort of person we look for, but there are some selective standards you'd have to meet. You'd have to prove yourself. You'd have to maintain a high degree of loyalty." A business card suddenly appeared in her manicured hand. "Think about it. And if you ever get tired of what you're doing, give me a call."

She placed the card on the bar, finished her drink, and left. I nursed my glass of wine a while longer, thinking. MSI had recruited me with an e-mail I'd initially mistaken for spam, until I'd had a bad enough day at work to follow up on it. Owen had noticed me from afar in a bookstore but had been too shy to approach. He'd seen me react to things that were magically veiled, which suggested I was immune to magic. From there, people from MSI had observed me until they were sure, and then had made the job offer.

But why would the Collegium recruit me now, after a

mild outburst in a meeting? Surely they didn't expect me to switch loyalties so quickly. Or was it a trap? Did they know I was investigating them?

The bartender put a glass of champagne in front of me. "I'm sorry, I didn't order this," I said.

"Your friend ordered it for you. She said you had something to celebrate."

I eyed the glass warily. The bartender had poured it after she left, so I doubted she'd poisoned or drugged it, and a spell or curse wouldn't work on me. It was probably safe to drink. And what if I was being watched? I wasn't sure yet what I should do, but I thought this could be the infiltration opportunity we were looking for. I raised the glass in a toast to whatever invisible eye was watching me and drank.

Owen was waiting for me on the sidewalk in front of my building when I left for work the next morning. "Sorry about yesterday," he said.

"No problem. I know you're busy."

"Is something wrong?"

"Wrong?" I'd thought I was putting up a good front, but if the guy whose head was usually lost in some old book had noticed, then I must have been radiating unease. "No, nothing's wrong. There's some stuff we need to talk about at the office."

I felt bad for making him suffer. He kept darting little glances at me as we headed to the subway station, and then he acted like he was walking on eggshells with me the whole way to the office. I figured that if I was being watched, any sense of unhappiness between us would only contribute to the impression that I was ripe for recruitment, and I didn't dare talk about this in public. I knew he'd understand when I got a chance to explain.

I was used to being able to speak freely as soon as we got in the office building, but knowing how many Collegium people worked there, and knowing that they were watching me, I couldn't tell him even then, which made him look more alarmed. "We should probably go straight to the boss," I said.

Only when we were in Merlin's office, with the door shut and with the privacy wards in place, did I say, "I think the Collegium is trying to recruit me."

"So, that's why you were upset," Owen said, sagging in visible relief. "I thought you were mad that I didn't want to go out to dinner with you last night."

I described my encounter with the mysterious stranger and what had led up to it. "So, what do I do? Kim's had no luck getting in, so maybe I could."

"I don't like it," Owen said, shaking his head. "They know your attachment to this company. I'm sure they'd assume you were spying. Maybe that's even why they approached you, to set a trap."

"I thought of that," I said. "I mean, I'd be the *last* person I'd recruit if I were them. On the other hand, I'd be a big prize. Turning me would help them against MSI."

"It would be very dangerous for you to put yourself in that situation," Merlin said, stroking his beard thoughtfully. "Even if they were recruiting you sincerely, they'd watch you to make sure you weren't a spy. You'd have to earn their trust over time before you gained any valuable intelligence."

"She did mention having to prove myself," I admitted. "I'm not sure I want to think about what that would entail."

"At least we know they couldn't make you turn someone into a frog," Owen said with a valiant attempt at a smile.

"Yeah, but they might ask me to betray the company somehow."

"I suggest that you disregard this offer," Merlin said. "Even if you were to eventually consider it, I think it would look more suspicious if you jumped at the first chance. However, perhaps it would not be a bad idea for us to begin giving you valid reasons to be more open to subsequent offers."

"You're going to make my life miserable at work?" I asked with some dismay. Not that I had a bad job, really. "What are you going to do, hire Mimi to oversee me? After all, she drove me to you in the first place."

"I was thinking more in terms of asking for more reports. Wouldn't it be premature for me to begin demanding an analysis of the return on investment of your marketing efforts and to criticize you when they haven't had immediate, miraculous results?"

"Have you been talking to Mimi?" I couldn't help but ask. "That's right out of her playbook."

"Does this mean we need to fight?" Owen asked.

He seemed to be joking—at least, he was smiling— but my stomach did a queasy flip-flop. I couldn't imagine that the Collegium would be keen on me being engaged to someone so high up in the company they were targeting. Even if they thought I could get sensitive information out of him, there would be a bigger risk of me remaining loyal to him and to the company. Everything about me suggested I was more likely to be a spy than a turncoat, and it would take a lot of effort to convince them that I'd turned enough for them to trust me. I couldn't see a lot of good coming out of me trying to use this as a chance to go undercover.

But as long as there was a chance, we played along. Merlin requested reports, and that gave me enough extra work to do that Owen and I barely saw each other during December. Every so often, I smiled wistfully at memories of the previous December when we'd first started dating. There had been Christmas shopping, ice skating... and, come to think of it, falling through the ice and being hounded by an incompetent fairy godmother. Ah, good times. Maybe it was for the best that we didn't have time for that this year.

I kept meeting with Kim, who was getting frustrated about not getting a job offer, especially when she heard that I'd had one. I went to the same bar alone a few times, but I never saw the mysterious recruiter.

Owen came home with me for Christmas, and for a week, we didn't have to worry about anything relating to the Collegium. There was no chance they were active in a small Texas town. We were both tired and a little crabby when we returned to New York. If anyone had been spying on us in the airport, I doubt they'd have assumed we were on the verge of breaking up, but if they were looking for signs of fractures, they might have been able to read something into the way we interacted. We spoke in short, sharp sentences, and there was little physical contact between us. Never mind that after spending hours shoulder-to-shoulder on an airplane, the last thing we wanted to do was touch another person.

When we returned to work after the holidays, Sam the gargoyle met us at the building entrance. "We've gotta talk," he said.

"What is it?" I asked.

"C'mon, up to the boss's office." It was hard to read his facial expression, considering he was made of stone, but I got the sense that he was really worried. Normally, he'd have teased us or asked how our holidays had gone.

Up in Merlin's office, Rod and Philip were already waiting, and Minerva soon joined us. Merlin activated the privacy wards, and he, Rod, and Owen did some other spell, like they were searching for bugs. Okay, I thought, this really was serious.

"Some events occurred during the holidays that have us concerned," Merlin began. "Two members of the Council and several corporate executives have gone missing."

"Are we sure they're missing and not just off on holidays?" I asked.

"Their families reported them missing."

"This sounds much like what happened to me," Philip said.

"The Collegium must be making a move," Rod mused. "I'll have to keep an eye on absentee reports today."

"We have no way of knowing it's the Collegium," Owen said. "Remember, it wasn't that long ago that the elves were abducting people."

"I have checked to make sure nothing of the sort is happening now," Merlin said. "Of course, there are many possible explanations, but I want all of you to be alert, and we should redouble our efforts to gain information."

"Should I call the number on that business card?" I asked, rather reluctantly.

"Business card?" Rod asked. I hadn't told anyone but Owen and Merlin about the attempted recruitment.

"Someone who may be Collegium approached me about working for them."

"That would be a very bad idea," Philip said, shaking his head.

"Which is why I didn't take them up on it."

Philip turned to Merlin. "I've heard about what they make their employees go through to ensure their loyalty."

"Like what?" I demanded.

"You don't want to know."

"Yes, I do, considering that they've approached me, and this may be our chance to infiltrate them."

"They make you betray someone you care about, and they'd probably make you turn on this company and the people in it. Instead of you infiltrating them so you could defend MSI, you might be the weapon they used to bring down the company. That's probably why they approached you."

I could feel myself go pale. "Okay, then, losing the card. But we need a plan B, and we need to find all those missing people. If they're frogs, how will they survive in this weather?"

Philip shivered. "I am fortunate that I was enchanted in the summer. By the time winter arrived, my frog instincts were strong enough that I knew what to do.

Someone enchanted in cold weather would be unlikely to find shelter before perishing."

I was just about to ask Minerva if she'd come up with anything when she said, "My people haven't been able to verify the whereabouts of anyone on the list. Several of them are definitely still alive, but I can't determine where or what state they might be in. We can try again in summer, in case they're frogs, and then we may be able to get a bearing on them so we can break the spell without having to kiss every frog in the city."

I felt so helpless, but there was little we could do right now. The halls of the sales department were awfully empty when I headed to my office, but that could have just been the first day back after the holidays. I shook my head. This whole thing was making me paranoid. Nothing much had changed in the company, but knowing there were people from a secret group there made it feel different.

Rod came to my office in the middle of the afternoon. I could tell who it was even before he spoke by the way Perdita's tone changed. Rod was what might best be described as unique-looking—not conventionally handsome, but if he made the most of his features and was smiling, he was striking in his own way. He had a habit of using an illusion to make himself more handsome, and while he'd mostly stopped using it in his social life, he didn't want to give it up at work because then people might not recognize him. As a result, my assistant was swooning over what she saw as movie-idol looks.

"It's okay, Perdita, you can send him in," I called out.

Rod entered my office, shut the door behind him, and

performed a privacy spell on the room. "I'm sure we can trust Perdita," I told him as he finished the spell.

"I'm not taking any chances," he said, his eyes grim.

That got my attention. "Whoa, what is it?"

He sat in the guest chair in front of my desk and handed me a sheet of paper. "The list of people who didn't show up today. None of these people are on approved vacation, none called in sick, and we haven't had any response when calling to check on them."

There were perhaps a dozen names on the list. I recognized several from Sales. "Is that unusual?"

"For the first day after a holiday? Not entirely. It's a bit higher than I would have expected, but I wouldn't have been all that alarmed if I hadn't known to be looking for anything. However, we crossed a number of names off the list we started with when we called around. *That* was the usual amount. There were some travel snags, oversleeping, illness." He pointed to the list. "These are the ones you might say have disappeared. But that's not all."

"Do tell."

"I cross-referenced these names with our list of Collegium associates, and they're mostly immediate supervisors of Collegium-related employees."

"Oh boy," I said. "That should suggest that where you didn't find that relationship, it might involve someone we don't know about who was hired during your tenure."

"Yeah, but that's a little harder to track, since there are a lot of employees under each supervisor, and it could be any one of them."

"So they're getting people out of the way to move their plants up into critical positions. It sounds like they're definitely making a move," I said. "We need to do something."

"But not you taking a job with them."

"No, of course not." But I couldn't help considering it, since it wasn't as though we had many other options. "What do you plan to do?"

"It's not up to me who gets promoted in each department, but I'm going to try to swing it so that as few as possible of the Collegium people get promoted into the empty slots. We have to let some in, or else it will be obvious that we're on to them."

"I just wish we knew what they were up to." I ran my fingers through my hair around my temples, then realized that was Owen's customary gesture of frustration combined with deep thought. We weren't even married yet, and I was already turning into him. "Maybe Kim will get some nibbles now that the holidays are over," I said, grasping at straws. "Since we pretended to fire her, they wouldn't ask her for loyalty tests against us, would they?"

"I have no idea how they work. But even if she got in, I wouldn't expect overnight miracles. No one's going to get in close enough to learn anything major. Those mafia undercover operations spanned years."

"Then is there a way to magically bug them? That's the other way the FBI went up against the mob."

"We'd have to know where to find them first."

"Which brings us back to getting someone inside. I'm supposed to check in with Kim tomorrow. Is there someone else we could pretend to fire if they don't want her?"

• • •

Kim was waiting at the bar when I arrived the following afternoon. She looked so dejected that I worried she was really feeling down about not being recruited and wasn't just acting bummed about being out of work. "No leads," she said with a weary sigh before I could ask. "It's a really tough job market."

"I'm sure you'll find something," I said, but I had a feeling that if they wanted her, they'd have grabbed her by now.

She downed her drink. "Yeah. Maybe. I don't know. But you can tell the boss how I'm doing. I'm sure he cares." If she was acting, she was doing a really convincing job. She even reeled a little when she climbed off her stool and headed off, leaving me alone to finish my glass of wine.

After I left, as I walked down the sidewalk toward the subway station, I reached into my pocket to get my gloves and encountered a piece of paper I didn't recall being there before. I pulled it out and read, "Turn left on Fulton."

It was a good thing I'd reached for my gloves when I had because Fulton was the next intersection. But should I follow the directions? It could be a trap. It would be a pretty weird trap, though. There were plenty of places someone could ambush me without sending me a written invitation.

I stopped at the street corner to wrestle with the decision. It could be dangerous. Or it could be a lead. When I looked up and saw a familiar gargoyle perched on top of a nearby lamppost, I made my decision and turned left. The gargoyle took off, flying behind me. If it turned out to be a trap, at least I had some backup. That's what

I'd tell Owen later if I got in trouble and he was mad at me for taking a risk.

The street was hardly vacant, so it wasn't what I'd consider a great ambush spot. I wasn't sure what I was supposed to do once I turned left on Fulton, so I kept walking. Just ahead of me, someone came out of a coffee shop with a paper cup in her hand. She had a shawl wrapped around her head and shoulders, obscuring her face, but that wasn't too odd in this weather. She joined the flow of pedestrian traffic as I passed and maintained a steady pace just behind me. If we'd been in cars, she'd have been in my blind spot.

"Don't turn around. Just keep walking," a voice said from behind me. I was pretty sure it was Sylvia, but I resisted the temptation to turn and look.

"What is it?" I asked.

"I'm about to need that exit strategy your people promised me. Pass that on, will you?"

"Okay."

"Your little ploy to get someone on the inside will never work. They're not going to hire that one. She doesn't come highly recommended. Too uptight. She's the type who would squeal to the authorities the moment she realized what was going on. So you can let her have her regular job back."

"That's good to know." Well, actually, it wasn't, because we didn't have much more of a plan than that, but at least we knew we could cut our losses and put Kim out of her misery.

"I hear they approached you."

"Maybe."

"No maybe about it. I know they did."

"Is it a trap? Do they know we're looking into them?"

"I don't know. But I figure it's on the level. If they wanted to get rid of you, they wouldn't have to hire you."

"What if they wanted my inside info on MSI?"

She gave a short, harsh laugh. "Oh, that's so cute. You think they don't already have inside info? As many people as they have there? There's practically nothing you could tell them that they don't already know. You're a case of if you can't beat 'em, join 'em, or ask them to join you."

"What makes them think *I* wouldn't go straight to the authorities? Foiling evil magic schemes is basically my hobby. Well, other than baking, embroidery, and knitting."

"I imagine they're going to make you an offer you can't refuse. You'd better be prepared for that."

"Who said I was going to take them up on it?"

"What choice do you have? Now, remember, I want an exit. Tomorrow, if possible. Same place and time, have someone ready to whisk me away into obscurity."

"Got it."

There was no response, but I knew better than to turn and look for her. I walked to the next intersection, then turned to make my way back toward the office. It was a pretty safe bet that Merlin would still be around. I still wasn't entirely sure he didn't live in his office.

Once I was back in the MSI building, I hesitated as I passed the floor where Owen's lab was, but decided to head straight to Merlin. This didn't really have anything to do with Owen.

As I expected, Merlin was still there. "Ah, Miss Chandler,

shouldn't you have gone home by now? Or did you have something to report from your meeting?"

I filled him in on what had happened, including Sylvia's warning about Kim not being hired. He made a call to the security crew to arrange Sylvia's escape, then faced me. "Are you considering the offer, then?"

"I still don't know. It may be our only chance, but it sounds like a slim chance. I don't know that it would be worth the risk."

"I agree. Let's wait and see, shall we? Perhaps you should help tomorrow, since you are a familiar face and you can spot any hidden magical people in the vicinity."

"Now, that sounds like my kind of assignment."

The next afternoon, I bundled up, since there was a chance I'd be spending a lot of time outdoors. I walked the length of Fulton Street, looking for any hidden magical people. "I don't see anything but our team," I said to Sam via the earpiece I wore.

"I doubt they're usin' anything but humans, doll," he said. "Let's watch the street and see if anyone suspicious sticks around. Then you describe 'em to me, and we'll see if they're veiled."

I made another pass up and down the street, but there was no sign of anyone who looked remotely suspicious— well, no more so than your average Manhattanite. I checked my watch. It was time. Sylvia ought to be coming by at any moment now.

But she didn't. We waited half an hour longer, but she wasn't there. Had she found her own way out, changed her mind, or was this yet another disappearance?

Four

Sam and I regrouped back at the office. "My people didn't spot any sign of her, comin' or goin'," Sam said.

"Maybe she changed her mind," I said. "She wasn't all that excited about having to leave. She put us off once before."

"Or maybe she was right about them being after her, and they got to her before we did."

"Let's hope not." It wasn't that I was so worried about Sylvia's fate. I just thought it was a very bad sign if something had happened to her. It would suggest that she was right about the threat we faced—a threat we were no closer to being up to defending against than we had been when she first approached us. All we knew was some people not to trust.

"Well, we tried, right?" Sam said with a shrug. "That's all we could do. We held up our end of the bargain. She's the one who didn't come through."

"Let me try getting in touch with her one more time."

"How do you plan to do that, doll? I thought the whole deal was that she got in touch with us."

"I can make it easy for her to contact us. I'll try going to the places where she's reached me in the past. If something came up and she aborted, that may be where she expects me to go so she can set up something else."

"I guess it's worth a shot," he said with another shrug. "But that's goin' above and beyond, if you ask me."

I headed to the bar where Sylvia had left the message for me. If she needed to contact me for another plan, that seemed like the best place to start. I ordered my usual glass of wine, even though what I really wanted was a cup of cocoa. I wondered how long I'd have to sit there before I could check my coat pockets.

Someone slid onto the stool next to mine, and I turned to see the woman who'd made the job offer. "We never heard from you," she said.

"I'm not interested."

"Just checking. But are you sure?"

"Why would you even want me?"

She laughed. "Come now, Katie, you know how rare people like you are. It's even more rare to find someone like you who's retained any sanity and common sense. You come very highly recommended. Our firm could really use someone like you who has a talent for getting things done."

I started to ask why she thought I'd turn on MSI, and then I realized that she'd never actually said she was with the Collegium. The business card she'd given me had been for a banking firm. This kind of recruiting happened all the time in the Wall Street area, I was sure. Someone from a rival company might approach another company's rising star and try to poach the talent. It didn't mean the rival had mob ties.

Of course, I wasn't so naive as to really believe that this was a perfectly innocent job offer. But I thought it best to play it that way. After all, why would I, a relative newcomer to the magical world, know anything about a super-secret cabal? "What kind of position are you talking about?"

"It would be the kind of verification work you're familiar with, only involving high-level financial transactions rather than making sure the right spells are stocked at magic shops. I understand you have a business background from the real world. We find that intriguing."

"I worked at a small-town farm supply store. That's hardly high finance."

"But it means you've actually worked with money in a real, tangible way, not just moving numbers around on a computer. You know what should be in contracts. You know how people should behave. I've heard a lot about how you apply common sense to your work, as well. You managed to work effectively as a verifier while your immunity wasn't working, from what I hear."

If Sylvia hadn't warned us about the Collegium, if this woman had just approached me like this, I might have been tempted. Yes, I owed MSI a lot, and I liked working with Owen. But we were going to be married soon, so we'd be living together. Did we have to also work together? Most couples had separate jobs. It might even take some strain off our relationship if we didn't have to be together so much.

But that *wasn't* what was really going on here, I was sure. If they were recruiting me into a Collegium front, they'd test my loyalty before I got access to any good information, so I wouldn't be able to do much as a spy, and I didn't want to actually work for them.

"I'm sorry, but I'm still not interested in changing jobs," I said. "I like where I am."

"That's not what I hear. You like the company. You hate your job."

"How could you possibly know that?"

"I'm very well connected," she said with a smile. She slid a business card across the bar to me. "Here, take another card. The offer stays open. Call me anytime."

She slid gracefully off the barstool and disappeared—well, not literally, in a puff of magical smoke, but I lost sight of her in the crowded bar. I finished my wine and went to retrieve my coat from the coat check. There was nothing in the pockets but my gloves.

After making myself visible in other places Sylvia had approached me, like the park and the subway, I became fairly certain that she hadn't vanished of her own accord. That meant she was right that they might get rid of her, and if she was right about that, then she was probably right about them making a move on MSI and targeting Merlin. We had to do something about it.

The problem was, I had no idea what we could do, short of firing everyone we suspected of being linked to the Collegium, and even then, I was sure there were others we didn't know about. Plus, they'd probably consider that to be the first shot in open warfare.

There was that one other option, the one we'd rejected

time after time as too dangerous and not very effective. But any information had to be better than no information at all. Even if I just went for an interview and saw who some of the players were and where they were located, we might be ahead of where we were now. I could always turn down the job.

But there was also the chance that I could get a lot more information than that. If I was so valuable to them that they were recruiting me—and Sylvia had said it wasn't because they thought I had inside information—then I might have a shot at getting the scoop.

I went straight to Merlin's office the next morning. "I don't think we have any other choice but for me to take this job with them," I said.

He gestured for me to take a seat. "I thought we agreed that it wouldn't do any good."

"Maybe it won't, but it's likely to do more good than doing nothing, and that's where we are now. We've lost Sylvia, apparently, which means she was right, and can we afford *not* to take action? Besides, I have a plan that might fast-track me into their trust."

"What would that be?"

"I'd have to make it look good, make it clear that I'm deserting you, that I might be mad enough at MSI to turn against you. When Rod first recruited me here, I ignored all his e-mails until I had a really bad day and a run-in with my old boss, Mimi. That was what spurred me to jump at any chance to get out of there. So I need something like that here—a chain of events that would make me abandon ship and run straight into their arms. Heck, I wouldn't be surprised if they don't try to arrange something like that, themselves. They have people on the inside who are apparently reporting on what's happening, so they'll know what I'm going through."

"I'm sure we can find some ways to frustrate you," he said, smiling slightly.

"And you're going to have to do it, too. I've had clashes with people in the company, but you've always had my back. For them to believe this, you'll have to give me a reason to be angry at you, personally."

"I suppose it would have to be unfair rather than warranted, but I believe it would look suspicious if I suddenly started being mean to you, with no warning or reason."

"We should probably do this gradually. Ramp up to it instead of changing abruptly."

"And what of Mr. Palmer? Have you discussed this with him?"

I shifted in my seat, not wanting to meet his eyes. "Not yet. I mean, we've talked about it in general, but I wanted to bring this up with you before I talked about it with him. It's not really under his jurisdiction, and I've been trying to keep him out of this whole thing."

"I would think he has a personal stake in the matter. Wouldn't it be odd for you to reject this company so strongly that you turn to an organization opposed to it while you continue planning a wedding to someone within the company?"

I bit my lip and tried not to groan. I'd thought about it, but then I'd tried not to think about it. That was the one hitch in the whole plan. I wasn't sure how I could pull off an attitude of "I hate MSI so much I want to bring them down, please tell me all your evil plans for doing so, in detail" while I was engaged to MSI's poster boy. "I may have to fake that, as well," I said, reluctantly admitting out loud what I'd been avoiding considering. "And what would sell my desertion better than breaking off my engagement?"

Merlin studied me with a stern gaze. "If you're going to take it that far, you absolutely must talk to Mr. Palmer about it before proceeding."

"Of course! I wouldn't just dump him and not let him know why."

"I meant that he needs to agree to it. It may be your choice to go undercover, but he will be making sacrifices, as well."

I nodded. "Okay. I'll talk to him. I'm sure he'll see my reasoning." Either that, or we'd end up having a fight that would make my departure from MSI very convincing.

I put off talking to Owen for as long as I could. I went back to my office, answered e-mails, did some paperwork, and made a pro/con list about my plan, outlining bullet points to show why this was our best possible hope and coming up with arguments to counter any objections I anticipated.

When all hands in the sales department were called to the Wacky Winter Warm-up party, I decided that facing Owen was the lesser of two evils and headed up to his lab.

He and his assistant, Jake, were standing in front of a whiteboard, arguing about some fine point of something written on the board. It was in a language I didn't recognize, and I'd learned to recognize a lot of languages from hanging around with Owen. Both of them held markers and were writing things above the words written on the board, going back and forth, each crossing out what the other had written and writing in something else. It was getting pretty heated.

Since Owen so seldom argued about much of anything, and him even raising his voice was a rare occurrence, I thought that this was the worst possible time to tell him I needed to pretend to break our engagement and quit the company in a huff of anger so I could go on a dangerous and potentially unproductive undercover mission. But before I could slip out of the lab, he noticed me.

"Katie! Is something wrong?" he asked.

"What? No! Why?" I wanted to kick myself because I couldn't have sounded guiltier if I'd tried.

"You look, well, frazzled."

"I barely escaped from a Sales party. It was pretty harrowing. What's going on here?"

"We're having a slight difference of opinion," Jake said. "And I still think you're reading that one rune the wrong way."

"This isn't an album cover, Jake."

"I know you've got all those fancy degrees and read this kind of stuff for fun, but that also means you've got some preconceived notions that keep you from seeing what's really there."

"But the spell doesn't make sense that way."

"Unless the spell's not meant to be about silence at all."

I boosted myself up to sit on the end of the lab table so I could watch the debate. It was too bad I didn't have any popcorn handy. "Silence?" I asked.

"Depending on how you interpret the runes, this could be a spell for dampening sound and creating silence," Owen said.

"Or it could be a direction to chant the spell internally, not making a sound," Jake said.

"Could it be both?" I asked. "It would make sense that you'd want to do a spell about silence quietly. If you need to dampen the sound you're making, it wouldn't do you much good if you had to chant a spell."

They looked at each other, both of them raising their eyebrows, then turned to face the board. "Maybe that's why we're reading it both ways," Owen said. "It's *meant* to mean both things. Look, that mark here is what changes the meaning."

"Yeah, that's why I thought it was a direction," Jake said. "So, a silent silence spell. Makes sense to me."

They turned back to face me, both smiling now, all traces of their earlier conflict gone. "I'm glad you came by," Owen said. "Sometimes it helps to get an outside perspective."

"That's me, having the common sense," I said. In my head, the words of the mystery recruiter echoed. She'd said that about me, too. "I guess everyone has a superpower."

"Did you need something other than a hiding place?" Owen asked.

Now that he was in a good mood again, I didn't have an excuse not to talk to him. "I need to check in with you about that thing we've been working on."

"I thought you were keeping me out of it."

"I wanted to run something by you."

"I'll keep working on this," Jake said, turning to write on the board.

I jumped off the table, and Owen escorted me to his office, then shut the door behind us and waved a hand to activate the privacy wards. "So, what is it?" he asked.

I'd spent enough time in the sales department to know you had to lay the groundwork for something like this. You couldn't just jump into the hard part. "Did you hear about Sylvia?" I asked.

"What about her?"

"She approached me yesterday, ready for us to get her to safety. She also said they're never going to hire Kim, so that plan's a dead end. Apparently, Gregor knows her a bit too well."

"So Sylvia's safe now?"

"Well, not exactly." I knew I needed to look him in the eye to sell this, but it was hard to do so. "She didn't show up for the extraction. We haven't heard from her since then. Either she changed her mind completely, or they got to her before she could get away. If it's the latter, that suggests she was right about everything else."

"I think all those other disappearances were another sign."

"Yeah, I guess." Now I really couldn't look him in the eye. I uncrossed my legs, then recrossed them. "Did I also mention that they tried recruiting me? At least, I'm pretty sure it's them. Obviously, they didn't say they were the Collegium. It was some financial institution I've never heard of. I turned them down, of course. They said they were interested in my common sense, and they'd let me do real verification work. Actually, they seem to know a lot about me."

"It might be some other company. You're getting

quite the reputation. Magical businesses all over the city would be glad to have you."

"I think the timing is pretty suspicious, though."

"Possibly. You're not even interested in looking into it?"

I started to wonder if he already knew where I was going with this. He had an uncanny sense that helped him predict what I was likely to do. I wasn't sure how much of that was magic and how much was that he really got me. "Well, that's the thing. I *am* thinking of giving them a call. If it's just another company, then no harm done, and hey, maybe I can even use it to negotiate a raise or a job I'd like better. And if it's not, then it may be our best shot at getting someone on the inside of the Collegium so we can learn what they're up to."

His expression became a lot less friendly and supportive. "I thought we agreed that you going undercover would be a bad idea because they'd never truly trust you."

"But that was before they started recruiting me. I think maybe I could trick them into trusting me if I made my departure look really good, if there was a good reason for me to be totally over MSI. I've been talking about it with the boss, and we figure that we could have things start to go downhill and then end with a bang."

"What about us? You'd still be engaged to me."

I really, *really* didn't want to face him when talking about this next part, but I forced myself to look him square in the eye when I said, "We'd have to pretend on that, as well. A nasty breakup would make it incredibly convincing. But it would be fake, really. We might even be able to find ways to see each other. We'd have to be careful, of course, but secret meetings could be kind of sexy. I wouldn't plan to stay there very long, just enough to learn something. Even if I learned some of their locations and people, that would help."

"Are you telling me this is what you're doing, or are you asking for my input?" His face was so stony that I couldn't read him at all. He made Sam, who was literally made of stone, look like Jim Carrey.

"Merlin said I had to talk to you before we decided anything because you'd be making a big sacrifice, too. I won't do it if you're against it. But think about it; this may be our only hope. How many people could be saved if I can find out what's going on? We don't want them having control of this company. You're the one always quoting that *Casablanca* line about the problems of two little people not mattering in the greater scheme of things."

"You'd be careful?"

"Duh!"

"You'd get yourself out of there the moment it looks like there's any danger?"

"Of course!"

"Katie, I know you. I can already hear it: 'But I'm so close!'"

"I've seen what delays did to Sylvia."

"I don't like it, but I won't stop you."

"Trust me, I don't like it, either. I just don't see how I have any choice. This may be our only chance ever to get someone inside."

"Or it really may be some international bank recruiting you."

"If it is, let's see what they offer. Maybe I can get a cool new job."

He grinned, then suddenly looked alarmed. "You are joking, right? You wouldn't really want to leave?"

"No, I wouldn't leave. But now I need to go let the boss know we're on so everyone can begin mistreating me and taking me for granted."

Implementing the scheme to give me an excuse to quit was both difficult and alarmingly easy. While Merlin and I could stage a dispute, there weren't many other people we were sure we could trust to be in on it, and that meant that whatever happened in my department had to be genuine. That was the hard part. The sad thing was, it happened anyway without any manipulation of events. All I had to do was actually express my feelings about the kind of stuff that happened all the time.

Take the meeting I had with Mr. Hartwell the next day. He was notorious about leaving people waiting, in spite of having a set appointment. Normally, I didn't let it get to me. I brought work I could do or something to read while I waited or, if I had another meeting, I asked his assistant to reschedule me. This time, when the time of the meeting arrived and he wasn't there, I got up and said, "Well, I guess the meeting wasn't that important to him, so it won't be a problem if it doesn't happen," then went back to my office. I had to move quickly to disguise the fact that my legs were shaking. I wasn't used to being quite that rebellious with authority figures.

There was yet another department party that afternoon—the "Let's Make a Splash Summer in January Luau"—and I didn't even pretend I was going to attend. A salesman wearing a grass skirt over his clothes stuck his head into my office. "Knock, knock!" he said. "Aren't you coming to the party? We have mai tais!"

"Unlike apparently everyone else around here, I have work to do," I snapped. "You know, I think our sales would improve dramatically if you devoted the time you spend partying to, you know, *selling*."

He blinked and flinched as though I'd struck him physically. "Well, if you're going to be that way about it."

I had to bite my lip to keep from grinning. So far, it seemed to be working. I felt my grin fading as I realized that creating a reason for me to want to quit and take another job offer didn't involve changing anything about my working environment. All I had to do to make jumping ship believable was react naturally.

I had to get back into character the next morning when a nervous Perdita came into my office. "Um, Katie, well, uh, Mr. Hartwell wants to see you, right away."

Without looking up from what I was doing—checking the weather forecast online—I said, "Okay."

She remained standing in the doorway. "He sounded pretty intense about it."

"When I'm done with this." After I noted the temperatures for the five-day outlook and had mentally planned my wardrobe accordingly, I got up and headed to Mr. Hartwell's office. My heart pounded so hard I felt like it was about to burst out of my chest like an alien, but I forced myself to play it cool.

This time, Mr. Hartwell was there, and he didn't look happy—well, as much as he could look anything with a face that could have been molded out of plastic. "Please, shut the door behind you," he said.

I tried not to gulp. I reminded myself that this was what I wanted, though having the door open would have been better so more people could have overheard. I shut the door and took a seat before he invited me to. "Did you need something?" I asked, maintaining an air of innocence.

"I understand you were busy yesterday."

"I was. And I don't appreciate having my time wasted."

That really took him aback. He was apparently planning to chide me, and now he was on the defensive. "Sometimes things come up."

"Then it would be considerate to communicate when things change instead of assuming that your time is more valuable than everyone else's."

"I'm sensing that this isn't about just one missed meeting. Are you unhappy here?"

I gave him a piercing glare. "Yes, I guess I am. I feel like I'm wasting my time. In fact, I'm going to apply for another internal position."

"Perhaps you should." His voice sounded harsh, and I realized what a big risk I was taking. I was burning a lot of bridges here, and if I wasn't able to get into the Collegium, I'd have to find a new job anyway. From this point, there was no turning back.

Five

Step two of Operation "Quit in a Huff" was complete. After the meeting with Mr. Hartwell, I went upstairs to Merlin's office and, with his door still open, I said, "You haven't yet replaced Kim. I'd like my old job as your assistant back."

"Does this mean you are unhappy in your current role?" he said, glancing up from the paperwork on his desk. "I would have thought that running the company's marketing efforts was a step up from being an administrative assistant."

"You would think that, wouldn't you? But that's not the way it seems to be working out, and I'm not sure I can survive another day in the sales department without becoming homicidal. We took down our primary competitor, so there's not much need for marketing. That job doesn't need my magical immunity to do it, so I feel like I'm wasting a valuable talent. And it seems I spend most of my time on what you might call 'other duties as assigned,' so I may as well be in a position where that's the entire job description." Even though I knew it was all an act, saying this to Merlin made my stomach queasy, and I could feel my face growing warm.

Actually, I wasn't sure how much of my reaction had anything to do with faking confrontation as it did with the sick realization that while I was playing a role, everything I said was absolutely true. Had I been holding all that in?

Merlin looked directly at me, and for a moment I thought I saw concern in his eyes, like he'd realized I was telling the truth. "I will consider it," he said.

"Do you have a timetable on that? Because I'm looking into some other options, and I'd like to know when I might know what my future will be."

"As I said, I will consider it." He dropped his gaze to his paperwork, and I got the message that I was dismissed. I turned and left his office, taking deep breaths to calm myself—deep, noisy breaths so anyone watching would know I needed to calm down.

"Are you okay, Katie?" Merlin's receptionist, a fairy named Trix, asked as I passed her desk.

I hated having to lie to a friend, and I was fairly certain she was trustworthy, but there was too much at stake, so I had to keep up the act with her. Besides, she was one of the better sources of office gossip, so if I sold it here, it was sure to make it to the Collegium people within the company. "I'm just having a crappy week," I said, blinking rapidly to make it look like I was fighting back tears of frustration.

"Did I hear that you're trying to come back up here?"

"Yeah. I think I was happiest here. Sales is such a zoo."

"That's their reputation. I don't know how you've been able to stand it. It would be great to have you back."

I held up fingers crossed for luck. "Let's see what happens."

"Maybe if I send out the right vibes, I can sway the boss."

"You do that," I said with a laugh, though I hoped it was just a joke and not something she really had the power to do. Getting what I wanted would ruin my scheme. I heaved a weary sigh. "Now, back to the salt mines."

Although I was trying to maintain an air of unhappiness, I felt pretty good about how things were going so far. Unfortunately, now I had to start the hard part: Destroying my relationship with Owen.

We'd been pretty much inseparable since I joined the company, first as friends and later as more than friends, so convincing the world that there was trouble in paradise wouldn't be easy. We were so well suited to each other that finding conflict would be difficult without either of us acting out of character. How would we convince people that we were falling apart so badly that I'd want nothing to do with him or the company he worked for?

I dropped by his lab soon after five to find him watching Jake giving a rambling monologue about music. Owen's lips moved slightly, and his fingers looked like they were squeezing something. Abruptly, the sound of Jake's voice cut off, even though his mouth kept moving. Owen mouthed some more words and spread his fingers, and Jake's voice returned.

"Hey, that worked!" Jake said.

"But it's not quite what we want here," Owen said,

frowning, as he bent over a notebook and jotted something. "It doesn't have the practical applications I'd like."

"I don't know, I could think of all kinds of applications for a mute button for people," I said.

"I know, right?" Jake said with a grin. "If movie theaters used this spell on the audience, it would improve the moviegoing experience dramatically."

"But the spell is supposed to be for stealth," Owen said, frowning. "Making others be quiet only makes it more likely that you'll be noticed in a more quiet environment."

"Unless you're sneaking around with someone who doesn't understand the concept of stealth," I said. "There's always that one person in movies who can't help but step on a twig or blurt out something at a bad time."

Owen made some more notes. "Maybe if we adjust this, and then do that, we can come up with something that muffles any sound the caster makes." After writing some more, he looked up at me. "Was there something you needed, Katie?"

I looked at my watch. "Well, it is after five, and you seem to be at a stopping point, so I thought maybe we could get some dinner. You asked for a rain check the other day, and it's not raining now!"

He looked pained, like he was actually physically ill, and my heart broke for him. I knew it had to be hard for him to even pretend to do anything that would look like it hurt me, and I felt awful for putting him in this position, but it would have been far worse not to bring him in on it. "Oh. But I'm not really at a stopping point. I want to test this next variation."

"How long do you think that will take?" I allowed the slightest bit of edge to creep into my voice.

"I don't know, an hour, maybe? It depends on how things go."

"Mind if I wait? This is kind of cool."

I could see the internal struggle in his eyes. He usually didn't mind me watching him work and even appreciated my insights, so telling me he didn't want me to stay would be a lie. He turned a shade of red I hadn't seen before. "I'm not sure how long it will take, so maybe we can have dinner some other time?"

"Well, I had some things about the wedding we needed to discuss."

"Then definitely some other time. I mean, when we have time to really work on it."

"So, that'll be when? Like maybe August?"

The sarcasm in my voice must have been pretty scathing because Jake took a couple of steps away from me before saying, "I, um, I'll just go get the bubble wrap so we can test the stealth mode, okay?" He beat a hasty retreat to the supply room.

Owen wrinkled his forehead. "Definitely before August. Aren't we talking about having the wedding in May?"

"Do you know when you might be able to squeeze me in?"

"I don't think I have anything scheduled this week. How about tomorrow?"

"I'll hold you to it. Now, have fun with your spell!" I thought I did a decent flounce on my way out of the office, and I made sure I looked like I was leaving in a huff as I passed the various offices and labs on my way out of the department.

The worst gossip in R&D had turned out to be an enemy mole who was no longer with the company, so I didn't have any absolute guarantees that word of my mild clash with Owen would spread outside the department, but I thought we'd given it a good show. In this case, while there was some element of truth in Owen's workaholic ways, most of the time it didn't bother me that much. We did need to plan our wedding, but normally I'd have happily stayed to watch the spell tests, and we'd have gone to dinner afterward. I supposed all this was a sign that we really were a good couple if we had to work to lay the grounds for a convincing breakup.

I had to remind myself to look unhappy as I made my way out of the building. "Hey, what's wrong, doll?" a voice from the awning over the entrance said. I looked up to see Sam staring down at me in concern.

I wasn't sure whether Merlin had clued him into the scheme, but since we were in public, I had no choice but to play along. "Oh, just a bad day, I guess," I said with a shrug. "Everything conspiring to go wrong, all at once."

"What, they don't properly appreciate you?"

"Doesn't look that way. But I'll live. Tomorrow's sure to be better."

When he didn't repeat the standing joke—that I wasn't entirely sure was a joke—that there was always room for me in Security, I was pretty sure he was in on it. Having a viable option would have ruined the illusion that I had absolutely nowhere else to turn.

"It's bound to look up," he said.

The next day, people in Sales were a little nicer to me, like they were making an effort, and there was even a small bakery box of cookies left on my desk. I tried not to groan out loud when I saw it. If people insisted on being nice to me, it would ruin everything. It's hard to dramatically quit your job in a fit of pique when people leave cookies for you, and these were the good kind, too—from one of those fancy gourmet bakeries. Just having the box in my office made it smell like fresh-baked cookies.

I sat at my desk and picked up the box, looking for some indication of who'd sent it. Was it a peace offering from Owen? An apology from Mr. Hartwell? There was a card tucked in the ribbon that bound the box, and I slipped it out.

The card was identical to the one the mysterious recruiter had given me. Sending gifts was upping the ante, and doing so to my office was particularly bold.

I got up and went out to Perdita's office. "Did you see who brought the cookies that were left on my desk?"

"You got cookies? That explains the smell. I thought maybe someone had a scented candle burning around here."

"You didn't see anyone come in and leave anything?"

"Nope. I think the place already smelled like cookies when I got here." She paused, then gave me a sheepish grin. "I don't suppose you're willing to share."

I handed the box to her. As good as they smelled, I'd suddenly lost my appetite. This might have been what I wanted, but while I knew I was likely being watched, it was unsettling to have proof of just how closely I was being observed. It was also proof that someone in Sales had to be a Collegium agent in order to get in and put something on my desk without anyone noticing anything odd.

No one in Sales gave me any reason to get upset that day, which I thought might help make things more realistic. My first opportunity for real conflict came at the end of the day, when I went to meet Owen for the dinner we'd planned. Or, really, pretended to plan, since I already knew it wasn't going to happen.

As usual, Owen was busy working when I stopped by his lab. "Ready for dinner?" I called out cheerfully.

He looked up at me, blinking. "Dinner?"

"You know, that meal you eat in the evening, after work? You said we'd have dinner today, since we have some things we need to work on for the wedding."

He turned pink, and I hoped that none of the other R&D people who were present could read him as well as I could because it was obvious to me that he was lying. If he tried to play poker, he'd end up living in a cardboard box, even as wealthy as he was. "Did I? Oh, I guess I did. Sorry, I forgot. Can we do it some other time? I've got a working group going on, so I can't just leave."

I glanced at the other people, who all were glancing back and forth between Owen and me. Owen might not have been a good liar, but he'd set things up well in making sure there were witnesses, including the one person in R&D we'd identified as being possibly linked to the Collegium.

That meant I had to play this well. "You forgot?" I said, letting my voice get a little shrill. "Really? You just *forgot* your fiancée? Now I'm worried about the wedding. If you can't remember to schedule time to plan it, are you going to be here tinkering with some spell while I'm wearing a white dress and veil and wondering where the hell you are?"

He flinched and turned redder. "Of course not. But this wasn't a wedding. It was just dinner, and it would be rude to bail on all these other people. If it was just me, I could drop things, but I can't. So how about tomorrow? For real? I'll put it in my calendar right now."

"Okay, tomorrow," I said through gritted teeth. "But I won't hold my breath." I whirled and stalked out of the lab before I could dissolve into giggles. I felt like an actress on a particularly bad soap opera, playing minor conflict as though it was Shakespearean drama.

When I got to work the following morning—late, because I figured it was a way to demonstrate unhappiness at work—Perdita was already at her desk. "Someone sent you flowers," she said. "They smell good, but not as good as the cookies. I wonder who they're from."

"Owen and I had a big fight yesterday, so maybe this is his way of apologizing," I said.

The flowers turned out to be a large bouquet of white roses. I knew there was supposed to be some kind of symbolism in that, but I couldn't remember exactly what. At this time of year, they either had to be imported or from a hothouse, and the scent was pretty strong.

I didn't really believe Owen had sent them because that would go against the act. I had a sinking feeling I already knew what I'd find when I opened the little envelope attached to the bouquet. Yep, another one of those business cards. It was a sign that the plan was working, but it was still kind of creepy to think that some secret organization knew that much about what was going on in my life. I thought this was pretty good proof that I wasn't being recruited to some magical finance company. Why would a bank know what was going on within MSI?

Midafternoon, Perdita called out, "You need to go see the boss."

I came out of my office. "Did they say why?"

"Nope. Trix just said you're wanted."

This was it, the stunning climax of our charade. I kept rubbing my hands on my pants as I went up to Merlin's office because my palms were sweaty. Trix nodded me toward Merlin's door when I arrived, and I made myself walk in as though I owned the place. "You wanted to see me?" I asked.

"Yes," Merlin said, resting his elbows on his desk and steepling his fingers. "I've given some thought to your request to return to your position as my assistant, but I've decided that Kim deserves to return. We've discussed our issues, and I believe that we've resolved them satisfactorily. She's a better fit for the position, and I think you contribute more to the company where you are."

"Seriously?" I blurted. "I only left that job to go on a special assignment for you, then didn't have a job to go back to because Kim had insinuated herself. You fired her, and now you want her back, over me? You know what? I've had offers. I can go where I'm appreciated. You can consider this my resignation."

Without waiting for his response (mostly because I didn't think I could look at him and keep a straight face), I whirled and stomped out, brushing right past Trix's desk. She jumped up and ran after me. "Katie, what's wrong?"

I stopped. "Actually, I think everything's great. I just quit. And it feels *sooo* good." Back at my office, I gathered the few belongings I had in there, grabbed the bouquet of roses, and walked out.

"Katie, where are you going?" Perdita called after me.

I stopped and turned back. "I just quit. You can probably handle my job. All the plans and documents you need are on my computer. Good luck!"

When I made it to the lobby, I was relieved to see that Trix had acted exactly as I expected and called Owen, who was already there, standing between me and the exit. "What are you doing?" he said, doing a decent job of looking alarmed. "You can't just quit!"

"I did."

"But there's paperwork and exit interviews, and that sort of thing."

"Rod knows where to find me." I moved around him to get to the door, and he kept pace.

"I'm sure we can work something out."

"I'm not sure you can. I'm always going to be a second-class citizen around here because I'm not really magical. I'm useful to you in a crisis, and then you forget about me."

He frowned. "Do you mean 'you' in terms of the company or me?"

"Both, I think. I'm certainly not a priority to either of you. And now, if you'll excuse me, I have places to go, people to see."

"Katie, wait!"

I kept walking, ignoring him, and I heard Sam say, "Sorry, kiddo, I don't think you're gonna sway her right now. That's gonna take lots of flowers and chocolate and making it clear what she means to you. Give her time."

I headed to that bar where the mysterious recruiter had approached me before and set my flowers on the table while I had a glass of wine. I thought it would look better if they came to me rather than me calling them. Given the hard sell and the public nature of my departure, I was sure I wouldn't have to wait long.

Except no one came over to me. I sat alone with my wine and my flowers, feeling drained. Even if it had been fake, I'd had to hype myself up to play those scenes, and now I felt the way I might have if they'd been for real. Eventually, the adrenaline wore off, and I was left feeling dejected. I gathered my flowers and headed home.

Nita was at home when I got there. "Ooh, who sent you flowers?" she asked as she pinned her name badge onto her vest and checked in the mirror to make sure it was straight.

"Believe it or not, some company has been recruiting me like crazy."

"Must be nice! Are you going to take them up on it?"

I set the bouquet on my nightstand and sank onto my bed. "Yeah, I think I might, considering I quit my job today."

She whirled to face me. "Really? You just quit your job, like that?" She snapped her fingers.

"Yeah, I did." I grinned. "And it felt really good."

"Please tell me you made a dramatic exit."

"Of course I did."

"I wish I'd been there to see it. I've always wanted to make a dramatic exit."

"You flew to New York without telling your parents you were leaving home."

"That's sneaking away. Sneaking is the exact opposite of dramatic. So, are you calling this other company?"

"Tomorrow," I said. "And, um, maybe we don't have to tell Gemma and Marcia until I have the other job set in stone. Especially Marcia. She'd have a cow if she knew I quit like that." I hadn't yet decided what to tell my other roommates, or how to tell them. It all depended on what happened next.

"Isn't her boyfriend your HR guy? I have a feeling she'll know soon enough."

"I don't think he's allowed to disclose stuff like that," I said. Rod was in on the scheme, since he had to know not to really put through all the severance paperwork, but I thought he was discreet enough not to say anything about it to Marcia.

I quit on a Friday, which meant I had to spend the weekend wondering what would happen while hiding what was happening from my roommates even as I was avoiding Owen. Since the odds were extremely slim that anyone from the Collegium would know what went on in my apartment, we didn't bother with any charades of him calling to talk to me and me refusing to take his calls. At the same time, I couldn't be seen getting together with him. Instead, we spent a lot of time on the phone. I felt like a teenager again, curled up on my bed with the receiver cradled against my ear, chatting with a boy.

By the time Monday rolled around, I was ready to make the next move. I told my roommates I was taking a mental health day, to explain why I let myself sleep a little late and wasn't getting ready for work. When Nita got home and went to bed, I read quietly in the living room, then went out for lunch to increase the chances of being approached.

By midafternoon, I was starting to think that I'd have to break down and call them. I was just about to head downtown to the usual bar when my cell phone rang. I didn't use it often, so I fumbled and nearly dropped it when I pulled it out of my purse. I flipped it open to see the display, and it said "Unknown Number."

Was this it, or was it some telemarketer? If they knew about how my day at work went, then surely they could get my cell number. I hit the "accept" button and said, "Hello?"

"Hello, Katie," the caller said. I thought I recognized the voice of the mysterious recruiter. "I understand you might be in a position to reconsider our offer."

"What gives you that impression?" I said, sitting on the nearest bench. This was it!

"You quit your job."

"Wow, word travels fast."

"We make it our business to know what happens in the magical world. So, are you interested?"

"Well, I might be open to talking."

"That's all we ask of you, to consider what we have to say. Now, since your schedule is open, how does tomorrow sound? Say, ten?"

"As you said, my schedule is open. Where at ten?"

"We'll take care of that. Just be ready and outside your building at ten." The call was disconnected before I could respond. "Okay, here we go," I said to myself.

I went home before calling Owen to let him know, since I didn't want to be seen immediately making a phone call. I thought it was incredibly likely that I was being watched. "I'm meeting with them tomorrow," I said when I reached him at his office.

"Where?"

"That's the thing—I don't know. They just said to be ready at ten."

"I don't like it. We know you can't trust these people. That's the point of all this."

"If they wanted fit me for cement shoes, wouldn't they have just grabbed me instead of sending me cookies and flowers?"

"Maybe it's some sick game they play with their prey. I'll get Sam to keep an eye on you."

"Be careful about it. If they get the slightest hint that MSI is watching me, it'll blow the whole operation, and I'm sure they'll be looking out for that sort of thing."

"There are gargoyles all over the city, and he can make it so they don't see him."

"They use immunes. That's why they're recruiting me," I reminded him.

"I don't like this at all."

"But it's necessary."

"If we don't hear from you by the end of the day, we'll come looking for you."

"I'll be fine," I insisted. I had to be.

The next morning, I went downstairs at the appointed time and stood on the sidewalk. I didn't spot anything out of the ordinary. If either side had any kind of aerial surveillance on me, it was good enough that even I didn't see it. Although I'd told Owen that it was risky because it might give us away, I felt rather uneasy about the idea of just heading off somewhere with these people without anyone knowing exactly where I was.

At precisely ten, a black limo pulled up in front of me. Its windows were so dark that I couldn't tell who—if anyone—was inside. The rear passenger door opened, and the recruiter appeared in the doorway, leaning forward so that her face showed. "Hello, Katie," she said. "Good, you're punctual. Please get in."

It was do-or-die time. With a deep breath, I entered the limousine.

Six

It wasn't the kind of stretch limo rented by kids going to the prom or used by movie stars. It was more of a classy businessperson's ride—a little bigger than a regular luxury sedan, with two rows of seats facing each other. The recruiter was seated with her back to the driver, and she motioned for me to take the forward-facing seat. As soon as I was settled, she tapped on the partition between her and the driver's compartment, and the car moved out into traffic.

At least, I felt motion. I couldn't see what was happening. The windows weren't just tinted. They were blacked-out. Even the partition was opaque. Basically, I was in a more luxurious version of a cargo van, which made me nervous. Was this a high-class kidnapping?

"It's probably a little early for champagne," the recruiter said with a smile. "But how about some coffee?" She studied me for a moment. "Let's see... a cappuccino? No, I've got it, a mocha."

A mug appeared in her hand, and she leaned over to

give it to me. I'd been planning to refuse, but the smell of the coffee and chocolate was enticing, and it was topped by a swirl of whipped cream and chocolate shavings. What mortal could resist?

I froze with the mug halfway to my mouth. Maybe that was the point, to make it irresistible. It was also a little unsettling just how well she knew what would be irresistible to me. She smiled wryly and said, "I suppose I can see why you might be leery. This is all rather odd—picking you up in a limo for a job interview, the blacked-out windows, and then I hand you the perfect drink. But I assure you, we mean you no harm."

"Isn't that what you'd say even if you meant me harm?" I asked. "I mean, you wouldn't say, 'We're planning to drug you and dump your body in the East River,' even if that's what you had planned."

Her smile wasn't all that reassuring. "If we were going to just dump you in the river, this isn't how we'd go about it. We wouldn't waste good chocolate on you if that were the case." The way she said it suggested that this wasn't purely hypothetical.

I supposed she had a point, and I was already in without a net, so I took a sip of the mocha, hoping I wasn't giving myself an embarrassing whipped-cream mustache. It was really good, I had to admit.

The car ran smoothly enough that it was hard to notice anything other than stops, starts, and turns. The sound from outside seemed muffled, as well. I'd thought about trying to mentally track the car's movements so I'd know where we were going, but I soon gave that up as impossible.

"Do you have any questions for me?" the recruiter asked.

"You mean, other than where are we going and why all the secrecy? I guess we could start with what job you're offering me, exactly. You talked about using my magical immunity, but how?"

"Eventually, you'd be something like an aide de camp to one of our rising executives—like a personal assistant, but not doing much administrative work. You wouldn't be typing memos or answering the phones. You'd be his eyes and ears to make sure magic isn't being misused. You might also help with research and in planning."

If it weren't a job with a potentially evil secret society, it actually sounded right up my alley. But there seemed to be a catch. "You said 'eventually,'" I pointed out.

"We don't just throw anyone in the deep end and see if they sink or swim," she replied. "There will be several candidates starting on more minor assignments so we can determine the best fit for the ultimate position."

"So, it's not guaranteed that I'll end up with the job you're offering me?"

"There is some competition for the position, yes," she said. "You'll need to prove yourself."

I'd been reading up on infiltrating the mob, and that made me nervous. What, exactly, would proving myself entail?

She laughed. "But don't worry, you won't be asked to whack anyone."

Had my thoughts been that obvious on my face, or could she read them? I was in big trouble if these people had ESP that worked on me. Then again, would we be going through this exercise if they could read my mind? They'd already know I couldn't be trusted. I concentrated hard on thinking, *I'm trying to infiltrate you to spy on you for MSI*, then waited for a reaction.

Either she didn't pick up on it or she was faking not picking up on it so she could draw me deeper into a trap. "The candidates who aren't selected aren't totally out of luck, though," she said, continuing conversationally. "If you've proved competent and loyal, you may be considered for the next executive who needs a right-hand person, and without having to go through the entire process all over again."

"It sounds like you take the vetting process very seriously."

"We consider ourselves to be hiring for life. This isn't just a job. It's truly a career, and it's better for us and for the employee that we get the best fit possible. We want our people to be in the ideal place for their personalities and talents so they'll be happy, and we believe in promoting from within."

That certainly sounded good. Or you could give it a more sinister spin and consider it just a nicer way of saying that the only way to leave was in a coffin. "What are the opportunities for advancement for someone in my position?" I asked, as though this was a normal job interview.

"You must understand that a nonmagical person has certain limits within our line of work, so I'm afraid to say that you would never reach the executive level on your own. However, if you're attached to the right person, you could rise with him—or her. Someone who proves particularly valuable may be requested by a more senior executive."

It sounded suspiciously like a workplace edition of *Survivor*. Not only were you competing for a job to start with, but you'd always have people below you wanting to move up. I was starting to see why they didn't want Kim. If Gregor had told them anything, then all the assistants to the more senior executives would have known they'd have targets on their backs. If this had been a real interview for a position I was truly interested in, I'd have been tempted to tell them to take me back home. Instead, I smiled and said, "That certainly gives you something to shoot for—and a reason to stay on your toes."

"That it does," she said with a smile.

I'd never paid that much attention to her when she'd approached me earlier, but now that she was sitting across from me in a car where I couldn't look out the window to see anything else, I had no choice but to study her. She was tall, slim, and attractive in an unassuming way. Her very light blond hair didn't have so much as a millimeter of dark roots showing, so either she was naturally blond or she could afford constant touch-ups. She wore a basic black suit that radiated expense—possibly beyond designer to custom-tailored using the best materials. Or else magically conjured. The bright red soles of her shoes that showed when she crossed her legs told me all I needed to know about them. I wondered if my potential paycheck would be in that range, or was she some kind of executive?

After apparently making a loop entirely around Manhattan and then driving crosstown a time or two, we seemed to go down an incline before coming to a stop. The recruiter sat still, making no move to get out or open the door, so I wondered if we were at our destination or stopping for some other reason. A moment later, the door opened, held by a uniformed chauffeur. "After you, Katie," the recruiter said.

I slid over on the seat and attempted to get out without tripping or otherwise doing anything awkward. When I was steady on my feet, I looked around to get my bearings, only to realize I was in a parking garage. There was no signage that I could see, no clue as to what building we might be in.

Sliding doors opened into a lobby, where a security guard waved us to a bank of elevators. There wasn't any signage in the lobby, either. I thought that was odd. It may have been the first office building I'd ever seen that didn't have anything showing the name of the building or its tenants.

The elevator only seemed to go up a few floors—though there were no handy buttons or lights showing which floor we were on—before stopping. "And here we are!" the recruiter said as the door slid aside to reveal a lobby that looked remarkably like the reception area of a posh spa—or what they looked like in the ads in fancy magazines.

There were lots of potted plants, what looked like natural light even though I couldn't see any windows, and comfortable chairs. Soft music played. I almost expected to be handed a plush robe and directed to a changing room. "Now, I'll turn you over to our evaluator, Marta," the recruiter said. She held out a hand for me to shake. "Good luck, and I'm sure you'll fit in great here."

"Thank you," I said, returning the handshake and making sure I gave her a firm grip.

Marta turned out to be a slender brunette with slightly Slavic features. "Hello, Katie," she said with a smile. "Please follow me." She led me from the lobby down a windowless sunlit hallway to a small room and gestured me inside. I'd compared the place to a posh spa, but this room really did look like a treatment room, without the massage table. "You can change in here," she said. "There are gowns in those bins, marked by size, and you can leave your coat and clothes in that wardrobe. You keep the key."

"Wait, what?" I said, sputtering. "I thought I was here for a job interview, not a spa day." I'd dressed very carefully in my best interview suit, and I hated the idea of leaving it behind to meet with a prospective employer while wearing some standard-issue gown.

Her pleasant smile withered somewhat. "We take security very seriously. No personal belongings—and that includes clothing—enter the secured areas. I assure you, your belongings are perfectly safe."

"You're making sure I'm not wearing a wire?"

She nodded. "Or carrying a charm, or anything else like that. Now, I'll be back in a moment. Would you care for something to drink?"

"No thanks, I'm good," I said. When she'd shut the door behind her, I paused for a moment. Did I really want to go through with this? But I didn't have a choice, and I'd made it this far. Fortunately, I had nothing to hide. I slipped out of my coat and hung it in the wardrobe, then sorted through the bins of gowns. They turned out to be nicer than hospital gowns, more like simple wraparound dresses with some sense of style. That made me feel slightly better about leaving my good suit behind. I'd just put my things in the wardrobe and locked the door when Marta returned.

"Good, you're ready," she said, giving me a critical look. She handed me a bottle of Perrier. "You might want this later. Now, come with me."

She brought me to another room that looked like an upscale police interview room—carpeted, with nice furniture and wallpaper, but still with a table, a chair on either side so people would have to sit facing each other, and a mirror that was probably a window. I swallowed an uncomfortable lump that had formed in my throat.

"Please, have a seat," Marta said.

I stood my ground, my arms folded across my chest. "Not until you tell me what's going on here. This is the weirdest interview I've ever experienced."

"It's nothing to be worried about, I assure you. In this phase, we'll be testing your magical immunity and your ability to use it to spot magical deception. Since you've been working for MSI, this should be no problem. It's merely a formality to get you to the next level, but we must go through the process."

Reluctantly, I took a seat, and she ran me through a battery of tests that were similar to things I'd experienced when I'd first joined MSI—seeing past what were apparently illusions to spot hidden words, having magic thrown at me to see how I'd react. After each test, Marta glanced at that mirror, and I wondered who was on the other side of it.

"Very good," Marta said when the battery of tests

was apparently over. "You passed with flying colors, as we expected. We'd heard rumors that you'd lost your immunity at one time and that you'd somehow gained magic, so we wanted to make sure you were truly back to normal."

"Yep, one hundred percent magic-free," I said. "And to be honest, I like it this way. Using magic wasn't really my thing. So, what's next?"

"You'll be meeting with some of the executives seeking assistants, for a personal interview."

I glanced down at the company-issued dress I wore. It wasn't as tacky as a hospital gown or as casual as a spa robe, but it still wasn't quite my idea of job interview attire. It looked more like something you'd wear to a cult indoctrination.

Noticing my dismay, Marta said, "Don't worry, everyone else who interviews here is dressed the same way. We're used to it by now."

"If you don't trust me enough to let me wear my own clothes, why should I trust you?"

"We have a lot more to lose. Let's just say we've been burned before."

"How will you ever know you can trust me?"

"We have our ways. Now, come."

We went back into the hallway and to another room that looked like a TV talk show set without the studio audience or the cameras. Come to think of it, there probably were cameras. They were just hidden, rather than those big studio things.

Two big swivel armchairs sat side by side, turned slightly to face each other. A small table sat between them. "Have a seat," Marta said. "The interviewer will be in soon."

She hadn't said which one was the hot seat, so I chose the chair closest to me. Once I was seated, I noticed that the wall opposite the chairs—where the audience would be if this had been a talk show set—was filled with a large screen. It looked like it could be a television, but I suspected it was yet another viewing screen. At least it wasn't a mirror. It would have been disconcerting to have to watch myself be interviewed.

About a minute later, the door opened, and a woman entered. She wore the same kind of chic black outfit worn by everyone else I'd encountered so far at this place, but she looked a little more down-to-earth than Marta or the recruiter. The woman checked the clipboard she held, then smiled and held her hand out to me. "Hi, Katie."

I stood to shake her hand. "Hi."

"Please, be seated." She perched on the edge of the other chair, resting the clipboard on her knees. "I imagine our hiring process seems a little odd to you."

"Very."

"You've done great so far. My name's Francine, and I'll be going over some basic questions with you." She glanced up at the screen, as though waiting for a signal, then asked, "What business experience do you have?"

I launched into a description of my present—make that, most recent—job, my previous positions at MSI, and then my nonmagical experience, both in New York and back home.

She nodded. "And how are you at dealing with difficult personalities?"

I couldn't help but laugh. "I grew up working in the family business, so that's been my life, and I couldn't even get away from them at the end of the day. And I've found that magical companies have a real tendency to attract people you might politely call 'unique.'"

We went back and forth like that on questions that could have come with any job interview, aside from the occasional mention of magic. It was certainly a more exhaustive interview than I'd had at MSI, where they'd been more concerned with persuading me that magic was real, and that I wasn't being pranked, than they'd been with checking my qualifications. The only qualification that had really mattered to them had been my magical immunity. Here, they'd tested that, but they really did seem to want to know what I knew and how I reacted. I suspected the questions were more about letting them observe me under fire than about getting information.

I felt utterly drained when the barrage finally stopped. Although she held a clipboard, Francine hadn't written a single word, which I thought confirmed my suspicion that there were cameras in the room. She glanced down at her clipboard, started to rise, then sat again. "Just one more question: What does loyalty mean to you?"

I had a feeling this one was the real test. "I've only worked for three places in my life—aside from campus jobs when I was in school," I said. "It takes a lot to get me to leave a company. I only left the family business to come to New York. I left my last two jobs when I didn't feel like my loyalty was appreciated or reciprocated."

"What about personal loyalty?"

"I currently share a room with my childhood best

friend, and my other roommates were my best friends in college. I guess you could say that when I commit to someone or something, I stick with them, unless they give me a reason not to."

"What about the other people in your life? You made friends at MSI, didn't you? And you're engaged to someone you met there."

I rubbed the blank spot on my finger where my engagement ring should have been. "Was engaged, I'm afraid. It didn't work out. I don't know that wizards and magical immunes can really mix like that. Or maybe we were simply on different paths." I shrugged. "I don't know. I just feel like he and all my other friends at MSI really let me down. I did so much for that company, for them, put myself on the line, saved them from so many disasters, and then when things settled down, it was like they didn't need me anymore. It was a real disappointment. When I left, they didn't even seem to care."

"I can assure you that we don't operate that way." She rose again, and this time she made it all the way to her feet. "Now, if you'll come with me."

I bit my tongue before I could complain about being sent to yet another room. This one looked more like a very small living room, with several chairs clustered around a low table. I didn't notice anything that looked like it might be a window to another room. If someone was watching, they hid it well. "In just a moment, the executive you'd be working with will be here to meet you," Francine said before shutting the door and leaving me alone.

I smoothed the skirt of my gown over my knees. If I'd made it this far, I hoped that meant that I'd made it at least into the group that would be competing for the final job. So far, I didn't seem to have learned anything useful other than that they were extremely paranoid.

The door opened, and a man in a business suit entered. He was young—maybe my age, but surely no older than thirty—and really quite good looking. He could have been a model in a Ralph Lauren catalog, with fresh-scrubbed, all-American blond-haired, blue-eyed looks, clear skin, and white teeth. He was definitely not what I imagined as a rising player in the magical mafia. He looked more like a member of the tennis team at an expensive boarding school.

He flashed those perfect white teeth at me. "Hi, Katie, I'm Roger," he said, shaking my hand, then gesturing for me to sit. "I'm having refreshments brought in for us so we can chat. I don't know about you, but I'm starving."

"Um, thanks," I said, feeling suddenly tongue-tied. I seemed to have reverted to my awkward teen years, unable to behave like a normal human being in the presence of a cute boy. I didn't know what was wrong with me. He wasn't my type, and Owen was far better looking to me. I chalked it up to the weirdness of the situation and the fact that I hadn't expected to encounter someone like him.

I forced myself to get a grip and stop acting like I was twelve, then thought that maybe I shouldn't stop it entirely. As far as they knew, I'd just ended an engagement, and here I was, faced with the poster boy for wealth and clean living. Acting a little flustered was to be expected.

The door opened, and a waiter entered with a small cart. He unloaded a coffeepot, cups, plates, and a tray of rolls and fruit before leaving. Roger poured coffee for both of us and gestured for me to help myself with the rolls. I was getting pretty hungry, so I took one.

After he'd sipped his coffee, he said, "I must say, I've been very impressed with what I've seen so far, Katie. I shouldn't be surprised, since we already knew a lot about you before we recruited you, but you've got a level of practical experience we don't often find in a candidate."

"You were watching that interview?"

"Well, yes. We find that we get better responses when a neutral party handles the interview and the executives observe. Then we can choose which candidates to meet face-to-face."

"And that means the candidates also don't see your face until you've decided you're interested."

"See, that's the kind of insight we need," he said, flashing those white teeth at me. Did he gargle with bleach to get them that white? "But, yes, that is a factor. As I'm sure you've been told a dozen times so far today, security is very important to us. It's easier to maintain a level of secrecy when outsiders know as little as possible. But congratulations, you've made it through all the layers, and I must say, there was some competition over you."

"Does this mean I'm hired?" I asked.

"We're at the point where it's down to a mutual decision. You needed to meet me to know if you even want the job, and I needed to meet you to be sure you're a good personality fit. Is there anything you want to know about me?"

"Well, what do you do?" I thought it was a pretty obvious question. Usually, you went into an interview already knowing what a company produced or did.

"I thought they explained your job description."

"Yes, my *job*. But since my job would be supporting your job, what do *you* do?"

"Mostly, I suppose you could say I move money around."

"So, finance?"

"Yes, finance."

"And the company? What does the company do, make, buy, sell, whatever? You haven't even told me the name of the business I'll be working for."

"We mostly deal in financial matters. And we're a consortium that doesn't have a branded identity. Trust me, even if I told you the name, it wouldn't mean anything to you. If we do our jobs properly, no one hears about us."

I smiled. "Now, was that so hard? I know security is important, but you can hardly expect anyone to take a job without knowing that much. I'd learn pretty quickly, anyway, in order to get my job done."

"True, I guess. Funny, but no one ever asks that question."

"Really? I guess they're all dazzled by the spectacle or stunned by the process."

"Most of our recruits haven't yet realized that they're immune to magic, so the testing goes a very different way, and then they're so distracted by learning that magic is real that they don't think much about what we really do."

"That's how it went when I joined MSI, which is why I know the questions to ask now."

"I can promise you one thing: I won't treat you they way they have. I will appreciate and utilize all your talents." He stared me directly in the eye as he spoke, his face a picture of sincerity. If it hadn't been for Owen, there was a good chance I'd have developed a hopeless crush. As it was, there may have been the slightest bit of a flutter somewhere inside me. Purely involuntary, of course.

"That's why I'm here," I said with a smile that I hoped looked as sincere as his gaze.

"Then shall we talk details?" He opened the folder he'd brought in with him and took out a sheet of paper, which he handed to me. "Here's our offer."

When I saw the number on the page under "salary," I could see why people didn't ask many questions. I didn't think I could ethically keep it, since I was here under false pretenses and I didn't want to compromise my true loyalties, but I supposed I would have to use some of the money to look like I was living with that kind of salary.

There were other benefits, including the car and driver to take me to work—probably so that I'd never find out where work actually was—and, oddly enough, a wardrobe. It clicked then that the expensive suits I'd noticed weren't just standard-issue New Yorker black working attire. The regular employees probably had to go through the same ritual of changing clothes and leaving their things behind, only they got tailored suits instead of a generic gown. Meals during working hours were included, as well, since we probably couldn't leave the office for lunch while not knowing where we were, and brown-bagging would mean bringing something personal that couldn't be allowed inside.

Then I noticed that there was company-owned housing for employees who made it past the probationary phase, and although there was nothing saying it was mandatory, it also wasn't presented as an option. In the New York real estate market, that alone would keep people in a job, if quitting meant having to find a new place to live, possibly with very little notice. It was kind of a pity that I had to pretend to be broken up with Owen, since having actual privacy at my place would be really nice.

"It's very generous," I said.

"As you said about your old job, if loyalty is expected, it has to be returned. We believe that if we keep our employees happy, they'll be loyal to us. Now, do you accept?"

Seven

I hesitated, and not just because I was still trying to avoid looking like I was eagerly infiltrating their organization. This wasn't turning out to be at all what I'd expected.

Then again, I hadn't really had a clear picture of what would happen. I guess I thought I'd get in, learn where their secret headquarters was and the identities of a few of the people, maybe smuggle out some documents or take pictures with a tiny camera cleverly disguised as a lipstick tube, possibly plant a hidden camera or listening device, and then quit once we had what we needed to either take them down or defend ourselves.

What I was getting into was going to be a lot more challenging and serious. It would be nearly impossible to smuggle anything in or out, I wouldn't learn their location, and I probably wouldn't get to work with anything sensitive for a while. I'd have to move out of my apartment, which would make it far more difficult to pass information to anyone with MSI, even indirectly. Would it be worth it?

Then again, if it was so tight, this might truly be our one chance to get inside. I just hoped it wasn't a trap. I took a deep breath and said, "I'm in."

Roger's smile was nearly blinding. "Good. I'm glad to have you. Now I'll turn you back over to Marta to work out the specifics."

He left, and soon Marta came into the room. I put down my coffee cup and stood, but she motioned for me to sit. "Don't worry, take your time. We're not going anywhere from here. I just have a little paperwork for you."

I'd been expecting to have to sign my life away, probably in blood, and swear an oath of loyalty, but I just had to sign a copy of the offer Roger had shown me and fill out the IRS paperwork—it seemed that the magical mob didn't want to get taken down like Al Capone. Perhaps they were saving the serious initiation for my first day of work.

Once the paperwork was done, Marta said, "Now I need to get a few measurements for your working attire. Please hold out your arms." I waited for her to get out a measuring tape, magical or otherwise, but she merely waved her hand while murmuring something under her breath. "There," she said with a satisfied nod when she was done. "We'll have new clothes for you tomorrow. Do you prefer slacks or a skirt?"

"I guess for work I like skirts, and the weather isn't going to matter, is it?"

"No. You can wear whatever you want to commute. Some people even wear their pajamas. Your changing room has a shower in it. However, if you're going to do that, we'll need to adjust your pickup time accordingly."

"That'll have to wait until I get the new place. My

roommates would notice that something was odd if I headed to work in my pajamas."

"Okay, I'll take you back to the changing room and then you can go home. We have you scheduled for an eight fifteen pickup in the morning."

She walked me back to the changing room, and I waited for some kind of veiled threat about keeping quiet, but nothing came. I supposed there wasn't much I could tell anyone so far, just that I'd somehow lucked into a job that would provide housing and a driver, but that required me to leave all personal items, including my clothes, in a locker before I went to work.

I changed and touched up my hair before leaving the room. Marta escorted me back to the reception area, where the blond recruiter waited. "Congratulations, and welcome aboard!" she said. "Ready to go?"

"Yeah, I guess. I have to admit, my head's spinning a bit."

"You'll get used to it." We took the elevator down to the basement lobby and got into the waiting limo. "Do you want to go home, or is there somewhere else we can drop you?"

"Home is good," I said.

We took what I was sure was a circuitous route back to my apartment building. When the car stopped, the recruiter made no move to open the door. She gave me a direct stare and said, "Of course, discretion is important. You are not to discuss your work with anyone."

"I have to tell people I have a new job."

"But you don't have to tell them details. You will also need to be very careful about your associates. We keep an eye on our employees."

"I'm pretty good at hiding things from my friends, considering my work has involved magic for about a year now."

Her smile thawed slightly. "Yes, it's like that. You were able to talk about your day at work with your friends without mentioning magic. You obviously know the drill."

She opened the door to let me out, and I stood on the sidewalk, watching the limo leave. What had I gotten myself into?

I wasn't sure how I could report to the people at MSI. After that warning about associates, I couldn't exactly run downtown to tell Merlin everything. I couldn't even go over to Owen's place after telling them that he and I had split up. I suspected I'd have to pass messages through Marcia, who could get them to Rod. And that would require telling Marcia what was going on.

Gemma came home first, but it was after the time I'd usually be home, so she didn't seem to notice that anything was up, and she was out the door a few minutes later with her yoga mat and gym bag. That was a bit of a relief because Marcia would be both more difficult and more important to the plan.

She usually worked pretty late, but she came home while I was making spaghetti sauce. "Mmm, that smells good," she said as she rounded the corner from the living room to the kitchen. "I hope you made enough to share."

"I did. Feel free to join me."

"No dinner out with Owen? Shouldn't you two be planning a wedding?"

"He's working on something."

"He's always working on something." She stretched her shoulders. "Would you mind pouring me a glass of red while I change? Then we can chat."

I had the table set before she returned in sweats, her face freshly scrubbed. "Actually, there's something we need to talk about," I said as I dished spaghetti out onto plates. I let her eat a few bites and drink some wine before I said, "I'm kind of involved in an undercover operation. Well, actually, I'm very involved." I gave her a quick briefing on all that had happened lately.

"Seriously? You're joining the magical mafia?" she asked.

"That's not quite what it seems to be. I mean, no Tommy guns and numbers running. It's just sort of secretive."

"So, more Illuminati than mafia?"

"Maybe. That's why I have to do this, to figure out exactly what they're doing and if we need to worry about it. They did turn Philip into a frog so they could steal his business, so they're definitely not benign."

"And you had to be the one to go undercover?"

"We tried with someone else, but they approached me."

"Are you sure it's not a trap?"

"No," I admitted. "But I've been assured that there's nothing I could tell them about MSI that they don't already know, so I don't know why they'd go out of their way to recruit me for that reason. I could see them trapping me if I'd approached them and they were suspicious of me." I took a long swallow of my own wine, steeling myself for this next part.

"But I'm going to need your help. When I said they were secretive, I was understating the case." I explained the car service to work, having to change clothes before work every day, and eventually having to live in one of their apartments. "It sounds like great perks until you realize that it's all about keeping you from knowing too much about the company, being able to smuggle anything in or out, and keeping you isolated from your old life. But I'm going to need some way to pass info to MSI, and you may be my best bet, since you're already known to be dating Rod. It won't look too fishy if I get together with my friend from college who's also my former roommate, and then if you get together with your boyfriend. I don't know how aware anyone is of whether you're in on the secret."

"Oh, so I'd be your contact! Cool! Yeah, I could do that."

"It'll be easier while I'm still living here, but then I doubt they'll let me see anything even remotely useful at first. Once I move out, we'll have to play it kind of casual— get together occasionally as friends."

"Surely they won't totally isolate you. They won't keep you from knowing where your apartment really is. Or will you have an apartment in the office building?"

I felt queasy as I considered the possibility. "I hope not. It probably is a safe bet that any apartment they give me will be bugged and watched."

"So no fun times with Owen, unless you want an audience, huh?"

I winced. "That's another thing. I have to pretend that I've broken up with him in order to make it look like I have no ties to MSI." When her eyes widened, I hurried to add, "He knows about it. We may come up with ways to meet. I hope."

"How long do you plan to stay there?"

"I don't know. Just long enough to find out what they have planned against MSI."

The problem was, I had no idea how long that was going to take.

I didn't dress up the way I normally would have for a first day of work, but I didn't go downstairs in my pajamas, either. I was a few minutes early, but it was still only about thirty seconds before a dark car pulled up to the curb. I wasn't sure if that meant the car was early or that they were monitoring my movements.

This car was an ordinary sedan rather than a limo—well, ordinary in the sense that it was the normal length. Once I was inside, I saw that it was anything but ordinary. Like the limo, the windows were blacked out. There was a partition between the backseat and the driver's seat, but there didn't seem to be any sliding window in that partition. If there was a way for me to communicate with the driver, I couldn't see it.

Unlike most sedans, there wasn't a bench all the way across for the back seat. There was a single seat and a kind of console. Actually, it looked like a coffee machine. There were even buttons that said "regular," "decaf," and "mocha." I pushed the "mocha" one, and a cup slid into position. Soon, brown liquid poured in from above it, making the car smell like coffee and chocolate. A squirt of whipped cream followed, then a dusting of cocoa powder, and then a light went off, indicating that it was done.

They might be evil, I thought as I took the cup, but I could get used to this.

Buttons on the door's armrest turned out to activate the entertainment system. I could select several local radio channels for news, or there were channels of different kinds of music, like on an airplane. I picked the "current pop hits" channel and settled back to drink my mocha.

The driver opened the door for me when we arrived, and I got the impression that I wouldn't have been able to open it from the inside. That was a little unsettling. A woman in what I now recognized as the Collegium's chic black uniform met me in the lobby. "Katie? Please come with me, and I'll get you settled."

She took me to a different elevator than the one I'd taken previously and inserted a card into a slot. "You'll get your own key card at orientation, and this will be the elevator you'll use," she said. I couldn't tell how high we went in the building—or how low we'd started—but my ears were popping by the time we stopped.

The elevator doors opened to reveal a bank of plain doors with small brass plaques on them. She led me to one, and when I got close, I saw that it had my name engraved on it. "Your palm print will open it," she said. I hadn't remembered giving them my palm print the day before, but I supposed they could have lifted it from any number of things. I wondered why they would have bothered instead of just asking for a print. I pressed my hand against the brass plate the woman indicated, and the door opened with a click.

Inside was a small dressing room. There was a closet on one side and a mirrored door on the other. In the middle was an armchair with a small table. The woman went over to the closet and opened it. "Your work wardrobe is in here. You should have everything you'll need."

She crossed to the mirrored door and opened it. "Here's your bathroom. There's also a shower, with toiletries provided." She shut the door. "You'll come here first thing in the morning and do whatever you need to get ready. Many employees just roll out of bed and into their cars, then get ready here. Adjust your pickup time if you plan to do that. You'll need to remove all your clothing and change before going to work. You can hang up or put away your own clothing here. When you're ready, you'll exit through this door." She pointed to one on the opposite side of the room. "At the end of the day, you'll go through the same procedure in reverse. Remove everything and put it through that slot into a hamper for cleaning. You're welcome to shower or do whatever else you want to do to get ready to go home. You may also bring clothing to store here, if you want to wear something different from what you wore to work. When you're ready to leave, hit this button by the door to signal your driver. It will light up when your car is ready. You may have the driver take you somewhere other than your home. We don't encourage pickups anywhere other than at your home. That will take prior arrangements. Do you have any questions?"

"None that I can think of now."

"Good. I will wait for you outside. Please get changed."

When she was gone, I opened the wardrobe and pulled out a drawer to find underwear and tights, all neatly folded. I took out what I needed and changed, hanging up my own clothes and putting my underwear in an empty drawer before I put on a suit jacket. There were several pairs of shoes in varying heel heights on the floor of the wardrobe. I picked a medium-high pair of heels and put them on, then turned to assess myself in the mirrored bathroom door.

I looked far more adult and sophisticated than I usually felt. It was a wonder what perfectly tailored clothes could do for a person. I touched up my hair, wondering what their policy on hairpins, ponytail holders, and the like was. Or jewelry. Was jewelry allowed?

I freshened my lipstick and put my purse in the wardrobe drawer before opening the exit door to join my guide. I thought I felt a slight tingle as I passed through the doorway, but I wasn't sure if it was magic or just nerves. I knew it had to have been magic when a bell clanged loudly. "What is it?" I asked.

The guide frowned at me. "You've brought something in from the outside. Didn't you remove everything?"

I surveyed myself, then realized I'd left my watch on. I held up my wrist to show her. "Sorry, I forgot."

"We have provided you with a watch, as well."

I returned to the room, removed my watch and put it in my purse, then put on the watch they provided. They really were serious about not bringing anything in, and I suspected they'd be the same way about bringing anything out. The alarm bell didn't ring when I left this time.

Now I had a chance to notice my surroundings. It was like being in the atrium of a large hotel. The ceiling above me was so high that I wasn't entirely sure if it was a ceiling or just the sky. Rows and rows of galleries surrounded the open space, and as I moved closer to the railing, I saw that there were many more levels below us. This side seemed to all be doors into changing rooms. On the other sides, the doors had windows in them, and it looked like they led to office suites.

"You'll be over here," the guide said, and I followed her around the corner and about midway down the next side, where she opened a door into a reception area. "You'll have some paperwork to do."

She left me in a small conference room, seated alone at a round table that had six chairs around it. A few minutes later, a woman who was either a well-preserved forty-five or a mature for her age thirty-five entered. She wore the uniform black suit, and her chestnut hair was slicked into a French twist. "Hello, Katie," she said as she took a seat across from me and set a file folder on the table. "I'm Evelyn, and I'm the office manager of this department. I have a little paperwork for you. You've already done most of it." She opened the file folder and flipped through the pages. "Yes, you just need to read and sign the employee policy and the nondisclosure agreement."

She shoved the pages and a pen at me. This seemed awfully mundane for joining a magical secret society. I'd expected a sacred oath, at the very least. This was just ordinary paperwork. My heart thudded in my chest as I read the nondisclosure agreement, since I knew I'd be violating it. Did it count as a lie if it was for the greater good? At least I knew the document couldn't be enchanted to force me to abide by it, since the enchantment wouldn't work on me. Crossing the fingers of my left hand under the table, I signed my name, then pushed the pages back to Evelyn.

"Excellent," she said with a smile. "Now, let's get you to your office."

She took me to what looked like a sunny little room. I thought for a moment that I might get my bearings on where the building was located within the city, but the view turned out to be of mountains. The window was fake, and I couldn't tell if it was on an interior wall or an exterior wall. "If you want a different view, let me know," Evelyn said. "You've got your computer there, and you'll be issued passwords and your key card at orientation. Now, can I get you anything? Coffee? Doughnut?"

"No, thanks. I'm good."

"Then I'll leave you to get settled. Orientation will start in an hour."

I wasn't sure what settling there was to do, since I wasn't allowed to bring anything into the building. There would be no potted plants or photos of my cat. Not that I had a cat. The only personalization was getting to choose the view outside my window, but then again, that was more than most people got, and the mountain sure beat the air shaft between buildings or the HVAC units on the roof of the lower building next door.

I still didn't know what, exactly, I'd be doing. All the orientation I'd received so far had covered the basics of getting to work. The orientation session was held in a room that looked like a small university lecture hall. About two dozen other people in black suits stared wide-eyed as an instructor rehashed the policies. It turned out that personal jewelry was, indeed, prohibited and could be locked in a safe in the changing room. I supposed it would have been too easy to slip a recording device in that way. Hair accessories could be ordered. After an exhaustive lecture on security and privacy, we lined up to be issued computer log-on information and company cell phones. This was the only item that could be carried in and out of the building. It was a tiny flip phone that fit easily into my pocket for carrying around the office. There were no desk phones, so the cell phones also served for intra-office communication. We were forbidden to give the number to anyone outside the company unless it was authorized for company business. I suspected it had GPS and possibly even surveillance capability and made a mental note to keep it zipped up in my purse when I was at home.

Even after the orientation session, I still wasn't sure what I was supposed to do with myself once I got back to my office. I logged on to my computer and found my internal e-mail, which was empty other than a "welcome" message. They'd told us in orientation that Internet access would only be allowed for business purposes.

I yelped and jumped out of my seat when the phone in my pocket rang. I fished it out and flipped it open. "Hi, this is Katie," I said, trying to sound smooth.

"Hi, Katie, this is Roger," came the deep voice in my ear. "Welcome aboard. I'd like to see you in my office."

"Sure. But you'll have to tell me where that is. I'm still finding my way around."

"Of course. I'd give you a map, but it wouldn't do you much good. This place can't really be mapped, but you're very close to me." If I wasn't mistaken, there was a seductive purr to his voice that gave his words a double meaning. I wondered what the fallout would be for rejecting the advances of a boss in the magical mafia. "Go to your office door."

I followed his directions. "Okay, I'm there."

"Turn right and walk down the hallway."

I barely stopped myself from saying, "Roger that," since his name being Roger would make that weird. I settled for, "Okay, turning right and walking."

"Keep walking." I did, walking and walking for what seemed like forever. Just how long was that hall, anyway? Then I heard an abrupt "Stop!" both in my ear and from nearby. I stopped and turned to look through the doorway of a corner office with a lovely view of London at night. Was it another fake window, or did this building contain portals to other locations? Roger sat grinning behind a desk inside the office.

I closed my phone, disconnecting the call, and entered. "Please, have a seat," Roger said, gesturing across his desk to a leather armchair. I felt like the chair swallowed me whole as I sat. The room had a peaceful sense to it, probably enhanced by the giant terrarium that nearly filled the wall behind the desk. All that greenery was soothing. Roger regarded me with a friendly smile and asked, "How's the first day going?"

"It hasn't really. I've just learned all the procedures for coming to work. I haven't done much else."

"All in good time. First, I thought we could chat. I'd like your input on something."

"Um, yeah, sure, I guess, though I'm not sure what help I'll be, since I'll probably wish I'd left a trail of breadcrumbs so I can find my way out of here."

"Oh, this is something you'll know a lot about. I was wondering, what's your opinion of Rod Gwaltney at MSI?"

Eight

Trying not to sound either too concerned or too calm, I frowned slightly and asked, "What do you want to know about Rod? And why? Are you considering recruiting him?"

Roger leaned back in his chair, the picture of ease. "In a sense, I suppose. He holds a pivotal position, as he influences staffing. MSI is critical to our business interests, as we're the two major players in the magical world and we're recruiting from a similar talent pool. That means he's someone I'd like to talk to. So, what can you tell me about him? I understand you're rather close."

I got the impression that this was one of those loyalty tests I'd expected. Could I win my way deeper into the Collegium without betraying a friend? Swallowing the lump in my throat while trying not to look like I was swallowing a lump in my throat, I said, "Yes, he's a good friend. He was the one who recruited me into MSI and one of the first people I got to know well on the job. He's also dating one of my roommates. What did you want to know about him?"

"Do you think he'd be open to a little, shall we say, inter-corporation cooperation? His predecessor used to work with us, and I'd like to reopen those ties."

"He might be." Were they trying to get Rod on the payroll so he'd hire Collegium plants at MSI? I didn't want to compromise him, but it would really help our operation if Rod became part of it, and it might give me more excuses to talk to him, maybe even from within the office. "I could probably sound him out a bit." I hesitated, worrying my lower lip with my teeth. "But there is some potential awkwardness, since I just broke off an engagement with his best friend. I haven't talked to him since then."

"What do you think would make him more open to cooperation? Money? Prestige?"

"He doesn't seem to be hurting for money, that I can tell. He does just fine with women. I think what he'd like is recognition and maybe the sense that he's making a difference, that what he does matters."

For a split second, Roger's pleasant smile became utterly terrifying, though I couldn't quite tell what had changed in his face to make it so. Maybe it was a predatory glint in his eyes. His lips might have thinned ever so slightly. Whatever it was, it made my blood run cold, and I became acutely aware that I was playing a very dangerous game.

"I think I can work with that," Roger said. "Thank you, Katie. You're already proving yourself to be quite an asset."

"Would you like me to talk to him for you?"

"Oh, no, don't worry about it. I'd rather not have you linked to this."

Of course, I was going to talk to him, as soon as possible, to warn him. It was too bad that I couldn't contact anyone on the outside while I was at work so I could get to him before Roger did. I smiled at Roger. "Okay, but let me know if you need me to put in a good word, or something."

"I'll do that." He opened a folder that lay on his desk and said, "Now, I'd like your magically immune eyes to help me out here."

We spent most of the rest of the day doing rather boring verification work, going over documents to check for embedded spells and veiled clauses—only, unlike my work at MSI, instead of looking for things others had hidden in contracts and other documents, I was apparently making sure that the right things had been hidden. I supposed I could see where having the *wrong* nefarious doublecross could ruin everything. I tried to remember any names of individuals or businesses in the contracts, but there were so many, and I didn't get time to pause and commit them to memory since I was reading along with Roger. The work was just as boring and tedious as it had been in my early days at MSI, though the setting was more pleasant.

I was a little surprised that someone deemed a rising star would be doing this kind of work himself rather than having me work with a secretary. It must be part of evaluating me for the job, I thought. I did catch a few errors, and I had to wonder whether they were accidental or intentionally put there to test me. He certainly came across as more pleased than chagrined when I spotted a problem.

I was even more surprised when he called a stop to the day's work at ten minutes before five. "I believe that's enough for now," he said, interlacing his fingers and stretching his arms out in front of him. "We can get back on this tomorrow. Now, do you need those breadcrumbs to find your way back to your office?"

"Down the hall and keep walking until something looks familiar?"

"That should work. Send up a flare if you get lost."

I didn't really need to go back to my office, since I didn't have anything there, but I thought it would look good to at least check in and see if I had any e-mail. I was skimming through subject lines of company-wide memos when I heard a light rap on my door. I looked up to see Evelyn.

"How did the first day go?" she asked.

"Okay, I guess," I replied.

"I suppose it is hard to judge from just one day. Do you have any questions?"

"Not really."

"Did anyone show you where to get coffee or lunch?"

"It hasn't come up yet."

"There's a break room just behind the room where you did your paperwork, and if you don't have anything scheduled during lunch tomorrow, I'll take you and the other new people down to the cafeteria so you can find your way around."

"Okay, thanks. That'll be great," I said.

"You probably don't need quite as much handholding

as the others, since you came from a magical company. We're having to orient them to magic at the same time as they're learning about us."

"I think that's going to happen no matter where you are when you learn about it," I said. "This place has some unique policies, but MSI was weird in its own way. Here, you can hardly tell magic is involved most of the time. There, they go out of their way to be as magical as possible." Come to think of it, I'd hardly seen any traces of magic here. A nonmagical person could visit these offices without having any idea that there was magic involved, other than the windows whose views didn't make any sense.

Evelyn smiled, and for a moment I had the vague sense that she reminded me of someone. I couldn't quite place it, though. Maybe she just had one of those faces. "I'm sure you'll be a big help to the others, which is another reason I wanted us to all have lunch together tomorrow."

"I'd be glad to help with the Magic 101 briefing," I said, though I did have to wonder if that would be a good idea, considering we were all apparently competing for the same job. My mission would stall out if I wasn't chosen, so should I help the competition? On the other hand, even if I didn't help, there was no guarantee I'd win, and if I'd made friends, maybe I could still get some info.

After I shut down the computer, I joined the flow of black-clad people out of the offices and to the changing rooms. The one with my name on it opened at the touch of my palm. I decided I might as well take advantage of the shower, since having decent hot water and pressure and no roommate waiting for the bathroom was a real luxury. After the shower, I got into my own clothes, hit the button to call for the car, and settled down to wait. As many people as I'd seen, I wondered how they could possibly manage to drive everyone to and from work. Or did everyone get the same treatment? Would that only last until I was fully trusted? Did rank-and-file employees have to ride a bus with blacked-out windows, like a school bus of evil?

The light flashed, and I headed out for the elevator to catch my ride home. I hoped Marcia was home first again because I needed to talk to her about Rod right away. I'd been with Roger all afternoon, and I hadn't seen him do anything to signal anyone else, so there was a chance I might be able to warn Rod before he was approached. I knew that without a warning, Rod would turn them down. Then again, that would make it seem more genuine when he accepted later. They didn't seem to stop at the first no.

Actually, I didn't wait for Marcia to come home. I shoved my office phone into my purse and shoved that under my bed, then shut my bedroom door and went out into the living room to use the apartment phone to call Marcia's cell. "I need to talk to Rod about something," I said. "Why don't you have him come over for dinner?"

"Okay," she said. "Is this about that thing you were talking about yesterday?"

"Yeah."

"I'll take care of it. We'll bring takeout. Are Gemma and Philip there?"

"Gemma left a note that she was out."

It was fortunate that our apartment was at the rear of the building so I couldn't stand at the window, watching for them. I worried that the Collegium would be monitoring me and the comings and goings at my apartment. Or was that inflating my own importance? Did they really care all that much what I did, or did they trust that their security measures were good enough to keep me from doing them any damage? Figuring that this was too important to take any chances, I turned on the TV so that my work phone would be even less likely to pick up any sound from our conversation. While I waited, I wrote down the names and other details I remembered from the documents I'd reviewed that day.

I just about leapt on Marcia and Rod when they arrived, I was so keyed up. "Has anyone approached you with any suspicious-sounding offers?" I asked Rod before he'd quite made it through the doorway.

"I'm doing great, Katie. Thanks for asking," he said, grinning. "And how's your new job going?"

"Since you're able to be that flippant about it, I'm going to assume that no, they haven't approached you."

Looking a little more concerned, he asked, "What's going on?"

"No, don't!" I shouted at Marcia, who'd picked up the TV remote. More softly, I added, "Just in case. They made me take a work phone home with me, and I'm afraid it could be a listening device. It's under my bed, but I'm not taking any chances." To Rod, I said, "The first thing my boss asked me was if I thought you were likely to be open to being recruited. Like we guessed, your predecessor was either Collegium or on their payroll, and they seem to want to make sure to get more of their people hired on. So you'll probably be approached soon."

"This is getting pretty serious, isn't it?" Marcia asked as we gathered around the dining table and Rod unpacked to-go containers.

"It was always serious," I said.

"So, should I turn them down or take them up on it?" Rod asked.

"You should probably turn them down at first. Make them work for it. But then it might help to at least pretend to play along with them. We might learn more."

"And we'd know exactly who in the company was Collegium. I'd have to hire some of them to make it look real, but at least we'd know."

"And maybe it wouldn't set off alarm bells if I stayed in touch with you."

He handed me a plate and the container of rice. "That's our Katie, getting something for us on her first day undercover."

"I'd say it's technically my second day, because just going on the interview counted as intelligence gathering," I said, dishing rice onto my plate.

More soberly, he said, "So it is worthwhile, you think?"

"Well, I'm not going to bring them down tomorrow, but I'm learning a lot."

While we ate, I summed up the work I'd done that day. "They seem to have their hands in a lot of businesses, magical and otherwise. The nonmagical people have no hope against them, since they wouldn't even know that they'd need magical immunes to check contracts. They're able to take over businesses left and right. Of course, I have no proof that this is actually something they've done. I just know that there are magically veiled contract clauses that could be used to do such a thing." I handed Rod the list I'd made. "This is all from memory, the best I could do. Since I can't carry anything in or out, I can't take notes or write it down when it's fresh."

"I'll make sure our verifiers are on high alert," Rod said, folding the list and pocketing it. "But we probably can't warn all these people without the Collegium suspecting you. It might even be a test."

I gulped. "Oh, right, I hadn't thought of that. If everyone mentioned in the documents I reviewed is somehow prepared for them, they might figure out it was me, even more so if they set it up that way. But I hate the idea of anyone getting bilked when we could have stopped it."

"I wonder how often that sort of contract double cross has happened," Marcia mused. "Even if people read contracts, would they memorize them to the point that they'd know there were whole new clauses in there the next time they checked the contract?"

"It's not just the Collegium that does that," Rod said. "That's why we have verifiers to check everything."

"But this is on a huge scale," I said. "They seem to be trying to build a massive conglomeration under their control."

"It does sound a lot like mob tactics," Marcia said. "Only with magic."

"And way more corporate," I said. "This doesn't look like any seedy backroom at a neighborhood social club. If it weren't for all the weird security measures and stuff like not even knowing where the building is, you'd think it was any other major multinational firm. And the people are actually kind of nice."

"Just don't go native on us," Rod said, laughing. "We don't want to have to deprogram you."

"No worries about that. I can already tell that they're up to no good. I just need to get in a little deeper to see what they're really trying, maybe learn more about how the organization works."

"The moment you feel uncomfortable or scared, get out of there."

There was something else I wanted to ask him, but I wasn't quite sure how, so I waited until we were done with dinner and Marcia was putting the leftovers in the refrigerator. "How's Owen doing?" I asked softly. "I know this is rough on him."

"He hasn't exactly said anything, but you know Owen. He doesn't say things. But don't worry about him. He's a big boy. After what you've watched him go through, it wouldn't kill him to see how the shoe feels on the other foot."

"I just want to be sure he knows that nothing I said was for real. It really was about the assignment."

He reached out and pulled me close in a brotherly hug. "You don't have to worry about that one bit. He knows."

The next day, I made sure I had nothing on me from the outside world when I left the changing room, and I made it without setting off any alarms. I found my office with only one slightly wrong turn, and there was a stack of folders waiting for me, with a note from Roger on the top, asking me to go over them and check them against a master document. I took that to mean I'd be working on my own. Perhaps one of my so-far unseen competitors was working one-on-one with him today.

But I didn't mind being left to myself, since that meant I'd have a chance to concentrate on memorizing names and other information. It felt like busy work, but it made the time pass quickly, and before I knew it, there was a light tap on my door. I looked up to see Evelyn. "Ready for lunch?" she asked.

I closed the folder I was working on. "Sure!"

"Come on, and you can meet the others."

First we went to the office next to mine, where an African American woman in maybe her midthirties was studying documents that looked similar to the ones I'd been working on. She looked up and rubbed her temples when we entered her office. "Lunch?" she asked, sounding grateful to be interrupted.

"If you're ready to go," Evelyn replied. "Trish, this is Katie, another one of the newcomers. Katie, Trish."

"Hi," I said, with a little wave.

"Does he have you doing stuff like this?" Trish gestured at the documents on her desk.

"Yeah."

"You know, there's a reason I didn't go to law school, but you've gotta wonder, what else is hiding out there." She shoved her chair back from her desk and stood, twisting to stretch her back. "Enough of that, and I may go nuts."

"It's best to take frequent breaks," I suggested.

We headed to the next office, where a slender blonde who couldn't have been too long out of school sat staring into space. "And this is Rebecca," Evelyn said.

"Bex," the young woman corrected. "Is it lunchtime already?"

"If you're ready."

She jumped out of her seat. "I'm starving. And you must be the other new people who'll probably get the job we're up for."

Trish and I introduced ourselves, and all of us headed for the cafeteria, Evelyn leading the way. "Of course, with most of the employees here having magical powers, a cafeteria is somewhat unnecessary, but we actually make it a policy to use as little magic as possible. That keeps our magical visibility low, and we can save our resources for other things."

The Collegium dining room looked like any corporate cafeteria, just with better food, no cashiers, and everyone dressed more or less the same in perfectly tailored clothes. Once we had our food and had settled at a table, Evelyn said, "So, what do you think of Roger so far?"

"Hard to say," Trish said with a shrug as she speared a lettuce leaf on her fork.

"He's cute," Bex said, smiling.

"I guess, if you fantasize about country clubs," I said, which made Trish smirk. "He hasn't yelled at me yet or forgotten my existence, and when he asked me to come to his office, he didn't make me stand there until he finished something else before dealing with me. That already puts him ahead of most bosses I've had."

"You and me both," Trish said, nodding.

"Why aren't you his assistant already?" Bex asked Evelyn. "You're the office manager, so it seems like you'd have the job."

"I'm not magically immune," Evelyn said. "That keeps me out of the running. I'm a member of one of the lesser families involved in the company, which gives me a job, but doesn't put me on the executive track, I'm afraid."

There were so many questions I wanted to ask about that, but I didn't dare, not yet, so I filed the information away for future reference. As far as I could tell, I wasn't supposed to know for certain that I was working for the Collegium rather than for some corporation.

I'd have thought that since we were all up for the same job and were in a mob-like organization, Trish, Bex, and I would have to guard ourselves from backstabbing by each other, but it didn't feel that way at all. Instead, we bonded over the shared experience of being thrown into this odd situation.

"Not too long ago, I'd never even heard of magic, and here I am now, working for basically the Citibank of magic," Trish said.

"I know!" Bex said. "This isn't at all what I imagined magic would be like. Where are the moving staircases and portraits that talk, and stuff like that?"

"MSI—the last place I worked—was a little more like that," I said.

"We try to keep up with the times here," Evelyn said. "Having magic doesn't mean you have to be stuck in the Middle Ages. The world is passing institutions like MSI by."

"Well, what do you expect when the CEO is more than a thousand years old?" I said, raising an eyebrow and feeling guilty for speaking ill of Merlin.

"Did they have all this security?" Trish asked. "I don't mind getting a fabulous work wardrobe, but I have to say, I've never heard of having to change clothes to go to work, unless you're in an operating room or making computer chips."

"Nothing like that there," I said, "but I wouldn't have been surprised at that place if they'd made us wear wizard's robes with moons and stars all over them."

"Did they sort you into houses?" Bex asked with a giggle.

"I'm kind of surprised they didn't," I said.

"Believe it or not, we do something like that here," Evelyn said. "You're sorted during the interviews and grouped into the divisions where you're most likely to fit, based on the executive running it."

Trish, Bex, and I regarded each other. Trish raised an eyebrow and said, "I don't know what that says about us."

"Maybe it just means that he has good taste," I said.

Later that afternoon, I finished my work and took it to Evelyn, as the memo on top had instructed. She thanked me and asked, "How's it going for you so far?"

"Fine, I guess. I'm sure my workload will change as I get further along."

"Of course! But what you're doing now is very important to the company. It's not just busy work or a test."

I ran into Roger in the hallway on my way back to my office, and he gave me a toothpaste-commercial smile. I thought I might even have seen a little glint off his teeth. "Did you already get through all those documents?" he asked.

"I just dropped them off with Evelyn."

"Outstanding! Then you can head out for the day."

It was nice to get to go home an entire hour early when I finished my work. That was rather unprecedented in my working experience. As soon as I made it home, I wrote down everything I remembered from the documents I'd read that day. I remembered a lot more because I'd had the time to really think about it, but I still felt like my list was incomplete and inaccurate. I just hoped it did some good, even though I doubted they'd given me anything truly critical.

Rod and Marcia came in together right after Gemma left for her spin class. I stopped myself from handing my information to Rod right away when I saw how grim he looked. "It looks like I've joined the club," he said, sitting heavily on the sofa.

Nine

"They approached you?" I asked eagerly. "How?"

"It was like with you—they came up to me when I was at lunch and handed me a card. Only they didn't ask me to apply for a job. The guy made it sound like he was with a recruitment agency and wanted me to give particular consideration to the job candidates he proposed. I told him to send me the résumés and I'd see what I could do, but I couldn't make any promises. He said it would be extremely beneficial for me to do what I could. I talked to the boss about it, and he agreed with you, that I should do it. I hate it, though." He shuddered and pounded his fist on his thigh. "I hate the idea of giving people preference because they belong to some group."

"Isn't that what happens with university alumni, and fraternities, and secret societies at Ivy League universities?" Marcia asked.

"They generally aren't giving kickbacks or threats. And I've tried to avoid that kind of bias when I hire. That's why we're a stronger company now. I've tried recruiting outside the usual areas, and that's given us some fresh perspectives and new customer bases. This is sending us back to the Dark Ages."

"Which is ironic, since they pride themselves on keeping up with the times," I said. I handed him the list of things I remembered. "Here's today's work. Was there anything in what I gave you yesterday?"

"Yeah, actually there was. Several of them were our customers who've recently canceled orders for spell development. Family members for two of the individuals recently went missing. The rest didn't seem to relate to anything we know of."

"It's possible that I didn't remember correctly," I said. "This list should be better, since I had a chance to concentrate more on remembering. Do you know what you're going to do about these things?"

"Right now, we're just watching and waiting."

"Don't wait too long. I have a feeling this is all part of some bigger plan, and we don't want to let them get too much done."

"But you don't know what that plan might be?"

"I've been there two days," I reminded him. "But while I have you, can you take a look at the company phone and make sure it's not enchanted? I need to know how safe it is for me to talk around it."

"I'm not as good at this sort of thing as Owen is, but I'll give it a shot."

I took the phone out of my purse and set it on the coffee table in front of him. He waved his hands over it, his eyes half closed, then shook his head. "I'm not picking up anything. It would be normal for them to be able to tell who you talked to and when, but it's not enchanted to spy on you when you're not using it."

"Whew," I said, sighing audibly. "That does make me feel a little better. They're still crazy paranoid, but at least I don't have Big Brother with me at all times."

It would have been nice, though, if I'd had a way to bug Roger's office. Then again, I couldn't tell that anything was actually happening there. I never saw him meeting with anyone, never noticed anyone coming to or going from his office when I approached it, never saw outsiders in our hallway. We may as well have been in our own isolated little pod rather than a part of a larger organization.

A week or so later, Trish brought that up when we were both getting coffee in the break room. "Have you ever worked in a place that didn't have meetings?" she asked.

"Only in my wildest dreams. Maybe we're just lucky, or else they don't yet trust us with meetings because we're still on probation."

"Yeah, but have you even seen Roger go to a meeting?"

"No, but his office is in another time zone." Possibly literally, since I felt like there was something funny about this building.

"True," she said, nodding. "I guess maybe I'm still not used to the whole magic thing."

My paranoia levels skyrocketed when I got an e-mail soon after returning to my office announcing a meeting in half an hour in the conference room. A moment later, Trish came into my office, glancing over her shoulder like she was making sure she hadn't been followed. "Were they spying on us?" she asked in a whisper. "Because this is just freaky. One minute we're all 'why don't they have meetings?' and the next minute they're announcing a meeting."

"Maybe it's a coincidence?" I ventured.

She wagged her finger at me. "Oh no, don't you try that. I can see on your face that you're just as freaked as I am. I wonder what this meeting is about. The first elimination?"

"Surely they wouldn't do that at a meeting."

"Or they're going to tell us how many companies they've been able to take over with these shady contracts we've been checking."

"If we're lucky, there will be cake."

And there was cake, just not in the way I feared. The "meeting" turned out to be a surprise Valentine's Day party for the staff. I'd entirely forgotten about the holiday—or perhaps had deliberately tried to forget, since I wouldn't be able to be with Owen. We'd never actually been together for Valentine's Day, since I'd been back home last year. It had been easy to forget the holiday because the security measures meant we didn't get the stream of florist deliveries or singing telegrams you'd see at any other company.

Roger made a brief appearance to hand each staff member a pink rose, then left the staff to celebrate. People who wanted to party weren't nagged about needing to get back to work, but those who got some cake and headed back to their offices didn't get a guilt trip about being antisocial. For an evil organization, they could have taught seminars in how to treat employees. I supposed it was easier to get loyalty by using honey rather than dire threats.

But I wasn't here to have the most pleasant working experience of my professional life. I was here to bring down an ancient secret organization, even if it offered prime benefits and cake. I just wasn't sure what else I could be doing right now other than passing on the names that came up in documents I was verifying.

I got my chance to learn more later that day when Roger called me to his office. I was surprised to run into Trish and Bex in the hallway, also on their way. So far, he'd kept the three of us separate when it came to work, like he was judging each of us independently rather than in direct competition. When we reached his office, he was on his feet and heading out the door. "Come on, there's a meeting," he said. He was missing his usual genial smile. I wouldn't say that he looked concerned, but he did look more intent and serious than he usually did. We had to hustle to keep up with him as we moved through the building.

I'd long since given up on figuring out the building's geography, but this trip was even more disorienting than usual. At one point, I felt like I'd gone from the top of a high rise to the bottom in a high-speed elevator, even as we just walked down a hallway. I glanced at the others and saw Trish put out a hand to steady herself against the wall.

Soon after that, we encountered a lot of other people heading in the same direction, converging on the same hallway from multiple angles. Whatever meeting this was, it was a big one.

I realized when we reached the conference room that "big" was something of an understatement. The room was more like an arena. On the floor stood a circular table with five chairs around it. The fifth chair was larger and more luxurious, almost a throne, and it sat facing the fan-shaped theater. There were four tiers of curved tables with executive-style chairs arranged along them and smaller chairs situated behind each of the executive chairs. I estimated there were about twenty executive seats on each tier, and it looked like the chairs were slightly smaller on each level. Behind the tiers with tables was auditorium-style seating for maybe a few hundred spectators.

Much to my surprise, Roger led us to the fourth tier of tables and took his seat, gesturing for the three immunes to sit in the chairs behind him. Assuming that the highest ranks sat at the bottom, I'd have figured him for being much higher. Then again, they'd told me in the interview that he was a rising executive. I supposed he was taking the advice about acting like he was already in the job he wanted seriously.

The room gradually filled, mostly from the top down. The higher-ranking people seemed to be waiting until everyone else was there before they made their appearance, which was another unexpected thing about Roger. I'd have thought he'd have at least wanted to be the last one on his tier to be seated, but he was among the first.

I soon saw why, though. "Keep your eyes open," he instructed us. "Let me know the moment you spot something fishy, whether or not it looks magical." He sat at high alert as the attendees filed in, apparently taking mental notes about everyone. He didn't seem to be particularly anxious, just very observant.

At one point, when the tiers were entirely full and

two of the seats on the floor had been taken, many of the people moved to rise, as though the judge was entering the courtroom. I glanced at Trish and Bex, who both shrugged. Roger was just starting to stand, and I leaned forward and said, "If you think someone important has just come in, they haven't."

He gave me a nod and leaned back in his seat, looking very much at ease. There was a lot of nervous shuffling throughout the room as people gradually realized they'd been hoaxed and made to look foolish. Across the room, a man one level down from us snickered. I could see Roger making note of him, and I had a feeling I wouldn't want to swap places with that guy.

The final two seats at the table on the floor filled—the ones flanking the big chair. The room then went very quiet. It was at least two minutes by my watch before a figure appeared in the doorway behind the big chair. Some of the people in the room stood. Others glanced awkwardly at each other. I whispered to Roger, "There really is someone there this time." He stood, and I figured the rest of us should, too, so I got to my feet. We didn't sit until that man took his seat, and he took his sweet time about it.

It was hard to get a good look at him from my position, and the lighting on him seemed to do more to blur him than illuminate him. There weren't any projection screens to make it easier to see him. I got the impression of a man old enough to have silver hair, of nondescript height and build. If this was the godfather of the magical mafia, I was a bit disappointed. Then again, when it came to magic, physical size and presence had very little to do with power.

When the godfather spoke, his voice rang throughout the room as though it had been amplified, though I didn't see any microphones. His voice was rough and harsh, with an accent that might have been British, by way of something else I couldn't quite place. He talked about the end of the previous year and financial results, the kind of stuff that could have been in any company's annual meeting. There was no sign that this was any kind of ancient magical secret society.

That was, until he got to the part about the previous year's key initiatives. That was an interesting way to phrase the big plan to bring Merlin back so he could be defeated once and for all. In fact, this godfather spoke like he'd learned English from reading business books. It was worse than Merlin had been when I'd first joined MSI and he was still getting adjusted to the modern world. Was this another ancient sorcerer brought back to life? I tried to form a mental image of him strong enough to be able to describe him later, but it was difficult when he was so nondescript.

When he finished summing up the failure, I realized I was on the edge of my seat. Would he actually say what their next plan was? I hardly dared hope it would be that easy.

And it wasn't. Instead of talking about next steps, he turned to the man on his right. "Would you care to explain the failure of this plan?" he asked.

That man gulped so audibly that I heard it. "There were factors outside our control," he said.

Like me, I couldn't help but think. I wondered if anyone in this room knew who I was or the role I'd played.

If they did, was my presence here considered a victory for Roger or a mistake? I supposed that would depend on the outcome, and I hoped it would be seen as a mistake when I brought this organization down. The way they talked about Merlin and Owen made me gnash my teeth.

The right-hand man didn't get much of a chance to explain beyond that before there was a puff of smoke and a flash of light, and then he disappeared. "I expect results," the godfather said. "The one who gets me results will get his seat." He rose from his throne and abruptly left the room.

Everyone scrambled to their feet, but he was gone before he could see who had stood for his departure. I had a feeling everyone else was mostly watching the others to see who might have a weakness. The people on the top tier focused on the tier below, probably trying to figure out who might move up a level when someone on the lowest tier moved into the vacated seat. Roger, however, eyed that empty seat. I had a feeling he wasn't going to bother with the intermediate steps. Either he'd jump straight up, or he'd eliminate the biggest threat on each level ahead of him.

The amount of magic in the air grew strong enough that it made the little hairs on the back of my neck stand at attention. Trish squirmed uncomfortably, and I leaned over to whisper, "It's magic. That's what it feels like."

"Really? I've been feeling this my whole life. I just thought it was someone walking over my grave."

"Yeah, that's the way it feels when strong magic is being used near you." I wasn't sure what they were doing. I didn't see any obvious pranks, like the one before the meeting, and no magical duels were breaking out among the attendees. They just seemed to all be testing each other.

Surprisingly, Roger didn't linger to indulge in the jockeying for position. He pushed his way past the others on his row and headed for the exit. We all had to scramble to keep up with him, he'd left so abruptly. I didn't want to risk him getting too far ahead because I wasn't sure I could find our office again without him.

We went through the maze of corridors, with another one of those elevator moments, before we got back to familiar ground. Roger asked us to come into his office with him. "Katie, you were there when their plan failed," he said when we were seated. "Why do you think it went wrong?"

Here was that loyalty test I'd worried about. I didn't want to give away any MSI secrets or tell him anything that would help. Then again, if anyone was going to get that chair, it would be best for me if it was Roger because that would take me closer to the heart of the organization. Better to give him a big boost than to have to spend years as he gradually moved up.

"Mostly, I think they chose the wrong people. I don't know how much of the plan came from here and how much was Ivor Ramsay, but Phelan Idris was kind of an idiot, and I think Ramsay had an overinflated sense of himself. He miscalculated severely in dealing with Merlin."

Roger gave a slight smile as he rubbed his fingertips together. "So, wrong people. What else?"

"The plan was maybe a bit too complicated? He went through all that song and dance to try to make Idris into a credible threat before he made his move, and that probably hurt his cause."

"How would you take over MSI?"

"If I knew that, I'd be there, running the place, instead of here," I said. I was being sarcastic, but he nodded as though it made total sense to him. And it probably did. That was the way he saw the world.

Roger then asked for our impressions from the meeting. Bex didn't have a lot to say; she seemed pretty shellshocked from the whole affair. Trish commented mildly, "I take it this place is pretty cutthroat—you really have to watch your back. That's what the pranking was about, right?"

"Everyone's looking for any advantage possible," Roger said with a shrug.

"Then maybe the way to set yourself apart is to not stoop to that level. That's a distraction."

"Right, right," he said, nodding.

When it was my turn, I really didn't know what to say. "I don't think your boss cares about that petty stuff. I doubt he noticed who stood when he entered. I think if I were you, I'd focus on what I wanted to achieve rather than worrying about competing with anyone else. There were some powerful people in that room. I don't know enough about them to know who's smart. But I wouldn't stop work on the day-to-day stuff while going after the big prize. If you don't land the big prize, then maybe you can still work your way up gradually."

He grinned, and I got the feeling his plan had just clicked in his head. That made me wonder what he was going to do next.

• • •

The ride home that evening felt longer than normal, but I wasn't sure if that was just perception, if we got stuck in traffic, or if the driver was trying to lose a follower by taking a different route. I stopped in the vestibule of my building to check the mail before going upstairs and was surprised to find a pink envelope addressed to me. There was no return address, and the address was a label printed on a computer. I might have tossed it as a piece of junk mail, but it had a real "Love" stamp on it rather than having been run through a meter, so I tore open the envelope as I climbed the stairs.

It was a Valentine's card with a cartoon dog on the front. I opened the card and had to stop halfway up the stairs to catch my balance because I recognized the schoolboy-perfect handwriting inside. Owen had managed to remember the holiday in spite of the circumstances. I felt bad that I hadn't done anything for him, but I was sure he'd understand.

But the message written inside wasn't a love note. It was a cryptic instruction to visit a bakery at a particular address. I wasn't sure what that meant, but I felt a surge of hope. Just in case, I ran up the stairs, dropped off the rest of the mail, and ran to my room to change into something a little nicer—cute enough not to feel out-of-place in a romantic situation, but not so cute that I'd look like I was going on a date. After touching up my hair and makeup, I ran out and headed for the address on the card.

Along the way, I tried to temper my expectations. It could have just been his way of giving me a gift. I'd find a cupcake there with my name on it, which wouldn't be a bad thing. It would be better than I'd expected when I started the day. Rather than let myself get carried away with romantic fantasies, I focused on being aware of my surroundings, making sure I wasn't being followed.

I reached the bakery and my heart sank when no one was there waiting for me. I approached the counter. "Hi, I was told I needed to come here," I said, realizing as I said it how odd that sounded.

But the guy at the counter didn't seem to think it was weird. "Are you Katie? Yeah, I've got something for you. Just a second." He went to a rack behind the counter and came back with a white box. "There's a card with it. Happy Valentine's Day."

I could smell the chocolate without opening the box. If this was all I got, it wasn't a bad consolation prize. I slid the envelope out from under the ribbon binding the box and found a small card inside. Instead of a romantic message, it gave another address a few blocks away.

That address turned out to belong to a florist, where a bouquet of red roses was waiting for me. The card on the bouquet gave yet another address, one that looked like an apartment number rather than a business. It was a newer building, and it had a doorman. I approached him at his post in the lobby, awkwardly moving the bakery box and the roses into my left arm so I could hand him the card from the roses. "I was told to come here."

He handed me a key and said, "Go right up." He was definitely expecting me. I didn't think he'd hand out keys to random people who showed up.

I went up on the elevator and found the apartment. Inside, there was a dining table set with china and more roses. Classical music played softly on a stereo. I set down the bakery box and roses and slipped off my coat, grinning like an idiot. There were two places set on the table, so this had to be a date.

But where was he? I cleared my throat, in case he was lying in wait to surprise me and didn't realize I was there. I noticed an envelope propped against an ice bucket with a bottle of champagne in it. The note said, "Have a drink while you wait." I got the bottle open and poured a glass, then sat down to wait.

I was starting to get worried that something had gone wrong when I finally heard the door unlock. I had a split second to fear that it might not be who I was expecting before Owen appeared in the doorway, carrying takeout bags. I jumped up and ran to greet him. It had been way too long since I'd seen him, and one sight of him made me realize how much I'd missed him. "This is amazing," I said, hugging him. "I can't believe you pulled this off."

"I wasn't going to miss another Valentine's Day," he said, beaming. "I didn't think you being undercover would count as an excuse."

"I might have let it slide just this one time."

He sighed. "Unfortunately, my plans are going to have to change. Someone seems to be watching me. I don't know if it's because of you or because of my position. I think I shook them, but we can't risk blowing your cover."

That dampened my good mood. "I think you're a target," I said. "You were a big part of foiling their plans before."

"Either way, I don't want them to be able to link you with me now. We'll have to take a rain check on the romantic dinner and get you out of here." He set the takeout bags on the table, and I put on my coat. I reluctantly left the roses where I'd set them, since they were rather unwieldy in case I had to maneuver, but on my way out, I grabbed the cake box. I might be deprived of my date night, but no one was taking my chocolate from me.

I paused to give Owen a good kiss before I left. "Thank you for thinking of all this. You made my day."

"We'll make up for it when all this is over. Now, go."

I had to wait a few minutes for an elevator, which made my walk-up apartment not look so bad. When I stepped out of the elevator in the lobby, I saw a couple of men in dark suits talking to the doorman. The doorman pointed in the general direction of the elevators. I hurried to step back on the elevator before the doors closed all the way and hit the button to take me back to the floor I'd left. I didn't know if the doorman was telling them about Owen or about me, but I didn't want to take any chances of walking right into them.

Owen opened the door just before I banged on it. "They're on their way up," I said. "The doorman seems to have talked."

He grabbed my arm. "This way." As we neared the elevators, he waved his hand, and I felt a surge of magic. I'd thought he was summoning an elevator, but we ran past the elevators and down the hall to the stairs. The sign said "roof access," and, sure enough, Owen headed up rather than down.

"Please tell me you've got a helicopter," I said as I followed him up the stairs. He was on the phone with someone, but I couldn't hear what he said over the sound of my panting.

It wasn't too tall a building by New York standards, only about fifteen stories, and we'd been on the eleventh floor. I was used to climbing stairs, but this was more stairs than I usually managed at one time, especially at a run. We burst out onto the roof, where a biting wind greeted us. I pulled my coat tighter around myself. "Now what?" I asked.

"They should be here soon."

I was afraid to ask who "they" might be. This wasn't the ideal weather for a magic carpet ride. But while we waited, it was my one chance to fill Owen in on what had happened at work. I told him about the meeting. "That may be why you're being watched," I concluded. "The way to move up is to get MSI, and you're key to that."

"It looks like Sylvia was right, then. They are coming after us."

"See, my mission was worthwhile."

Sam landed on the roof before Owen could respond. "He'll be here in a jiffy," he said. "Need me to scope out the ground below?"

"I'm afraid they're in the building," Owen said. He turned to me. "I'd better go back down and be in that apartment. My spell may have slowed down the elevators, but they should be up soon. I'll have to act like it's a surprise for the person in my department who was letting me use her apartment. If you hear any rumors about me dating someone in the company, you'll know that this is what it was about."

"Thank her for helping. I hope she enjoys the dinner and flowers. I'm keeping the cake."

He grinned. "I thought as much. Enjoy it!" He leaned

over to kiss me. "Happy Valentine's Day." And then he was gone.

I watched him slip through the doorway and back into the building, and when I turned around to face Sam again, I thought about chasing after Owen. The biggest gargoyle I'd ever seen had just landed on the roof. "Katie, meet Fred," Sam said. "Fred, Katie. Fred'll get you out of here just fine."

I gulped as I looked at the stony beast the size of a pony. "How?" I managed to ask.

"Just climb on board," Fred said in a voice so deep I felt the roof vibrate under my feet.

Tucking the cake box under my left arm, I grabbed the back of Fred's wing and pulled myself up. It was surprisingly comfortable once I got settled. I suspected that comfort wouldn't last for long when we hit the air, and I wasn't wrong. The wind was cold in my face, and it wasn't long before I could no longer feel my fingers and toes. Fortunately, we weren't far from my place, and Fred dropped me on the roof. He waved a hand to unlock the door to the stairs for me. "There you go!" he boomed.

"Thanks for the lift," I said—or tried to say. My teeth chattered too much for the words to make much sense. I slid off his back and barely caught myself when I landed. I staggered to the door and into the blessed warmth of the stairs, which weren't heated, but which were out of the wind, which made them feel tropical when compared to the rooftop. I was a little more thawed by the time I reached our floor, but I banged on the apartment door rather than trying to work the key.

Marcia opened the door and let me in. "Where have you been, and what happened to you?" she asked.

"Owen attempted to surprise me for Valentine's Day," I said. "Things went awry. Hot cocoa, please, and then I can explain more."

Without arguing, she put a kettle on, and I sank into one of the dining chairs. I opened the cake box to find that the cake had been somewhat smashed, but it was still chocolate, so I was okay with that. I ran a finger along the edge of the box to get the icing that had smeared off. That revived me enough to say, "It was a nice try, but we'll have to be more careful. He's being watched. Or I am. Anyway, I had to make a daring escape. And now I need chocolate."

She set a mug in front of me. "You've got to admit, your Valentine's Day was more exciting than a card and candy."

"A card and candy can be pretty nice, though."

A couple more weeks into my assignment, Roger called me into his office in the morning. "I need you to come with me," he said.

"Okay, sure," I replied. "Where?"

With a smile, he said, "You don't need to worry about that. I'll get you there. Once we're there, I need you to be my eyes and ears. Observe everything."

He led me to an elevator that took us to that basement lobby, where a limo waited. Once we were inside, I said, "I don't know if I'm dressed for the weather outside. My coat's in my changing room."

"Did you think we didn't consider that?" he said,

gesturing to the seat next to me. I looked down and realized that the folded black material beside me was an overcoat.

We rode for some time in the blacked-out car. I was getting used to the sensation of not knowing where I was, but with Roger, going to a meeting during the day, it became unsettling again. I found myself wondering how often this was likely to happen and whether I'd be subject to the same magical screening as when I normally came and went. Would I have a chance to pass on anything or bring anything back?

But first, I supposed, I had to see what this meeting would entail. The car stopped, and both Roger and I put on our coats before getting out. I found myself in lower Manhattan, not too far from MSI. I nearly tripped over my own feet when I saw the name of the company we were visiting. It was the firm on one of my lists that MSI had managed to steer away from the Collegium. Now it looked like the Collegium wasn't going to take their departure lying down.

Ten

"Follow my lead and do as I say," Roger said as we entered the lobby. His friendly smile never faded, but his eyes were cold and hard and his voice had a grim edge to it. He approached the receptionist. "I need to see Mr. Bartles immediately," he said.

"May I ask who you are?" she said, raising the phone to her ear.

"He'll know," Roger said. He stood looming over her while she relayed the message to her boss.

"He'll be right with you," she said, hanging up the phone.

A man I assumed was Mr. Bartles came rushing into the lobby before she even finished speaking. He was pale, and beads of sweat glistened on his forehead. The poor man looked utterly terrified. Although I'd noticed the hint of danger in Roger's eyes, I still found it hard to reconcile this reaction to him with the man I had to admit was probably the best boss I'd ever had. Roger was mostly so very nice. He wasn't at all the image of the leg-breaking thug.

"Roger, I was meaning to call you," Bartles said, wringing his hands. Either he had an unusually high-pitched voice for a man or he was so strained that his voice shot up an octave. He cleared his throat and added in something closer to the tone I expected, "Please, come to my office so we can talk."

Roger followed him without a word, and I went along with them. Roger gestured for me to sit in the guest chair while he remained standing. Bartles headed toward his own desk chair, but hesitated and ended up standing, facing Roger. "I was meaning to call you," he said, his voice straining to a higher pitch again.

"I understand you met with MSI," Roger said sternly.

"Yes, they got in touch with me. We're a valuable customer, so you can't imagine they'd let me go without an effort."

"You could have told them you weren't going to change your mind."

Bartles clenched his hands and glanced around, as though looking for help. "I felt I owed it to them, and they did point out some, er, irregularities in the contract you offered me."

Roger raised an eyebrow. "Irregularities, you say?"

"Well, yes. Their verifier spotted some veiled clauses."

"You let their verifier look at our contract? And then you believed what they said?"

"I, um, well, you see..."

I was utterly terrified that Roger was going to make me look at the contract and swear that it was all aboveboard. I didn't think I could do that, not even to save an undercover operation. At least if things went wrong here, I could flee on foot to MSI. I might lose my purse and house keys and anything else locked in my changing room, but I'd be away.

While I was eyeing the distance to the room's exit, Bartles surprised me by finding his inner fortitude. He stopped stammering, pulled himself up straight, and said, "Yes, I did believe them. They've never lied to me. You had hidden language that would have allowed you to gradually take over my company, and you'd enchanted the document to make it utterly binding—on me, but not on you. You could have broken the contract at any time. That's not how the people I want to do business with behave."

Roger's smile seemed genuine. I thought for a moment that he was going to be reasonable about this, but then he waved his hand, and Bartles disappeared. In his place sat a small frog.

I managed to swallow my scream of shock. I'd seen someone turned from a frog back into a human, but this was my first time to see it go the other way around. Roger bent and very gently scooped the frog up and put him in his pocket, then rifled through the papers on Bartles's desk, found what was apparently the Collegium's contract, waved his hand at it, and a signature appeared on the bottom.

"There, that's settled," he said with a satisfied nod. "Come, Katie, back to the office."

I followed him, wondering the whole time whether I should just jump ship, here and now. I couldn't be a part of this. I didn't know exactly why he'd brought me, whether he'd have made me fake a verification if Bartles had been amenable or if he was testing me, showing me what they did and watching my reaction. Maybe both.

I felt like I had a few seconds in the walk from the building to the car when I might have been able to make a run for it, but I reminded myself that the whole point of this operation was to stop things like this from happening for good. Quitting because I was queasy about being involved with one incident wouldn't help anyone. Besides, if I wanted to quit, it would be far easier, if less dramatic, to simply not show up for work the next day, when I had all my stuff with me. I got into the back of the limo with Roger and the frog.

I didn't know where to look, whether I should make eye contact with Roger or stare into space. Unfortunately, looking out the window wasn't an option. "I imagine that was a little unsettling," Roger said after a few minutes of uncomfortable silence. His voice sounded warm and gentle.

"Yeah," I said, unable to hold back the "no duh" tone in my voice.

"I assure you that it was necessary, and he will be treated humanely. I'll show you."

"What did he do to deserve that?"

"He went against his word. This merely holds him to the terms of our agreement, and I'm sure he'll eventually see it our way."

What could I say to that? Roger might be friendly and pleasant and great to work for, but I was starting to suspect that the man was a sociopath. The rest of the ride felt awkward to me, a sensation that wasn't helped by the constant croaking coming from Roger's pocket.

When we arrived at our building, instead of going straight to our office suite, Roger took me from the entrance lobby to the floor of that atrium our offices opened onto. A garden filled the floor, with plants, trees, and a small stream flowing into a pond. It looked like a frog's dream habitat, and most of the lily pads had frogs sitting on them. Roger removed the frog from his pocket and gently placed it on one of the lily pads.

"It would be cruel to let them out into the wild at this time of year," he said. I bit my tongue to keep myself from telling him that turning people into frogs was already pretty cruel. "They wouldn't be able to hibernate properly, and it takes time for the frog instincts to take over, so they wouldn't even know what to do. We'll release some of them in springtime."

I looked around at all the frogs in the atrium garden. Were these just the people turned into frogs since the first freeze, or whenever it was that frogs would have gone into hibernation? I counted at least twenty. This likely explained where the missing people had gone. Was one of them Sylvia?

Now I knew that what I was doing was worthwhile. I had to bring down the Collegium so I could save these people and keep anyone else from sharing their fate. Not that I'd been very successful so far. In fact, one of these people was here because I'd tried to help. If I hadn't shared that list with MSI, maybe they wouldn't have intervened, and then Mr. Bartles would have only lost his business without the indignity of being turned into a frog.

But it would only drive me crazy if I thought that way. Maybe MSI would have talked to him again, anyway, and now I had proof of what they were up to. I'd have to remind myself of that as I continued this operation.

I couldn't be sure if it had anything to do with what I'd just witnessed, but that same afternoon, Evelyn sent me an e-mail with links to listings for available company apartments for me to look at. Had I won my way into the company by not running screaming from Roger, or was this his way of sucking me further into the company, now that I knew too much?

Much to my relief, they were real apartments with actual addresses, not units in this crazy office building, so I wasn't being completely warehoused away from the rest of the world. All of them were well beyond what I'd normally be able to afford—the kind of dream apartments the young singles lived in on television sitcoms. There was a midtown high-rise flat, a SoHo loft, a cozy West Village studio, and an Upper West Side basement apartment in a brownstone. None of them were close to where I currently lived, so they'd separate me from my friends—which might have been the point.

The West Village apartment was smallest, but it was closer to my current stomping grounds, and I'd always liked that neighborhood. It had almost a small-town feel, with its twisty streets and more human-scaled buildings. I might not feel quite so alone in a smaller place. I replied to Evelyn that I would like to see that one, and she responded with an appointment that afternoon.

For this trip away from the office, I had to go through the usual leaving-work routine of changing clothes, since I'd be going straight home from the apartment. The drive there seemed to take about as long as any other drive home from work, but I couldn't be sure if that meant anything. For all I knew, the office building could have been on Union Square, blocks from my apartment, and we just drove around in circles on the way there.

A woman in the requisite black Collegium uniform met me outside the apartment. I sent the driver on, saying I could make my own way home from there. I couldn't help but breathe a sigh of relief when he agreed without protest. At least they weren't trying to control absolutely every aspect of my life. The apartment was as cute as it had looked on the listing, and it was furnished in a way that was almost exactly my taste. I wasn't sure if they had somehow done that just for me, based on what they'd learned about me, or if it merely went with the apartment, and the apartment was my kind of place.

It was small, with one main room serving as living room, bedroom, and dining room. The sofa folded out into a bed, and the coffee table was at a height that made it work as a low dining table, with ottomans that could be pulled up around it. The bathroom had been updated, so it had modern fixtures, and the kitchen was almost as large as the one in my current apartment. There were French doors and a small balcony overlooking the narrow, tree-lined brick street.

"I'll take it," I said without hesitation. In fact, I was rather worried that I wouldn't want to go back to my old place when this operation was over. Then again, I'd be marrying Owen very soon, and his place was far bigger and much nicer than this. I wasn't sure why I kept forgetting about that—maybe it was just too painful to dwell on it when I was separated from him.

The woman handed me a set of keys. "Here you are, then," she said.

I blinked, startled. "You mean, it's mine, now?"

"Whenever you like. You can take your time moving in, but we'd really like you to be living here full-time starting next week."

When she was gone, I sat on the sofa, trying to get a feel for the place, but then I was too antsy to just sit there. I searched for bugs in the obvious places where they always were on TV—lamps, picture frames, vases of flowers—and looked for anything that might be a camera. Then I realized that if there was surveillance equipment, my search wouldn't look good. But what did they expect me to think, given their paranoid security? Surely anyone in my situation would have checked, whether or not they were undercover operatives.

I walked a few blocks to catch an L train across town to my old place. On my way into the station, I noticed a man walking beside me. We had to part at the turnstiles, but then he matched me almost stride-for-stride on the stairs. I glanced over and did a double take, nearly stumbling, when I recognized Owen. He caught my elbow to steady me and hissed, "Don't act like you know me."

I assumed that meant he was in some kind of magical disguise. Even without a disguise, he was bundled up in a coat with an upturned collar and hat pulled low so I could barely see his face. "Thanks," I said, the way I might have to any stranger who'd helped.

"Don't mention it. Are you okay?" He hadn't yet released my arm, like he was reluctant to let go. Only when we were at the bottom of the stairs did he move slightly aside, but then when the train arrived, he got on the same car. The evening rush crowd pouring into the car gave us an excuse to stand close together, our shoulders touching.

In fact, we were close enough that I could lean slightly and whisper in his ear. "They got Mr. Bartles," I said. "You may have persuaded him to stay, but they went and turned him into a frog and magically forged his signature. They've got an atrium full of frogs."

He looked at me, the alarm evident in his eyes. "You need to get out of there," he whispered.

"I can't, not when I'm finally getting something. They gave me my apartment today, so I must be in. I may start learning more."

"That's what you were doing in the Village? Sam gave me the heads-up that he'd spotted you."

"Oh, so I'm being watched?"

"As much as we can. We've been trying to follow that car on your way to work, but we lose you every time."

"Even the gargoyles can't keep up?"

He shook his head slightly. "No. I think there's some kind of obscuring spell."

"It's too bad you don't have magically immune gargoyles, though I guess that would be impossible."

The train slowed as it neared Union Station. "I'll get off here, since it's more crowded and confusing," he said. "Take care of yourself."

"You, too," I whispered, but he was already gone, melting into the mob shoving their way off the train. As he passed me, he gently patted the small of my back, and I tried to etch the sensation into my memory to get me through the coming days.

• • •

The apartment came furnished with high-end linens and cookware, so there wasn't much I needed to move other than books, clothes, and personal items, but I still brought my pillow with me, along with a suitcase full of clothes and other necessities, when I went to work the next morning. I figured it would be easier to move by limo than by subway or cab. I could stash stuff in my changing room and then have the car take me to the new place after work.

The apartment must have meant that I'd made it to whatever the next step was because when I was called to Roger's office for a meeting, Trish was there, but there was no sign of Bex. Roger, as genial as ever, gave us a warm smile and said, "Congratulations, you've both demonstrated the kind of ability and drive that I'm looking for, so you'll be continuing in consideration for the position as my personal assistant. The assignments in the coming days may be more challenging, but you'll also have more autonomy and more privileges."

I resisted the urge to glance at Trish and see how she was taking this. Since it wasn't safe to talk about such things, I wasn't sure how much she knew about this place now. Had she watched someone be turned into a frog? Was she on board with that sort of thing and eagerly seeking the job? We weren't close, but we had become work friends. I hoped things didn't get more cutthroat from this point on.

I was also worried about Bex. Since she was a magical immune, I doubted that she was down in the frog pond, but what had happened to her? Had she seen the frog thing and decided she was out, or had she not made the cut? Did they let people quit? We never learned anyone's last name, which made it difficult, if not impossible, to have someone look her up for me and make sure she was okay.

As Trish and I left Roger's office, I chanced a sidelong glance at her and caught her doing the same to me. Both of us turned our attention ahead. What did you say in this sort of circumstance? "Well, may the best woman win!" I said, perhaps a bit too cheerfully, when we reached my office.

"Yeah," she said, but not with much enthusiasm. There was a slight crease between her eyes and a tension in the way she held her shoulders, but I couldn't tell if she wasn't keen on wishing me well or if she was ambivalent about moving ahead in the company. I was barely to my desk when she returned to my office. "Look, I know this place is weird, but I think it would be a good idea if we could find each other away from work. If I disappear, look me up, and if you do, I'll do the same. My last name is Douglas, and I live on Eleventh. I'm in the book."

Could I trust her? My gut told me I could. "My last name's Chandler, but the phone at my place—well, my old place—is in Gemma Stewart's name."

She raised an eyebrow. "They're giving you an apartment? I guess you got the job."

"I have roommates who have some ties to MSI. I think they wanted me out of that situation."

"Yeah. Maybe." But she didn't look too convinced.

I soon saw that making it up a step was going to mean a real change. Roger asked me to stay late one night, and after everyone else had left for the evening, he asked me to go to the archives to find a particular ledger that had been lost. "I think it might have been hidden under a spell," he said. "You should be able to see it, if that's the case." I got the impression that he didn't want anyone else to see what he had me looking for, and thus the nighttime work.

He sent me off on my own, with directions and an access card. It was my first time to go anywhere other than between the changing room and the office or the office and the cafeteria without an escort. I was beginning to suspect that this building didn't entirely exist in any one place but maybe was a mix of buildings in far-flung locations connected by portals. There were a lot of tall buildings in Manhattan, but none this tall and this big devoted solely to one company. That's the kind of thing people would notice. They might or might not notice gargoyles that weren't always where they were supposed to be or people with fairy wings, but they'd notice a giant building.

I found myself living that moment in the *Beauty and the Beast* film when the Beast gives Belle the giant library when I stepped into the archives. It was yet another space that shouldn't have fit into any building I knew of in the city. The rows of shelves went up nearly as high as the atrium, with winding ramps connecting the levels.

Unfortunately, these weren't fun books. They were records. I could probably have found evidence for all the Collegium's bad deeds in this room, but I reminded myself that I wasn't trying to find evidence to take them to court. I was trying to find out what they planned next. That meant I had to figure out what Roger wanted, why, and what he planned to do with the information.

He'd given me a general area where I was likely to find what he needed, which was good because otherwise I'd never be able to leave the archive. I was on the lowest level, where I thought I saw a couple of stone tablets carved with runes. As I climbed the ramp, I saw a shelf of cubbyholes, each filled with a scroll. On the next level I passed were giant leather-bound books. I climbed higher and higher, pausing every so often so I didn't get dizzy, and at each level the books looked newer.

I was looking for the turn of the century—that is, the nineteenth century to twentieth century. These books were mass-produced ledgers and ordinary-looking cloth-bound books. Roger had narrowed it down to a single floor, but there were still a lot of books to look at.

I glanced at the note he'd given me. The book was supposed to be marked with a series of letters and numbers. I scanned the spines and saw that the books were in order. If the book was missing, it likely wasn't where it should have been, but I thought it wise to check there first. A magically veiled book could be in the right place and still be missing.

I stood with my hands on my hips and surveyed the shelves around me. It might have helped if I had any idea of who had hidden the book, and why. Was it merely misplaced, or was it actually veiled? If it was veiled, then that was meant to hide it from most people, but surely if it was still in the archives, they'd have wanted someone to find it eventually. Otherwise, wouldn't it have been destroyed?

I thought about how I would hide something like that and tried reversing the numbers on the label. I didn't find anything in that location. I stared at the call numbers awhile longer, then had an idea. If I correlated each letter to a number, and each number to a letter, then reversed the letter and number sections to make it look like the other call numbers, then...

Wishing I'd brought a pencil with me, I did the decoding in my head, trying to keep it straight, and went to the right spot on the shelf. And there it was!

Since I was all alone, I let myself punch the air and whoop in triumph. The code was blindingly simple, when you thought about it, but combined with magical veiling that would keep any wizard from being able to read the proper label, it must have served its purpose.

I reached for the book, and sparks flew, making me jump backward with a squeak of shock. The sparks hadn't hurt me, but there must have been a protection spell that would have kept anyone susceptible to magic from being able to touch it. I tried again, forcing myself to ignore the sparks. "Just what about you is so secret?" I mused, using the kind of tone I might employ to calm a distressed animal. Then I realized I was actually petting the book.

Whether the spell had dissipated once I took the book off the shelf or whether the soothing really had worked, the book stopped spewing sparks. I knew I should probably take the book straight to Roger, but he hadn't said not to look at it, so I opened the front cover. It gave off one last spark, then settled down with something that was almost a sigh.

I couldn't tell that there was anything special about it. It just looked like an accounting ledger to me, with columns of names and numbers. Why would anyone go to great lengths to hide this? I supposed perhaps that this could have been someone's second set of books, or maybe this was a list of people the Collegium was leaning on for kickbacks. Make that had leaned on, since this had all happened about a hundred years ago.

I flipped the page, and on this one, it wasn't just names and numbers, but rather a whole page of writing. The handwriting was difficult to read, but it looked like a list of events, with paragraphs of explanations. I couldn't tell if it was a plan for future activity or a record of past activity.

Before I could get too far into it, I heard footsteps approaching. Hastily, I slammed the book shut and gave a satisfied nod. "Yep, that's the one I was looking for." I smiled as I passed the approaching person and walked like I was a woman on a mission. I had to resist the urge to look back to see where the woman went. What was someone else doing here at this time?

I was itching to read more of the book, but I could hardly do that while I walked through the hallways, and there was no way I'd get away with taking it to my office first before handing it over to Roger. I still couldn't figure out what he wanted with a hundred-year-old record book, why finding it was a secret mission, or why this book had been magically hidden.

Reluctantly, I brought it straight to Roger's office. "Here you go!" I said. "I think this is the one you were looking for."

He looked up at me, and his eyebrows rose. "Already?"

"It was in a pretty logical place, once I cracked the code."

His smile looked hungry. If he'd been in a cartoon, drool would have trickled from his lips. "You don't realize how long I've wanted to find this book," he said, his voice husky. If he'd sounded like that when talking to me, I'd have said he was trying to seduce me. As it was, I thought I should probably give him and the book some alone time. He shook himself out of his lustful daze and said, "I'm impressed. I should have sent you in earlier. You have no idea what this means to me."

"Well, here you go," I said, stepping forward to hand the book to him.

He reached out for it, and the moment his fingers came in contact with it, a burst of light blew him backward, tipping over his chair. I didn't feel anything, even though the explosion happened right in my face.

I immediately dropped the book on the desk and rushed to check on Roger. He'd been thrown out of his chair onto the floor. There was a trickle of blood on his forehead, and he wasn't moving. I guessed that he'd hit his head on the corner of the filing cabinet behind his desk.

At this time of night, I wasn't sure if there would be emergency personnel on hand, and since he was doing this at night without wanting anyone to know what we were up to, I figured he wouldn't want me to call for help. But what if he really had been badly hurt?

I knelt beside him and gently shook his shoulder. "Roger? Roger?" I asked.

Much to my relief, his eyelashes fluttered, and soon he groaned. "What happened?" he mumbled.

"That book seems to have some kind of 'keep out'

spell on it," I explained, "it created a blast that knocked you backward when you touched it, and then it looks like you hit your head. Do you have medics we could call?"

He sat up straight, then had to squeeze his eyes shut for a second. "No, I'll be fine. Don't call anyone." He gave me a shaky grin. "It looks like you'll have to handle this book for me."

"It must be really valuable if it's that well-protected," I said. "Though that kind of security does kind of render it useless."

"Unless you've got the right people on board. It belonged to the last person to rise unnaturally rapidly in the company, and no one knew quite how he brought in that kind of money. I'm hoping it will reveal some of his secrets. But perhaps we'd better tackle that in the morning."

Sure enough, I'd barely made it to the office the next day before he called for me. When I reached his office, he reminded me of a child on Christmas morning whose parents slept late. He was so antsy with anticipation that he could barely stand still. "Come in. Please, sit down," he said eagerly, gesturing for me to take his chair at his desk.

I sat down and pulled the book toward me. "So, what do you want me to read? The whole thing?"

"Let's start at the beginning and see what's there."

He leaned over my shoulder so he could read as I turned pages. While he read silently, I skimmed the page. My eyes caught on the name "Meredith," which was Sylvia's family. The page detailed what her great-grandfather had done to Philip Vandermeer—on the orders of this book's author—to secure funding for other operations.

"Yes, that should do nicely to start," Roger said. "Vandermeer was released, but now I can get that company for myself."

I tried not to gulp audibly. I had to warn Philip. But how?

Eleven

My mind raced, desperately trying to come up with a way to get out of there. Maybe I could fake a case of food poisoning, or a sudden-onset migraine so bad that I had to go home and lie down immediately.

Then again, there was no reason Roger had to act right away. Surely he'd read the rest of the book and put together an overall plan that fit the current situation. He wasn't crazy enough to run off and carry out step one before he made the rest of the plan. I leaned over the book. "Ready for me to turn to the next page?" I asked, my fingers touching the corner.

Much to my relief, he had me keep going. There were spells on the next page that he read over my shoulder. I was somewhat familiar with spells from my own brief experience with magic and from spending so much time with Owen, but I still wasn't totally sure how the first one must work. It had something to do with transportation. The second involved a spell done on an object to make it a beacon. It didn't look all that exciting to me, but after he read it, Roger's eyes sparkled with excitement.

"Thank you. That will be all for now," he said. "Leave the book on my desk open to this page." I did as he asked and returned to my office. Maybe this was my chance to warn Philip, but I still couldn't think of a way. Any phone calls out would be monitored, assuming they went through. I only had e-mail access to other people within the company, so that wouldn't work. A couple of hours later, I was just about to resort to that sudden-onset migraine plan, figuring I'd been at work long enough to make it seem plausible, when Roger appeared in my doorway. "I need you to come with me," he said, a manic gleam in his eye that had me really worried. What was he up to?

I barely managed not to groan out loud. It was too late to escape. All I could do was hope that it was some other errand we were on that had nothing to do with Philip.

I had to hurry to keep up with Roger as we left the office. He called for a car while we made our way down to the lobby, and a limo waited for us. For me, the ride was intensely uncomfortable. Did he know I knew Philip? Probably, given that they seemed to have researched me thoroughly. But why was he making me come along? I didn't think my presence would make any difference in the outcome. Was this one of those loyalty tests, to see how I'd act when one of my friends was the foe? I reminded myself that this excursion might not have been related to what we'd just read in the book, but I had a hard time believing it.

By the time the car stopped, my stomach was churning, and I was afraid I'd throw up. If I looked nearly as green as I felt, Roger would have been sure to keep his shoes out of range. Then again, they were probably company shoes, and he didn't care what happened to them because his own Italian loafers were in his changing room, assuming executives had to go through the same security procedures as we did.

My heart sank when we got out of the car and I saw that we were, in fact, at Philip's business. I'd visited this building before, when I was helping Philip find out what had happened to his family company. It hadn't changed much since it had returned to its original ownership. It still looked and even smelled like old money, with heavy antique furnishings, paneled walls, and thick carpets.

Roger approached the lobby receptionist with a smile that would have looked genuine even to me if I hadn't known what lay behind it. "Hi, I'm here to see Mr. Vandermeer," he said.

"Do you have an appointment?" the receptionist asked.

His smile remained friendly, even as his eyes hardened slightly. "Yes." I felt the tingle of his magic being used.

"Sorry, that doesn't work on me," she said, raising an eyebrow, and I had to bite my lip to keep myself from grinning. I was impressed that Philip had thought to hire a magical immune.

Roger's expression returned to nonthreatening blandness. "Oh, sorry, but I thought it was worth a try, it really is urgent. You see, Katie here is the one who needs to see him. She's a good friend. Tell her, Katie."

Now I knew why he'd brought me. My name would

get us past the guardian at the gate. I wanted to refuse to play along, but did I really have a choice? Not if I wanted to get to the bottom of this. "Yes, tell Philip it's his friend, Kathleen Chandler." I never used my full name, so I hoped Philip would get the clue.

The receptionist pushed some buttons, then said into her headset, "I have a Kathleen Chandler and an associate here to see Mr. Vandermeer. She says she's a friend." There was a long pause, then the receptionist gave me a smile. "You can go on up. You know where his office is?"

"Yes," I said. "Thank you!"

My sense of dread grew as we went up in the elevator. Philip knew about my mission, knew who I was working for, so he should know that if I was there on a weekday, it had something to do with the Collegium. I didn't habitually visit him at work. Everything about this visit should have come across as weird.

I braced myself when the elevator stopped and the doors opened, ready for whatever defense mechanisms Philip had in place. But all I saw was the executive lobby, with furnishings even fancier than in the main lobby below. Maybe Philip was trying not to blow my cover, I thought as I stepped out onto the plush carpeting. If he acted like he knew me visiting was a problem, that would reveal that he knew something.

Philip came out of his office to greet us even before the receptionist could say anything. I thought there was a wariness in his eyes, so I was pretty sure he knew something had to be up. "Katie, it's good to see you," he said. "Though it is a surprise. Was there something you needed?"

"I'm afraid I used her name to get through the door," Roger said, all smooth geniality as he reached out a hand for Philip to shake. "I'm Roger. I work with Katie, and I really wanted a meeting with you. Can we talk?"

Philip glanced at me, and I wasn't sure how to signal him. The entire situation was very "run, while you still can," but if I did anything to indicate that, I'd give myself away. I wished I knew Morse code, so I could have blinked a message.

It didn't matter much, anyway, as Roger didn't even wait for an answer. He just barged into Philip's office and took a seat in one of the guest chairs in front of Philip's massive desk. That left Philip and me facing each other in the doorway. "Be careful," I mouthed silently, and Philip nodded before turning to head to his desk. I followed and perched uneasily on the edge of the other guest chair.

"What can I do for you, Roger?" Philip asked once he was seated.

Still being so friendly that you'd never guess that he was basically the devil, Roger said, "I'm sure you've got your hands full getting back in the swing of things after being away for so long, not only getting used to an entirely new era, but also getting caught up with the business. The world's changed a lot in the past century."

"It has, indeed," Philip said.

"Well, I'd like to offer my help to you, in exchange for some help I could use from you."

"What sort of help?"

"I know that when the interim leadership of your company got ousted, you probably lost a lot of business because the Meredith family had certain...connections."

"Yes, I noticed. Though most of the business we lost wasn't actually all that profitable for the company. The connections, as you put it, were more of a liability than an asset."

Roger's pleasant mask faded ever so slightly. "I think you'll find that there were other benefits related to those connections. We can call them intangibles. The company might not have remained in operation without those particular benefits. Now, I can bring a lot of business your way, as well as provide you with those intangible benefits, in exchange for a line of credit. You see, I'm going to require some funding to carry out certain plans. Those plans could benefit both of us in a big way."

"We do offer lines of credit to certain qualified clients," Philip said evenly. "Usually, though, we require those clients to have accounts with us. If you'd care to open an account and fill out an application, we'll see what we can do about a line of credit. What sort of business are you in?"

I found it very hard to keep a straight face. I never would have guessed that Philip had it in him to be this cool. What really surprised me was that Roger laughed. "Oh, come on," he said. "Can we stop playing around? I know you know exactly who I represent and what I can—and will—do. Do you really want to go through that again? Now, do you want to work with me here, or what?"

"The passage of time—much of it spent on a lily pad—has not changed my stance toward your organization," Philip said. "My answer remains the same. I will not do business with you. I will not give you money. Now, good day."

Roger rose, braced his hands on the edge of Philip's desk, and leaned forward. The effect was somewhat ruined by the fact that the desk was so huge, he could only loom from a few feet away, which probably wasn't quite as intimidating as he'd hoped. "How well do you know the people working under you? Because if something should happen to you, your business is mine, anyway."

I winced, waiting for the inevitable frog spell, but instead, Roger just whirled and stalked out of the room. I jumped up and hurried to follow him. The atmosphere in the car on the way back to the office was tense. Since I'd already watched him turn someone into a frog, I didn't think I could play dumb with him. But then I didn't think any normal person would dare ask him questions while he looked that angry. Or would a normal person question his threats to a friend?

Really, a normal person would have fled after the first frogging. Or possibly even after the "our security is so tight, you'll have to take off your underwear and put on our company-supplied undies to enter the office" routine. The red flags had been flapping furiously in the gale-force winds from the initial interview. The hypothetical "normal" person would be long-gone by now, so it did no good to gauge my actions by that yardstick.

Back at the office, we spent another couple of hours with me turning pages and Roger reading over my shoulder. I didn't think the book's plan for world domination was all that groundbreaking. It just made sense to get funding, hire staff loyal to you, then infiltrate the key magical organizations. There were some more spells in the mix, and while I thought I could remember the gist of the plan, there was no way I could memorize the details of spells to share with Owen. I did get the impression that Rod would need to be extra careful about the people Roger made him hire. It sounded like these new hires would be personally loyal to Roger rather than ordinary Collegium plants.

I felt like I'd done a day's hard labor by the time I left the office. The car ride home seemed to take longer than ever, but I wasn't sure if that was merely perception or if it had something to do with traffic, or if perhaps they weren't taking me home, after all. I was greatly relieved to step out of the car and find myself in front of my new apartment.

As I juggled bags to open the front door, I noticed something stuck in the door frame—a small slip of paper. Curious, I pulled it out and held it in my hand with my keys as I carried everything upstairs to my apartment. There was another door to unlock there, and finally, I was home. I let the bags drop so I could read the note. In Owen's handwriting, it said, "I could really do with a bookstore browse."

Since it was still early in the evening and Owen never got away from work on time, I took the time to hang up the clothes I'd brought over and put out some of my personal items. It was starting to look like my home rather than impersonal corporate housing. That done, I spiffed myself up a bit, put on my coat, and headed across town to the Strand, hoping that was the bookstore Owen meant. All those dense rows of bookshelves were tailor-made for secret meetings and the chance to talk without being observed.

Once in the store, I browsed my way casually toward a

more remote corner and waited for something to happen. I'd pulled a big book full of colorful pictures of gardens off the shelf and was flipping through it when I heard a soft voice from the other side of the shelf say, "Good, you got my note."

I peered through the gap on the shelf the book I held had occupied and saw Owen looking back at me. "And I'm glad I picked the right store."

"Where else would I have gone?"

"Exactly. You would not believe what happened today." I filled him in on everything, from the book to the visit to Philip's office. "Maybe you could put a security detail on him, or something," I concluded.

"Wouldn't that give it all away?"

"Roger already threatened him. Wouldn't security be appropriate?"

"Good point, though I suspect he'll have thought of the same thing himself."

"And Rod should know that anyone Roger wants him to hire isn't just Collegium—or may not even be Collegium at all—but rather is personally loyal to Roger. There's no telling what he'll do if he sees this as his chance to leapfrog ahead. Pun very much intended."

I couldn't see his whole face through the gap between books, but the part I saw looked worried. "I think you've done what you set out to do. We should get you out of there."

"But I'm just starting to get to the good stuff!" I protested. "All that time, going through the motions, and now I'm in. I'm seeing his plans firsthand. This is where the assignment really gets going. We'd lose everything if

I left now." I knew that was exactly what he'd said I'd say, but it was true.

He was silent for a long moment. I was about to say something when he put back the book that fit in the gap he was speaking through and pulled out another one. Now I could see even less of him. "Oh, excuse me," he said, moving up against the shelves as someone passed behind him. That made me look around to see if anyone was on my aisle. No one was, but I put back the book I was flipping through and took one opposite the gap Owen had just opened.

"We've got to stop meeting like this," I quipped.

He didn't smile. "That's what I was just saying."

I dropped my voice to what I hoped was a sexy purr. "You've got to admit, these clandestine trysts are kind of romantic." I reached my hand across the tops of the books on the shelf below the one we were speaking through. After a moment, he noticed what I was doing and put his own hand across to take mine. It seemed like it had been forever since we'd touched. I felt like the soundtrack should be swelling with sad, romantic music as we made a desperate connection across the barrier that divided us. Then I remembered the Elf Lord's scheme that had put us in the middle of a romantic movie and made myself forget the mental image. We didn't need to go through that again. Funny, though, we always seemed to end up having these moments in bookstores.

"You're crazy, you know that?" he said, but I could hear the smile in his voice.

"I thought that was my line about you. You're usually

the one taking crazy risks. At least I'm not making myself be bait."

"Be careful, and the moment you feel like you're in any danger or that they've figured you out, get out."

"I will," I assured him. He gave my hand one last squeeze, so tight my knuckles popped, before slowly releasing it. Finally, only our fingertips were touching, then he was gone. The book reappeared in its slot, and I was left alone on my side of the shelves.

With a sigh I didn't even bother trying to conceal, I put the book I held back on the shelf. To cover for the time I'd spent browsing in that section, I bought a book of fashion photography. I hoped it might give me wedding dress ideas without looking like I was doing anything to plan a wedding.

The new apartment felt rather empty when I went home. I was so used to having roommates that it was odd having no one at all around. I had to wonder just how alone I was. Was the place bugged or under surveillance? As paranoid as they were about security procedures at the office, surely they'd do something to watch people away from work, or did they think that the office security covered it all?

Roger called me to his office as soon as I arrived the next morning. He was standing slightly away from his desk, and he gestured toward the book that still sat where we'd left it. "Would you mind taking this and transcribing it for me?" he asked. "I'd like to use my desk again, and I'd like to be able to read the information at my leisure without needing someone to turn the pages."

"No problem," I said, picking up the book, which let off a couple of sparks that made Roger jump backward.

"I know it'll be tedious, so I don't expect it overnight, but if you could get sections to me as you do them, that would be great. Oh, and it's probably best if you do it by hand and not on the company's computer system."

I tried to keep my smile firmly in place. "Okay, but I'm not making any promises about my handwriting."

It was frustrating knowing that I'd be making a copy of this book and had no way to smuggle any of it out. Did the scanners detect something as minor as paper? Couldn't you make a grocery list at work and take it home?

On the other hand, I thought, as I started work deciphering the difficult handwriting, the very act of writing it down would mean I remembered more of it. I was mostly worried about those spells and what they might do. That's where I needed to get them precisely. Change one little squiggle in a magical formula and something else entirely was bound to happen.

Trying to memorize as I wrote helped me remain conscious during the boring work. As I'd thought the day before when Roger was skimming the book, the plans didn't seem all that earthshattering. There was nothing in here that needed to have been hidden away and magically protected. I suspected that the spells were the key.

I studied the first one carefully, committing it to memory like I'd have to recite it in front of the class. There were only a couple of symbols involved, and I pulled my watch aside to copy them onto my wrist, where the band would hide them. I was pretty sure I'd left the office with ink stains on my fingers before, so I hoped I could get away with it.

By the end of the day, I'd written out ten pages and my fingers were starting to cramp. I took those pages to Roger. "Here's the first day's work," I said. "If you don't mind, I'll take a break now. I'm worried that I'm getting sloppy as I get tired."

He flipped through the pages and said, without looking up, "Sure. These are great. Thanks."

"I'll get back on it tomorrow."

"Mmm hmm."

I had a feeling I could have added, "And I'll use glitter ink tomorrow," and he wouldn't have noticed, so I slipped away.

In the changing room, I was careful when I removed the company watch and put on my own, then I held my breath as I left the room, terrified that alarms would start blaring, letting everyone know I was walking away with valuable information. But nothing happened. I didn't even have to use my prepared excuse that I was planning to get a tattoo and those symbols looked cool.

As soon as I was home, I checked my traps and found that either no one had entered or they'd done a great job of not disturbing anything. Feeling a little more secure, I sat down to write out the spell that I'd memorized and copied the symbols from my wrist. Now I had to find a way to get it to Owen. I called Marcia. "Hey, are you up for dinner? I miss you guys."

"Can't handle it out on your own, huh? We got takeout since Nita's off tonight, and we have enough to feed an army, so come on over."

It would be difficult to talk freely with Nita there, but

it would also look less suspicious—more like I really was getting together with my old roommates and less like I might be passing on valuable information.

Nita met me at the door with a hug. "I can't believe you abandoned me!" she said. "How's life on your own?"

"It's quiet," I said. "Sometimes that's good, sometimes that's bad. But it's only been a few days."

"You'll have to have a party the next time I'm off in the evening. I'll even make samosas. Now that Mom's speaking to me again, she sent her recipe."

As we gathered around the table and served ourselves from containers of Indian food, I asked Gemma, "How's Philip doing?"

The tiny crease that formed between her eyebrows told me she knew at least something about what was going on. "He's doing fine. He's under a lot of stress right now, though."

I nodded and hoped she knew that it wasn't my fault.

Nita, oblivious to the tension, chattered happily about what was going on at work and compared the food to the way her mother made it back home. Soon, the rest of us got caught up in her good spirits, and it felt like old times, the group of us hanging out together at home.

After dinner, while Gemma and Nita were clearing the table, Marcia moved to sit by me and whispered, "I take it there was something you needed to tell me or give me."

"Yeah, this." I took the spell out of my pocket. "I want Owen to take a look at it. It's from that book I've been having to read—he'll know what that means. I memorized the spell and copied the symbols, so I'm pretty sure it's accurate. I'm curious about what it does. That's the only reason I can think of for this book to have been hidden the way it was. Everything else is hardly groundbreaking."

She took the page and slid it into her own pocket. "I'll get it to Rod. I was going to head over there later tonight, anyway."

"Thanks."

"How are you holding up away from Owen?"

"He finds ways to see me," I said, feeling myself blush. "But it's not like when I was able to see him every day, all the time."

"Hey, maybe absence will make the heart grow fonder."

"We were already pretty fond of each other."

"Yeah, but now being together will be a big deal rather than just another day at the office."

It was hard to concentrate on my work the next day when I was so distracted by wondering what Owen would make of the spell. I tried memorizing another one and wrote more symbols on the inside of my wrist. Writing those symbols while whispering the words under my breath might have been dangerous if I'd had any magic in me. Being immune to magic came in handy at times.

I looked for another hidden note outside my new building when I got home, but I didn't see anything. I was sitting on the sofa, writing out the new spell, when I glanced up and barely bit back a scream when I saw a monster staring through the window. A second later, I realized that it wasn't a monster. It was just a gargoyle perched on my balcony. I got up and opened the French doors to allow him inside.

"Thanks, doll," Sam said, shaking the snow off his wings. "It was gettin' cold out there. I got a message for you from Palmer." He cleared his throat, then said in Owen's voice, "Excellent work, Katie! I'm doing some analysis of that spell, but if it's what I think it is, it's more dangerous to the Collegium than it is to us. I think it's a key to something important they may have hidden. That, and not the plan, may be how that person a century ago took over." Sam cleared his throat again and said in his normal voice, "Got that, doll?"

"Yeah, I did, thanks. And let me guess, he's still there working on it."

"You know him so well."

"Do you mind waiting a second or two? I got another spell today, and I'm just finishing writing it out." Only then did it occur to me that maybe we shouldn't have been talking openly in here. "Oops, this might not be a safe place to talk."

Sam waved a wing. "Don't worry, sweetheart, I got it covered. I've been in the security game a long time. I barely say hello to the neighbors without warding. But I wouldn't have conversations with anyone else here, if I was you. I'm not pickin' up on anything, but better safe than sorry."

I finished writing the spell, folded it, and handed it to Sam. He didn't have pockets, since he didn't have clothes, but the piece of paper vanished somewhere. "I'll pass it on to him straightaway. Good work, kiddo. When you come back, you're comin' to work for me, got that? I don't want to waste these skills of yours."

"It's a deal," I said.

I'd barely closed the French doors after he flew away before my personal phone rang. It was Gemma. "What happened to Philip?" she demanded. "I can't seem to reach him."

Twelve

Aware of what Sam had just warned me about, I kept my voice neutral and said, "Oh, were you expecting to hear from him?" as I picked up my coat and slid my free arm into it. I switched the phone to my other ear and put on the other sleeve while I slipped on the nearest pair of shoes, then ran down the stairs and out into the street.

Meanwhile, Gemma told me the whole story, how Phillip had been at work that day, but went missing without anyone noticing him leave. "What do you know about this?" she demanded.

"Nothing!" I said. "I know Roger threatened him, but I hadn't heard anything about him going back there. I thought Philip knew to beef up his security. Owen was going to look into how MSI could help."

"They said he did have security, but it's like he vanished into thin air from inside his office, where he should have been safe. And no, they didn't find any frogs in there."

"When I saw Roger turn someone into a frog, he took

the frog with him. They've got a frog pond in the building atrium so they're safe in cold weather." I meant it to be reassuring, but I had to admit that it probably didn't come out that way.

"Can you get to him?" Her voice sounded strained with panic, pitched a little too high.

"I don't know. I don't have access to most of the building, and they seldom let me out of my office without an escort. I don't know if that's a place anyone's just allowed to go, or if only certain people can. Even if I could get to him and figure out which frog it is and break the spell with a kiss, I still wouldn't be able to get him out of the building."

I could hear her taking a few long, deep breaths. "Okay, right, that makes sense," she said, sounding a little steadier.

"Look, this is why I'm doing this," I reminded her. "He's not the only victim. I'm trying to find a way to take these people down. Then we can free everyone and make sure it doesn't happen to anyone else again."

"I know. And I know it's not your fault. He wouldn't have been as prepared as he was if it hadn't been for you."

"I'm doing what I can, and trust me, it's a little frustrating to be so constrained."

After I ended the call, I popped into the nearest corner shop and bought a packet of cookies, in case someone was watching me and wondering why I was walking down the street, chatting on the phone, on a snowy evening. Besides, I needed chocolate and carbs in the worst way. That much wasn't a cover.

Later that night, I was lying in bed, trying to still my

brain enough to get some rest, when I spotted something glowing outside my window. I rolled over and sat up to see a sparkling arrow. Puzzled, I got out of bed and went to the French doors, opening them and stepping onto the balcony. Owen stood in the street below.

I didn't need him to tell me what to do next. I rushed back inside, threw on my coat over my pajamas, and shoved my feet into shoes before running downstairs.

When I was just a few feet away from him, he knelt and touched the ground. I felt a surge of power, and then the world seemed to stop. The snowflakes froze in the air around us. He straightened as I reached him, and I stepped right into his embrace as he caught me and kissed me. I hadn't realized just how much I missed that, so I let myself enjoy it for a long moment, even though I was pretty sure he hadn't come here and pulled a magical stunt he wasn't supposed to do just so we could have a makeout session.

"You're brilliant!" he said when he finally came up for air.

"Oh, so that's what this was about," I teased. "And here I thought it was because you loved me."

"That, too," he said with a saucy grin. "But you really are brilliant. Whoever this guy was who took over the Collegium a hundred years ago, it wasn't because he had a clever plan. It was because he'd figured out some interesting magic."

I snuggled against him, my head on his shoulder, and he responded by wrapping his arms tightly around me. "How interesting?"

"Like I had Sam tell you earlier, the first spell is a kind

of magical key for getting past any magical safeguards within the Collegium. It would have been easy for him to have pulled a coup once he had a power base, since he'd have been able to go right to the top ranks and take them out."

"I'm guessing that the second spell is even more interesting, if you came straight here to talk about it."

He tightened his hold on me and kissed the top of my head. "Yes! It's a universal access code that breaks down all kinds of security. With that spell, someone could transport himself straight into a warded room."

"Transport right into a warded room?" I asked, a sick feeling growing in my stomach. "You mean like 'poof!' right past guards and spells, and stuff?"

"Yes, but the trick is that you have to plant a beacon in the location, and you lock onto the beacon to transport yourself. I've already got a team in security figuring out a way to counter it so we can beef up our wards, but I'm not too worried, since you have to get in to plant the beacon before you can transport, and that's unlikely."

"That's how they did it, then," I said.

"Did what?"

"They got Philip. We think." I told him what Gemma had told me. "And I'm the one who got him into Philip's office so he could leave a beacon. That's what that visit must have been about."

"It's not your fault. You're doing what you have to do, and you had no way of knowing you were giving him that kind of help."

"I should have, though. I knew I was reading some serious spells. But maybe I should hold off on giving him more spells from the book until you've checked them. He can't even touch the book, so it's not like he can check to make sure I'm giving him the right information. It's also possible that some of it's veiled."

He shoved me just far enough away from himself that he could brace his hands on my shoulders and look me in the eye. "That's a great idea! Do that! How much of the book has he actually looked at directly?"

"Only the beginning. And I know he can't touch it. It blew him across the room the last time he tried. I've been shutting it when I leave for the day, so he can't read the page it's open to. There may be other immunes around he can use, but he seems to be keeping this between him and me. He won't even let me type the transcriptions using the company computer."

"Okay, then, leave out the spells until I've had a look at them. This may give us an edge." He pulled me back to him and kissed me. "Now, I'd better go. I shouldn't sustain this suspension for too long." He gave me one more lingering kiss before he released me.

"Bye. I love you," I said.

"I love you, too. Hurry and bring down these people so we can get back on track."

"Will do." After a jaunty salute, I hurried back to my building. Only after I was inside did I hear normal sounds resuming. By the time I was upstairs and looked out the window, he was gone and snow was falling, already erasing our footprints. Come to think about it, there was only one set of footprints, leading back to my building. Had he been testing that transportation spell?

• • •

On my way to my office the next day, I couldn't help but look over the railing in the atrium. The frog pond was so far below that I couldn't even tell that's what it was from this level. Was Philip down there? I hated to think of him being stuck like that again, and in spite of what Owen had said, I feared it was my fault. I shouldn't have been handing Roger spells. Or maybe I should have altered them slightly when copying them.

That gave me an idea. On the page I needed to start with, there was a long, complicated-looking spell, and I sensed magic coming off the page, which suggested that it was either veiled or its appearance was altered, so no one without the right spell—or without magical immunity—would be able to read it. I changed a few things as I copied it, making sure I memorized the correct version. I'd spent enough time verifying spells for Owen that I knew ways to change it while still making it look authentic. I marked the symbols on my wrist under my watch, as usual. This spell was harder to memorize than the previous ones, but copying it helped.

Roger wasn't in his office when I dropped off that day's work, so I hurried back to my office to check the book for what his next step likely was. He'd already taken over the Vandermeer company. It looked like next he needed to recruit "soldiers" loyal to him, using the funds he got from the Vandermeer firm. I wondered where one would go to hire magical thugs. Would he get them from within the Collegium, or would he find wannabes?

That was a question for Rod, I thought, so as soon as I was home and had written out the spells I'd memorized, I called Marcia. "How's Gemma holding up?" I asked first.

"She's upset and burying herself in work. And what about you?"

"Me?" I asked, a little surprised, since I wasn't the one we were worried about, but then I realized that she was giving me an opening in case I wanted to arrange a meeting. "I'm okay, I guess. A little lonely all by myself over here."

"Why don't you join Rod and me for dinner tonight?" Marcia said. "He'd love to catch up, and I guess that's been awkward with you and Owen being broken up. He's not choosing sides, but he would like to see you."

"Sure, that sounds great," I said.

"Okay, how about his place at eight?"

I was spoiled by having had a crosstown subway station practically at my front door and a major station with multiple up/downtown lines a few blocks away, so while my new neighborhood was cute, it was somewhat limited in easy transportation options. And then I remembered that I was making money now and had an apartment that was paid for. I walked a few blocks to a busier street and hailed a cab, feeling utterly decadent doing so, which was weird, considering I was driven to work in a luxury sedan.

At his apartment, Rod greeted me with a hug. "It's good to see you," he said. "Marcia's on her way. So, what did you want to talk about?"

I handed him the spell I'd copied. "Here's the latest thing for Owen. And what do you know about how someone would go about recruiting magical thugs?"

"You're not planning a life of crime, are you? Those Collegium people must be a bad influence."

In spite of myself, I grinned. "You never know. But that's the next step in Roger's grand plan for world domination, according to the book. He's got the funding after taking out Philip. Now he's supposed to use that money to hire soldiers who are loyal to him rather than the Collegium, so that should mean he's recruiting from outside."

"Well, in my job in Personnel, I've never had much occasion to hire thugs. We prefer to fight with our brains and our powers. But I think what you might find is that he'll hire creatures."

"Like the ones Idris had working for him—those skeleton things, harpies, and the like?"

"And there would certainly be some unemployed ones. I know he created a thing or two, which would have faded when he quit supporting the spell, but yeah, most of his allies were goons for hire. They'd be loyal to whoever was paying the bills."

I couldn't help but make a face. Those things had been awful to deal with. They'd followed me around, and I could see them while other people couldn't. "That must be where he was this afternoon, out recruiting."

Rod scratched the back of his neck and looked uncomfortable. "That would explain the call he made to me today. I don't think he's just hiring thugs. He wants talent, too. He wanted to know if I knew of anyone who might be amenable."

"Maybe this is our chance to infiltrate his group further."

"That was what the boss said, so I gave him a few people I know are loyal and who have been briefed. It's not full-time work, just as-needed. I'm pretty sure they're not coming under the Collegium umbrella. They won't be going to work in that fortress of theirs."

Marcia arrived, which put the conversation on hold while Rod served dinner. He was a decent cook, probably from his playboy days when he'd been desperately trying to impress women. For a little while, I was able to forget my concerns and enjoy being with friends, but by the time he served dessert, we were back to business.

"I really feel like it's all coming together," I said. "We at least know what Roger wants and have the scoop on his plan to do it. Now we've got Owen checking out his spells before I give them to him, and sometimes I'm adjusting them. We just need to catch him in some way that will stop him."

"And stop the Collegium," Rod reminded me. "We might stop him and still have to deal with them. But we've altered our wards, so that spell of his can't work on us, even if he could drop off a beacon somehow."

"Will that clue him in that I've passed the spells on?"

"Why should it? He's getting them from a hundred-year-old document. I'd hope we'd have updated our security since then."

"Good point."

"You do realize how crazy all this sounds," Marcia said.

"Welcome to the magical world, my dear," Rod said, leaning over to kiss her cheek. "And what would you think if we were infiltrating the mafia to protect ourselves?"

"I'd think you were crazy because that's the FBI's job. Don't you have magic cops?"

"Kind of," Rod said. "But I'm not sure how much we can trust the Council enforcers, especially with a couple of Council members having recently been replaced. Jurisdictional boundaries are rather fluid in our world. If you know about a problem, you deal with it."

"It sounds like the Wild West to me," Marcia said, shaking her head. "And don't you have undercover specialists? Why send Katie?"

"We tried sending someone else," I said. "I was the one who got recruited. Though I suspect that may have been a Roger thing—he thought he'd get some inside scoop on MSI from me, and then I know some other highly placed people in the magical world."

She took a sip of wine. "Well, I have to say, a job where they give you a West Village apartment and drive you to work every day doesn't sound all that bad. Not to mention providing the work wardrobe."

"On the other hand, I'm totally cut off from the world while I'm at work. I can't even put a photo of my parents on my desk or carry out a grocery list I jotted down while I was on a phone call. And I don't know where my office is."

"Okay, that part is weird. That's worse than when I worked retail when I was in college and they had to search my purse before I could leave every day. I guess if you're untrustworthy, you don't trust anyone else."

After we'd helped Rod clean up from dinner and started to head out, he caught me at the door. "Do I have to tell you to be careful? Cooperate with them and do what they say, even if they're doing something you have a problem with. Remember the big picture."

"That's how I'm sleeping at night," I said grimly.

• • •

I managed not to jump in shock when Roger called me the next morning, but I still couldn't help but tense up all over. Had he figured out that I'd given him a bogus spell? I hoped my voice didn't shake as much as it felt like it did when I answered.

"Can you come to my office right away?" he asked, rather brusquely.

"Of course," I replied as my heart hammered in my chest. He was a raging psychopath, I was pretty sure, but he was usually rather pleasant and friendly. If he was that terse, something was wrong. I tried taking a few of the yoga breaths Gemma had taught me—slow in and out through my nose—but they didn't do much to stop the panic attack. I told myself that if something was really wrong, he'd have kept me out of the building, or he'd have had me dragged out of my office. Would he really bother calling me in before chaining me in the dungeon, or whatever it was he did to people he couldn't turn into frogs?

I felt a little better when he looked up at me and smiled as I entered his office. Even better was the spread of coffee and pastries set out on his desk. I didn't think he'd serve me Danishes before sending me to my doom. If he did, he was a bigger psycho than I thought.

"Please, come in and help yourself," he said with a gesture toward the food. I didn't need encouraging. It was only midmorning, but I was starving because I hadn't had time for breakfast. There wasn't a lot of leeway in the morning when a car picked you up at a precise time, and I was used to roommates waking me when they got up. It was hard to oversleep when there was that much activity in the apartment. It had been ages since I'd needed an alarm clock, and I wasn't adjusting well.

Once I'd taken a Danish and poured a cup of coffee, he gave me a smile so nice I could almost forget what he really was. "How are you liking things here so far?" he asked.

"I have to say, it's been the best working environment I've ever experienced," I replied, quite honestly. Yeah, there was the weirdness of having to change clothes, and all, but no one yelled at me, I got to arrive at nine and leave at five, there weren't a lot of pointless meetings, and Roger hadn't ever changed his mind about an assignment he'd given me after I'd done it and then blamed me for not doing it right in the first place. It didn't say much for the management I'd dealt with that a psychopathic mobster with plans for world domination really was the best boss I'd ever had.

"Good," he said, still smiling. "Do you enjoy your work?" Before I could answer, he laughed and said, "Okay, that's a stupid question. The work I've given you so far is incredibly tedious. Copying documents by hand would be way below your skill level if it weren't for the fact that you're the only one who can touch that book. You might even be the only one who can read it properly. But I promise, there will be more interesting work for you in the coming months." With an even bigger grin, he added, "Stick with me, kid, and you'll really go places," in a reasonable Humphrey Bogart impression.

That gave me a pang. Owen loved Humphrey Bogart films. Because of this operation, I'd missed spending the winter snuggled up with him in front of his fireplace, watching old movies. I forced myself to smile at Roger because the last thing I needed was him asking me why I looked so sad.

More seriously, Roger said, "What I'm saying is, you're the candidate I've selected for the permanent position as my right hand. You've got valuable connections, you're smart, you're efficient, and you've proven yourself to be loyal. Congratulations, and welcome aboard."

"Um, thanks," I said, trying to sound more enthusiastic than I felt. This was what I wanted—getting closer to the heart of the matter. It was just not my idea of fun to have to spend that much time with someone like him.

"You'll be getting a new office closer to mine. It'll be bigger. And you'll have outside communications access, as you'll need that to make appointments and take calls for me." That was an improvement, I thought. I didn't even have to fake the smile in response. Not that I'd be able to talk to people at MSI, but in a crisis, I might be able to call one of my friends and give them a prearranged danger signal.

I nodded in acknowledgment, and he continued. "As I'm sure you can tell from the transcription you've been doing, I'm gearing up for a big operation, and I'll need your help every step of the way. However, I should warn you that there may be some risks." He waved a hand at his office door, shutting it, before saying, "What I'm working on isn't exactly sanctioned by the company. It's in line with their ultimate goals, but I intend to do it on my own before they can get to it. That should secure my rise, and when I rise, you'll come with me. But if it doesn't work, if

I fail, you'll fail along with me. You won't have any future with this company apart from me. If my plans don't work, you'll be out—or worse. I feel like I should make that clear to you before we go further."

"What do you mean by 'worse'?" I asked, because I figured any normal person would.

"There may be consequences. You've seen what happens to magical people—or even normal people—who get in our way. Magical punishments wouldn't work on you, of course, but there may be other consequences. Is this a risk you can accept?"

I gulped. "I believe so."

He grinned again. "Good. I can assure you that I have no intention to fail. I've got the tools I need, and my plan is already in place. You and me together, I think we might even be unstoppable, and then the sky's the limit. We won't only take over this place, we'll take it in new directions. We'll rule the magical world!"

I braced myself, waiting for the bolt of lightning and clap of ominous thunder that usually accompanied proclamations like that. Unfortunately, the real world usually wasn't very cinematic, so nothing happened. His eyes did have a crazy gleam to them, and the "Mwa ha ha!" was implied in his tone. I also thought I detected a slight crackle of magic around him.

"That sounds exciting," I said, mustering all the enthusiasm I could.

"Yeah, you'll really be able to stick it to those people at MSI. They'll regret letting you get away from them. Let me know if there's anyone in particular you want me to deal with, like that ex of yours."

It was a good thing I already had my eager mask on because I wasn't sure I'd have been able to hide my feelings quickly enough otherwise. "That—that won't be necessary," I stammered, even as I felt like a steel band had gone around my chest. More flippantly, I added, "I want him around to see how successful I am without him. That wouldn't be any fun at all if he were a frog down in that pond."

He laughed. "I can see your point. I'll admit, I do have one ex down there, but it's far more satisfying being successful in front of the ex who's still dealing with wardrobing—and that's as far as she'll ever go. But the moment you want him taken out, you just say the word. What about your old boss?"

"Which one?" I asked. I did have one former boss I wouldn't mind having turned into a frog, even if she wasn't magical. I mean, if I needed to give a name to prove my loyalty, I'd be willing to sacrifice and let them have Mimi. But I suspected that wasn't where he was going with this.

"You know the one I mean."

"Merlin? Good luck with that. You know what he did to the last person who took him on."

"Oh, when I'm done with my plans, he'll be easy prey for me. What would you say his greatest weakness was?"

"Well, he is a bit behind the times," I said, which was sort of true. He'd been in a magical coma for about a thousand years, only reviving a couple of years ago, so he'd missed a lot of development. But he'd also done a really good job of catching up. I didn't tell Roger that, though.

"I think I can work with that," Roger said with a

satisfied nod. "But that's not my next step. I have other things to put in place first. Go ahead and finish your coffee—take your time—and then I need your help with something."

I didn't want to think about what that might be, but at least it sounded like Owen and Merlin were off the agenda for today. I finished my coffee and Danish, feeling like I should be hurrying because Roger watched me the whole time. If he wasn't tapping his foot impatiently, he was giving off the vibe that he was.

As soon as I finished, he stood and said, "Great! Come with me." He called for a car while we walked to the elevator.

He didn't start talking to explain himself until we were in the car, traveling away from the office building. He did something with his hands that created a glow around us before he spoke. "As you can imagine, I won't be able to do this alone, and I won't be able to use company personnel unless I've recruited and vetted them myself. So we're doing some recruiting, and I want you to help me evaluate the applicants. I believe you're familiar with their work."

I nodded, figuring that these were the people Rod was giving him. I hoped they'd been briefed on my role so they didn't think I'd turned traitor when they saw me with Roger.

"They're not always what they seem," he went on, "and you'll be able to tell me what I'm getting."

The car stopped, and when we got out, we seemed to be in another underground garage. Or maybe we were inside a warehouse building. Whatever it was, it was big and cavernous, and there were windows high above that let in a small amount of light. By the time it reached the ground where we were, the light was faint.

I got the impression that we were surrounded. In the near-darkness, I couldn't see them, but I could hear sounds coming from all angles, and there was a sense of movement.

Roger formed a glowing light in his hand and launched it to hover above us. I couldn't stop myself from recoiling when I saw what that light revealed.

We were surrounded, all right. Creatures out of nightmares appeared from the shadows—creepy skeletal monsters and leather-winged hags. "What's she doing here?" one of the harpies rasped, pointing a gnarled talon at me.

Thirteen

These were all the creatures who used to work for Phelan Idris, the first foe I'd faced when I entered the magical world. I'd had many a run-in with them along the way. They couldn't harm me magically, but they could do physical damage, and they were just plain creepy. I wanted to back away and hide behind Roger, but I forced myself to stand my ground and stare at them defiantly.

"She works for me now," Roger said.

"Does she?" the harpy said with the kind of grin that gave me the impression she'd just shoved a child into her oven to roast.

"Yes, and if you'd like to work for me, you'll leave her alone." He turned to me. "Can you see what they really are?"

I couldn't help but make a face. "Unfortunately."

"Tell me what you see."

"Well, there are a bunch of harpies. I'm not sure what the skeleton creatures are supposed to be. They used to stalk me when they were working for someone else."

Roger turned back toward the creatures. "Who, exactly, were you working for? Who hired you and paid you?"

The harpy, who seemed to be the spokeswoman for the group while the others just hung around and looked menacing, said, "That nerdy boy, what was his name?"

"No one else? No one older?"

"He was the only one we saw."

Roger nodded in satisfaction at that. "I'm willing to hire you to work directly for me. You'll be paid in cash, part up front, part when I'm sure you're doing what I want."

"And what would you be hiring us to do? We specialize in ominous lurking."

"None of that yet. I want you on standby for specific tasks. I'll give you targets and objectives."

"Killing, maiming, or just threatening?" the harpy asked as she examined her claws.

"We'd start with threatening and possibly work our way up, depending on how the target reacts. So, are you in?"

They huddled, which was not a sight I really wanted to see. It created a tight ball of ugly evil. "What do you think? Were they good at threatening?" Roger asked me softly.

"Good enough, I suppose," I said with a shrug. "I got used to them."

"But you're hardly ordinary. I suspect it would take a lot to scare you."

"If you're going after magical people, they're probably even harder to scare. They're more accustomed to this sort of thing."

"I hope I can accomplish my objectives by merely unsettling them at first. That might make them more receptive when I offer to protect them from these threats."

Really? He was planning to run a protection racket? This *was* the magical mafia, I thought, trying not to grin and shake my head. But I guessed if it worked in the nonmagical world, it would work with magic.

The creatures finished their discussion and turned to face Roger. The harpy spoke. "We'll start at a hundred dollars an hour when we're actually working. Each. Five grand a week retainer for the group."

"Two grand a week retainer, and trust me, you'll get plenty of hours in," Roger countered.

The creatures huddled again, then the harpy said, "Done. But we want the first week's retainer up front."

"That's not a problem," Roger said. "I'll have the cash to you by the end of the day."

"Not now?" the harpy whined.

"I don't carry that kind of cash. Shall we meet here again, or somewhere else?"

Her hideous face twisted into something I assumed was meant as a smile. "I could always drop by your office to pick it up."

"You know that's not going to happen."

"Don't worry, we'll find you. That's what we do." Her cackle echoed in the vast space, and there was a rustling as all the creatures disappeared into the darkness.

Roger took a handkerchief out of his pocket and wiped his hands, even though he hadn't touched any of the creatures. "Disgusting things," he muttered. "But they are the best at what they do." He refolded the handkerchief and returned it to his pocket. "Now, shall we go? We've got another stop to make."

When we were inside the car, Roger snapped his fingers, and the windows became transparent. As the car left the warehouse, light poured into the interior, and I found myself sighing. It felt so good to feel sunlight and to know where I was. Judging by the angle of the skyline, I figured we were somewhere in Brooklyn. We drove across the bridge to Manhattan and stopped in front of the kind of restaurant where corporate bigwigs probably did deals over three-martini lunches.

"Hungry for lunch?" Roger asked.

"Um, I guess," I said. I hoped this was strictly business and that he wasn't putting the moves on me. Or was this kind of place his equivalent of grabbing a sandwich at the corner deli, no big deal?

A doorman helped me out of the car and an attendant inside took our coats. "There will be someone joining us," he told the hostess, and I relaxed a little. If someone was joining us, then this was business.

Once we were seated, he declined the wine list and ordered a soda for himself and an iced tea for me. I might have been miffed that he hadn't consulted me, but he was right about my order. After the waiter left, he said, "I'm looking at a potential team member today, and I'd appreciate your insight. Let me know if anything seems off, for one thing. And you might know something about them."

Now, I figured, we'd be meeting with those people Rod was sending to us. Much to my surprise, Minerva Felps swooped toward our table, her colorful scarves flying out behind her. "You must be Roger—and no, I didn't know that because I'm a seer. I know it because you set up the meeting. And hello, Katie! It's good to see that you've landed on your feet. The way you were treated was atrocious." I would have said she was laying it on a little thick, but that was the way she always was.

She let the waiter seat her, ordered a gimlet, and turned to face Roger again. "I'm a little confused because you're not planning to offer me a regular job. You just want me to freelance for you on the side. But I can't quite get a good read on what sort of work you're doing, or even who you work for."

I was surprised to see just how taken aback Roger was. It did take getting used to Minerva, but if he was recruiting a seer, surely he knew what he was getting. It would have been more alarming if she hadn't already known what was going on.

"I'm glad to hear that my defenses are working," he said. He paused while the waiter brought our drinks and distributed menus. "But I'm impressed that you got that much. You must be the real deal."

"Do you think I'd be where I am now if I wasn't? So, you want a little freelance scrying done for you?"

"I'm doing some long-range planning, and I want to get a sense of possible outcomes."

"Personal or professional?"

"Both."

"That I can do for you. Not here, of course. That takes solitude, quiet, and preparation. And you'd have to drop those defenses for me to get an accurate read."

I bit my lip so I wouldn't grin. It would be a big help to

us if Minerva was able to read his future. I sincerely hoped that she really was on our side because I was toast if she wasn't. A real seer who'd tell him the whole truth would surely tell him he had a traitor in his midst. Minerva hadn't been on any list we'd put together of potential Collegium allies, and I doubted Roger would have wanted to talk to her if she had been.

"I'm sure that can be arranged. I'll have Katie get in touch with you later to set up a meeting."

She tilted her head to the side, studying him, for a moment. "I can tell you that things are in flux around you. There are a lot of variables at work that make your future very hazy."

"In a good way or a bad way?"

"It could go either way."

"Tell me what I'm thinking now."

"You're testing me to see how accurate I am, and you wonder if I could give you a read on Katie, here. Sorry, no can do. It won't work on her. And I'm a seer, not a clairvoyant, so I can read your future. I can get a sense of your fate. I can find lost people. But I can't read your mind."

"I thought you just did."

"Only because it was painfully transparent. Heck, I bet Katie here could have read that one off you, and she doesn't have a drop of magic in her."

The conversation ended when the waiter returned to take our orders, and then we made small talk over lunch. Under Minerva's casual questioning, I learned far more about Roger than I had in the whole time I'd been working with him. For instance, his father had apparently been a big player in the company he worked for (I assumed he meant the Collegium) but had fallen afoul of someone in the hierarchy. His mother used to work for MSI, a long time ago. He'd been top of his class at Harvard and had an MBA, in addition to being a trained wizard. Basically, he was the preppie from hell. He played golf and tennis, summered at Martha's Vineyard, where he kept his sailboat, and all those little things that sounded like something out of a movie. He was single, not even dating, because he was focused on his career and his last two relationships had ended badly (he didn't mention the frog to Minerva).

I watched and listened in awe. I'd never have had the nerve to ask him those sorts of questions, but she got away with it by acting like she already knew the answers and was checking her facts. I couldn't tell whether or not he realized just how much he was being manipulated. It was all rather brilliant, and I was getting a clearer picture of why he was doing what he was doing. He was trying to get back for what had happened to his father, and maybe avoid getting himself into a similar situation.

We ended the lunch with a promise to get in touch with Minerva, and as soon we were back in our car—the windows blacked out again—Roger asked me, "Do you think she's worthwhile?"

"I've never known her to be wrong."

"How loyal do you think she is to MSI?"

"From my understanding, she worked directly under the previous president. So her loyalty may be more to him than to the current boss." I thought that he could read into that what he wanted. The statement of fact was true, but I'd presented the interpretation as merely a possibility.

He leaned back against his seat, a smugly satisfied smile on his face. "I don't see how she should have a conflict of interest, unless she sees what I plan to do to that company and to her boss and she has to decide what to do with that knowledge. Not that I'd give her the chance to tell anyone." He said it so casually that unless you'd seen what he did to people who crossed him, you might not have realized he was making a threat. It sounded like it was no different to him than talking about picking up milk on the way home. I forced myself not to shudder.

We had to stop this guy, preferably in a way that totally neutralized him. I almost felt sorry for the higher-ups in the Collegium, with him gunning for them. Somehow, I doubted he'd put them carefully in an indoor frog pond. He'd probably throw them right out into the street to be run over by a truck.

When we returned to headquarters, Roger took me straight to my new office. I no longer entered past Evelyn's office or went through the reception area. I had a direct path from the gallery around the atrium to Roger's immediate domain. He hadn't been kidding about my new office being larger. It was bigger than my apartment, with a large L-shaped desk and a full-sized sofa. The window had the same London view as from Roger's office next door, which made me wonder yet again if it was a faked view or a real one. Maybe there was some kind of portal in the hallway, and we really were in London.

"What do you think?" Roger asked, sounding strangely eager to please.

"It's beautiful."

"If you want some decorations, something to personalize

it, talk to Evelyn. She can let you choose some paintings and plants."

"Okay, great. And now I guess I'd better go back and get that book."

He grinned. "Yes, that's one thing we couldn't bring for you. I'll let you get to work."

I didn't hear from Owen again for days, which was probably smart on his part because it kept us from doing anything that looked suspicious, but I still missed him terribly. Friday night, I was copying out the spell I'd memorized that day and trying to decide if I should cook something or call my friends to go out when the front door buzzer sounded. "Pizza delivery," a voice on the intercom said, and I grinned because I recognized that voice.

"Come on up," I said, hitting the button to unlock the door, then I flew to my own door and flung it open.

When Owen reached my floor, I saw that he'd really immersed himself in the role. He wore a jacket with the logo of a neighborhood pizza restaurant and a ballcap with the same logo. He carried an insulated case. I started to speak, but he held a finger to his lips, and I nodded, stepping back to allow him inside. "That'll be twenty-seventeen, with tax," he said.

"Let me get my purse," I said.

We both paused for a moment, after which he said, "Thanks, miss. You have a good evening." He opened and shut my door, then he waved his hands, doing something complicated with his fingers. When it was done, he said, "I knew that silence spell would come in handy eventually."

I let him put the pizza down on the coffee table before

I threw myself into his arms. "I've missed you so much," I said, showering him with kisses.

He laughed as he staggered backward under my assault. "Really? I hadn't noticed." He wrapped his arms around me and kissed me back.

After that had gone on for a while, I asked, still clinging to him, "What kind of pizza is it?"

"Canadian bacon and mushroom."

"It would be a real pity if we let it get cold."

"And we should probably talk. I don't think I can get away with staying too long without someone wondering what's going on. They'll either notice the pizza delivery guy hanging out for a long time or the fact that you've been silent for ages."

"I'm starting to wonder how much they really are watching me," I said as I unzipped the pizza bag. The aroma of hot pizza filled the room, and I inhaled deeply. I took out the cardboard box and opened it, then removed a slice. "Roger acts like he trusts me completely. He may be just arrogant enough to think that he'd know if I had the potential to be disloyal."

Owen took his own slice of pizza, and we both sat on the sofa. I handed him some of the paper napkins from the pizza bag. "You don't know what his bosses might be doing," he said. "They may have figured out that he has his own agenda and might be watching you to see what that is."

"Then they're going to think I'm the pizza delivery guy's fantasy customer," I said, running my toes up his calf.

He turned bright red and smiled. "I hope you didn't give that spell you gave me to Roger."

"I wasn't sure if he saw that page, so I made a few alterations before giving him anything. I've left out the rest so far this week."

"Good, because it's kind of scary."

"Worse than turning people into frogs?"

"How about turning them into portraits? If you see anything hanging on the walls in that building, you might want to give it a second look. It could be the people who were running the Collegium a century ago—and I don't mean pictures of them."

"Is it reversible?"

"It might be, but that's not contained within the spell. Frankly, figuring that out is low on my priority list right now."

"I have more spells for you." I finished the slice of pizza I was eating, wiped my hands on a napkin, and picked up the page I'd been working on. "There's this one," I said, handing it to him. Then I rose slightly to dig under the sofa cushions. "And these. I hope they're at all accurate. It's hard doing this sort of thing from memory."

"You're doing great. The ones you've sent so far could be really useful. If we could find that building to get inside, we could get straight to the core of things with one of those spells."

"I'm not sure it's just one building. In fact, I think I'm working in London right now. It's like the building is just a collection of portals to other buildings."

He raised an eyebrow. "Really? That's interesting. I've heard of things like that, but haven't seen it implemented. It would make travel a lot easier."

"Yeah, too bad it seems the only way out is to come back to New York. I don't know if there are exits everywhere."

"I'd think there would have to be. Otherwise, why do such a thing? As it is, it would be the ideal way to escape to another jurisdiction if there's ever a raid. That must be what the spell does, give you access to all those portals. If we could just get something into the building with you, we might be able to track it better."

"Or plant one of those beacons to transport directly. But it wouldn't go any farther than my changing room, or the alarms would go off. I'm not sure that knowing where the changing room is would do you much good."

"What about when you leave the building with Roger during the day?"

"We don't seem to go through the same security process when returning, but I haven't tried to bring in anything from the outside, so I don't know if I just haven't noticed because I haven't set off the alarms. I'm never out of his sight, though. Picking up anything would be tricky. You haven't had any luck finding a way to get past the disguise spells on the car to follow it?"

"Nope, and we gave it another shot after that lunch you had with Minerva. She says your boss is terrifying, by the way."

"Yeah, I'm starting to get that feeling. She picked up something?"

"She used words like 'apocalypse.'"

"Yikes!"

"Which is why I don't want to take any risk of putting you in danger."

"Well, at least they can't turn me into a portrait."

"There are ways to remove your magical immunity. If you notice symptoms, don't go back there, and let us know right away. We can hide you."

"I don't think he'd do that. He needs my immunity."

"But if he starts to have any doubts about you, he might not care so much." He took the pages I'd given him, folded them, and slid them into the front of his jacket. "And now I'd better get out of here."

"So soon?"

"It's risky enough just coming here. I'm not going to put you in more danger." He picked up the pizza bag and headed for the door.

I hurried after him to give him one last pizza-tasting kiss. "I can't wait to see what you come up with next."

"I wish I didn't have to come up with anything." After one more quick kiss, he dissolved the silence spell and was gone.

I returned to the sofa and took another slice of pizza. I supposed that if Minerva was using words like "apocalypse" to describe Roger's potential future, it would all be worth it when we stopped his evil scheme, but for now, it was pretty tough.

Monday morning, Roger had me call Minerva to set up a session. I had to make it look innocent on both ends of the conversation, since he was hiding his actions from the Collegium and he thought she was secretly moonlighting on MSI. It was my first contact with the outside world from within the Collegium, and I heard enough clicks on the line to know that the call was definitely being monitored. We set the appointment for that evening at the Plaza hotel.

"Do you mind working late tonight?" Roger asked me when I let him know the appointment was set. "I'd like you to be there. I'll need an objective opinion of what happens, and you can take notes so I have a good record of what she tells me."

"I don't have any plans this evening."

"Good. You can have dinner here. Get whatever you like. There's a salon and spa on the lower level, if you'd like to get a massage or something while you're killing time."

"Ooh, that sounds nice," I said, but I wasn't really thinking about the massage. I was thinking about an excuse to go to the lower level, where the frog pond was.

I wasn't sure what I'd do there, since even if I found the Philip frog and kissed him, I wouldn't have a way to get him out of the building, but I liked the idea of being able to get there. Maybe seeing me would make him feel less alone, assuming he was aware of anything like that. He'd never said much about what it was like to be a frog.

I found the spa number in the company directory and called to make an appointment for a massage right after work. When I'd finished that day's transcription for Roger—mostly a lot of rambling about how the Collegium should be run—I headed downstairs. The spa opened from the atrium where the frog pond was. If I hadn't seen Roger delivering his victim to the pond, I'd have thought it was just part of the spa ambience, a bit of nature brought indoors. It became a little less tranquil when you knew it was basically a prison.

I took a moment to stand on the edge of the pond, scanning the surface for frogs. One did hop in my general direction, moving from rock to lily pad to log, but it was hard to tell if it was merely hopping around, or if it was trying to get to me. "I'll help you as soon as I can, Philip," I whispered.

"Katie?" a voice behind me said, and I turned to see a sturdy woman in a lab coat.

"Oh, yes, sorry," I said. "I was pretending it was spring."

"It's easy to do that here, isn't it? Come on inside, and I'll show you the changing room."

I undressed and put on the plush robe they provided. Then I had a moment of panic when I realized I'd have to take off my watch. The symbols from the spell I'd memorized that day were written on my wrist, and they were obviously in ballpoint ink, not a tattoo. Rather than take the risk, I scrubbed the marks off in the room's sink. I figured I could always rewrite them. There was still some ink left on my wrist, but it didn't look like I was smuggling company information out.

After the massage—the kind of perk I'd hate to lose when I went back to MSI—I went upstairs to find dinner waiting for me on my desk. Before I ate, I paused to quickly rewrite the symbols.

Finally, it was time to go. I wasn't sure how this would work—did I dress in my outside world clothes before leaving, then go straight home from the hotel, or did I wear my work clothes, come back here after the meeting, change, and then go home? I wouldn't be able to go straight home from the meeting, since my house keys were in my changing room.

Roger answered that question when he handed me a small black bag. "Here are some things for overnight. You'll be staying at the hotel. The room where we're meeting is booked in your name, and you need to stay there to make it look legitimate."

"How are you going to explain your presence?" I couldn't help but ask.

"Don't worry, your reputation will be safe. I'll sneak in. No one will know I've been at the hotel. Minerva will be visiting you there, as a friend."

It turned out that I was alone in the car on my way to the Plaza. As the doorman helped me out of the limo, I worried that I didn't have my purse to be able to tip him, but I found a convenient roll of bills in the pocket of the coat that had been waiting for me in the car. Roger might have been kind of crazy, but he was a compulsive planner.

The suite waiting for me looked like the kind of place where a princess might feel at home. The furniture was ornate, the carpet plush, and there was a crystal chandelier overhead in the sitting room. I took my bag to the adjacent bedroom and opened it, finding a few toiletries, a hairbrush, a pair of black silk pajamas, a change of underwear, black slacks, and a black sweater. As I hung up the clothes, I thought about how when I was done with this operation, I was going to wear colors so bright you'd need sunglasses to look at me.

I was arranging the toiletries in the bathroom when I heard a knock on the door. I opened it to find Minerva. "Not bad," she said, eyeing the room. "Your boss may possibly be Satan himself, but he does treat you well."

"I had a massage earlier today in the company spa."

"Really? That's a perk I could get behind." She abruptly turned and opened the door to reveal Roger standing there, his hand raised to knock. "And here you are," she said, stepping back to allow him to enter. "Have a seat and make yourself comfortable while I get set up."

She hummed to herself as she took candles out of her bulky tote bag and lit them with a wave of her hand. Next, she removed a metal bowl and handed it to me. "Go fill this with water, please."

I did so and brought it back to her. She placed it on the little round table and gestured for Roger to sit in one of the antique-looking chairs. She took the other chair, and I perched on the edge of the sofa, watching both of them.

"Okay, I need you to close your eyes, Roger," she said, "and open your mind to me."

He did so, and she waited a second or two before she leaned over the bowl. Then she immediately sat upright, saying, "Whoa!"

Fourteen

I knew that Minerva would tell me what she saw if she intended for me to know, so I held my tongue and watched her. "Yeah, everything's all in flux," she said. "Lots of chaos here. It looks to me like you're the biggest variable. Your future depends on particular decisions you make."

Without opening his eyes, Roger said through gritted teeth, "That's why I'm consulting you. What decisions should I make?"

"I'll need to drill a little deeper. Give me your hand."

He lifted his hand from the table, and she removed her large flower brooch, then poked his finger with its pin. He yelped and opened his eyes for a second. "Hey!" he complained.

"Sorry, I needed some blood, and it would have had a different quality if you'd been bracing yourself for it." She grabbed his hand and moved it over the bowl, squeezing his finger to release a few drops. The blood swirled into the water. I wondered if that had been necessary or if she was messing with him. With Minerva, you never really knew.

She let his hand go and leaned over the water again. "Okay, what you have planned is the only path to success I see for you. If you don't do it, you won't go anywhere. You won't fail, but you won't soar. However, this path is also a sure route to failure."

"So if I carry out this plan, I'll either succeed or fail in a big way, but if I don't, I'm stuck?"

"That about covers it. At the moment, I'm seeing equal possibilities for all three outcomes. No, wait, the sit still one is fading. I guess you've made your mind up there."

"You can already see it?"

"It's already causing ripple effects in the universe. Now that you've made that decision, I can get into more specifics on the other possible decisions you're facing. Let's see... Your biggest threat isn't what you think it is. I can't tell you what it is, just that your focus is in the wrong direction."

I suspected she was talking about me. I hoped he didn't interpret it that way, or that he was too arrogant to consider that I might be a threat. He'd probably just focus on someone else within the company.

"One of your foes is ancient, another new. You'd do better if your life were more well-rounded. You should have allies from a variety of walks of life. No, not allies, friends. Not having friends could be a problem for you. Allies who join with you for a purpose won't have your back when you fail. Friends might. Stay at home next Saturday night. Sorry, that one's kind of random, but the tree I see for that decision leads to potential disaster if you're away from home."

"But you haven't told me anything in particular to do," he complained.

"You wanted me to scry you up a no-fail plan to get everything you ever wanted? Anyone who tells you they can do that is lying. Ignore what those phone psychics say on late-night infomercials. They just want your credit card number. I'm telling you that I see a lot of branches in your fate—one thing happens if you make one decision, another thing with a different decision."

"Then tell me which decision I should make."

"It's not that specific. Just that you have a lot of potentially life-changing decisions happening in the next few weeks. You are at the critical time in your life."

"So I should act now?"

"I'm telling you that you *will* act now, one way or another. The choices you make in these weeks—even if the choice is to not make a choice—will change the rest of your life. But I can't tell you if those choices involve quitting your job to sail around the world or not ordering the bad sushi that will send you to the hospital so that you can't take any action."

"Do you see me as successful?"

"That is definitely one of the potential outcomes. You could have everything you ever wanted. But that's a potential. You have to make all the right choices to get there, and each choice creates a bunch of other choices. Basically, what I see is a big tree, and all the little twigs at the ends are less defined."

"What's the choice on the trunk? The big one that starts the branching?"

"To do what you have planned for tomorrow, or not.

One way, your plan starts to fail. The other way, you might have a chance of succeeding."

"But which choice leads to which outcome?"

"Sorry, I only see potential outcomes, not what gets you there."

I was dying to know what he had planned for tomorrow. Unfortunately, I was likely to learn about it too late to do anything about it.

"Is that all you have for me?"

"Is there anything else you'd like to know?"

He hesitated a long time, his forehead creased. Finally, he asked, "Can you tell me the fate of my company?"

"You'll have to give me something to work with to read it. Do you have anything on you that represents your company?"

He opened his eyes to reach into his breast pocket and take out a business card. He handed it to her, and she held it briefly, her eyes closed, before waving it over the bowl. She glanced inside, frowned, and waved it again. "Sorry, I'm getting nothing. Is this card for real? Because the results I'm getting suggest that it's just a front."

I bit my lip and hoped Roger didn't glance at me. I was pretty sure Minerva was only doing this to make him admit he was Collegium.

He paused for a moment before unfastening the tiny tie tack he wore. "Maybe this will work."

"Let's give it a shot." She waved it over the bowl. "Hmm, looks like your fate and its fate are bound together. If you succeed, your company will thrive. If you fail, you could bring it down with you."

"And if I don't act?"

"If you don't act, it carries on as before."

I could see the egomania flare up in his eyes. "So, it all depends on me! I knew it was my destiny."

Minerva gave me the slightest of glances out of the corner of her eye, with a hint of a smirk. He'd completely disregarded the part where if he didn't engage in his plan to take over, the Collegium would do just fine. But hey, failure was what I wanted, so who was I to point out the flaws in his thinking?

"Anything else you want to know? Stock tips, sports scores?"

"No, none of that. You've been helpful." Beaming brightly enough to light up the room, he pulled a roll of cash from his breast pocket and handed it to her. "Thank you. I may call on you again."

"You do that," she said, tucking the cash somewhere in the voluminous folds around her body.

"Then if we're through here, I'll leave. Katie, I'll see you in the morning. Feel free to order anything you want from room service."

When he was gone, Minerva said, "Want to take him up on it? I could do with a drink."

"Why not?" I found the room service menu and we ordered drinks and some snacks.

After they'd been delivered, Minerva performed what I recognized to be the silence spell. "That little thing sure does come in handy," she said. "You'll have to thank your fellow for that."

"You'll probably talk to him before I do," I said, unable to stop myself from sounding a little morose.

"Yeah, I bet it's a big change going from him to spending

all your time with that piece of work." She gestured with her head in the direction of the door where Roger had departed.

"Believe it or not, he's not bad to work for," I said. "I've only seen the psycho side of him a few times. Otherwise, he treats me well, anticipates my needs, and gives me credit for my work. There's just that teeny problem of what he does to anyone who gets in his way."

"Well, we've got countermeasures for any of those spells you've found, so we're making progress. Let's see, what else was I supposed to tell you?"

"Did you get any kind of clue what choice he has to make tomorrow?"

"Sorry, I really didn't get any more than I told him. I just know that if he does one thing, he'll fail, and if he does the other, he might still have a chance of succeeding." She drained her glass. "It does seem like actions tend to give you the exact opposite result from what you'd think. Which is why prophecy like this is so tricky. The thing you do to avoid the outcome you're afraid of is usually exactly what makes it happen. That's why we mostly only use our gifts for finding things or for spotting trends. Trying to dig into outcomes for an individual only leads to trouble. Shakespeare knew what he was doing when he wrote all those tragedies about prophecies bringing about someone's downfall."

Once she'd left, it felt a little weird being all alone in a luxurious hotel suite. I'd have been tempted to call Owen if I'd had my own phone with me. I didn't dare do so on the company phone, and I was afraid that any numbers I called from the room would end up on the bill.

Still, it was a luxurious hotel suite that I didn't have to pay for. I wasn't sure when I'd ever get to stay in a place like this again. Then I remembered that I was marrying a millionaire. Owen tended not to live like a wealthy person, other than his house, so it was easy to forget. I imagined he probably wouldn't spring for something like this on a regular basis, but we might do it for special occasions. I made a mental note of how nice this place might be for a wedding night.

If I ever got to go back to my real life to plan and have a wedding. But Minerva had said the critical time would be in the next few weeks, starting tomorrow.

I went to work the next morning eager to learn what Roger's critical decision would be. I didn't see him around when I arrived, so I got busy transcribing more of the book. The author was beyond the part where he laid the groundwork and was getting into implementation. He'd used the spell from earlier in the book to enter the offices of people he wanted to take down, pulling off coups from within. I shuddered at the account. It seemed like he'd been developing his spells when he wrote the first parts, but didn't use them until later. Maybe Roger should have waited until he had the whole book before he took action, I thought, but I figured that was up to him. He certainly didn't ask for my advice.

I took those sheets to him at lunchtime and found that he still had that manic gleam in his eyes. He glanced at what I'd brought him and beamed so broadly they'd have to tell him to tone it down for a toothpaste ad. "This is it!" he said. "It's what I'm supposed to do today!"

It was another one of those moments when I expected to see a bolt of lightning and hear a clap of thunder. I unconsciously took a step away from him, but he was so caught up in his excitement that he didn't seem to notice.

He jumped out of his seat. "Come on, Katie, let's go. We have people to visit."

Visit? So he wasn't going to just poof into places and take them down? I barely kept up with him as he hustled down the hallway, his phone to his ear. "I think we'll drop in on some of your old friends," he said once we were in the elevator. "You should enjoy this, coming back in a position of power after the way they treated you."

"Yeah, that'll be awesome," I said, trying to sound enthusiastic rather than terrified. There was no way I could think of to warn MSI. I couldn't call them. Maybe Minerva had let Merlin know what she'd seen the night before and they'd be on guard for a potentially pivotal day.

Roger didn't seem to notice my unease. He was too caught up in visions of grandeur, possibly mentally writing the threatening speech he planned to give Merlin. Meanwhile, I was fretting about how many people knew I was undercover. It could blow everything if someone said the wrong thing at the wrong time. But then it would also be difficult for me to repair trust if someone who wasn't in on it saw me with Roger. I wasn't sure why he was bringing me with him, unless he really thought that he was doing me a favor by letting me confront my former employer.

The trip didn't take very long, so perhaps Roger was so eager that he'd told the driver he didn't need to make laps to throw me off. I'd almost have said it might have been walking distance, though it was hard to judge in all the stopping and starting that came with driving in Manhattan.

I certainly wasn't mentally or emotionally prepared when we came to a final stop and the driver opened the door for us. It felt weird to enter the MSI building like this, not as an employee, but as a potential enemy.

Sam was at his usual post on the awning overlooking the front entrance. He didn't acknowledge me, which made me wonder if he was visible to Roger. That question was answered when he followed us inside, gliding silently, and Roger didn't turn around or otherwise react.

Seeing the vast, cathedral-like lobby brought tears to my eyes. I'd really missed this place, and I couldn't wait to come back for good. I just had to finish this one little assignment, foil an evil scheme, and take down the magical mafia. Piece of cake.

The security guard in the lobby came across as being more like an old-fashioned butler, but I knew he had great power at his disposal. Roger swept right past him to the main stairs. "Excuse me," the guard called out, but Roger ignored him—until he ran smack into an invisible force at the first landing and nearly fell down the stairs. I didn't realize it at first because the barrier hadn't stopped me. I only turned and looked back when I heard the swearing.

"Now, who are you, who are you here to see, and upon what business?" the guard asked.

"I'm no one you want to trifle with, old man," Roger said, his voice an icy snarl.

"And you're here to see...?" the guard continued, totally unruffled.

"Merlin. I'm here to see Merlin."

"Just one moment, and I'll let him know you're here." He pushed some buttons on his console, then said, "A person not to be trifled with is here to see Merlin." A pause, then, "Yes, I'll send him right up." He smiled at Roger. "Up at the top floor. He's expecting you."

His mild politeness enraged Roger even more. I thought for a moment that he might do something to the guard, and Sam must have agreed, for he swooped down to rest on the guard's desk, ready to add his own firepower to the guard's defenses. Fortunately, Roger got his rage under control and refocused himself, whirling about to storm up the stairs, brushing past me on the landing.

Sam took flight again, following us all the way up to Merlin's office. Trix had apparently been warned, for she was playing it as cool as the guard had. "Right in there. He's expecting you," she said, though I thought her voice shook a little. She glanced at me, as if for reassurance, but I didn't dare respond. I got the feeling that Roger barely remembered my existence at the moment, but we were too close to success to risk it all on the wrong expression at the wrong time, so I kept my face steely and closed.

The last person I expected to see in Merlin's office was Owen. Did he just happen to already be there, or had he rushed in when the guard called from downstairs? I didn't even let myself look at him because I didn't think I could do so without giving myself away. At least if I avoided looking at him entirely, Roger might read that as post-breakup iciness.

Merlin stood from behind his desk and greeted Roger

with a smile. "Well, hello there. To what do we owe the pleasure?"

Roger was really taken aback. Nothing ruins a good bluster like a refusal to be combative. "We need to talk," he said.

Merlin gestured toward a chair. "Please, have a seat. Can I get you some tea?"

Frowning in confusion, Roger sat. Then he blinked, as though just realizing that he'd followed Merlin's command. "Um, no thanks," he said.

"Miss Chandler, it's good to see that you found another position," Merlin said, resuming his seat.

I sat next to Roger. "It was good to find someone who valued my talents," I said, remembering that I was playing the role of disgruntled former employee. "If I'd known you weren't the only game in town for immunes, I'd have jumped ship a long time ago."

"I'm sorry you feel that way," Merlin said smoothly. Switching gears, he turned to Roger and added, "May I introduce my colleague, Owen Palmer? He's our theoretical magic genius in research and development. We were just discussing an old spell he's analyzing."

Owen started to rise from his chair. "If you'd like me to leave..."

"No, I'm glad you're here," Roger said. He'd regained some of his equilibrium and was back with his usual cool sense of control.

"So, what was it you wanted to discuss with us, Mr.... ah, you appear to have us at a disadvantage," Merlin said.

"You can call me Roger."

I found myself shivering at the degree of chill in the

room. None of the three men were going to let on that they felt the slightest hint of discomfort at the situation. I hadn't had a good demonstration of Roger's magical abilities, but Merlin and Owen were two of the most powerful wizards ever, and Sam was lurking silently nearby. If it came to a fight, I'd bet on the good guys winning.

But I suspected Roger was well aware of that. Direct confrontation wasn't really his style. He was here to feel out their weaknesses, I was sure, as well as probably to drop off a beacon he could use to come back magically when he thought they wouldn't be expecting him. That was, after all, the next step in his plan for taking over. Was this the pivotal incident Minerva had seen?

"What did you want to discuss, Roger?" Merlin asked, still conveying an air of geniality even while radiating dislike.

"I know there were some, shall we say, issues with your predecessor," Roger began.

"Do you mean his plot to bring me back so he could defeat me?" Merlin said with a smile that I found just a little bit frightening.

"Yes, that. But do you know that he maintained certain business relationships that were mutually beneficial? I'd like to restore those relationships."

"Ah, I believe you're speaking of the Collegium. I'm not sure why we would want anything to do with such an organization. I founded the group that grew to become Magic, Spells, and Illusions, Incorporated, to counter the earliest phase of the Collegium, though we called it something different back then."

"I can understand if your knowledge of our organization

is a bit archaic, given your circumstances," Roger said. "I know the early years tended to focus on dark magic and trying to manipulate rulers. Now, we're more of a business conglomerate with interests in a variety of industries. That's where we can benefit you."

"In what way?"

"We could bring you new clients. We can insure that you don't face competition."

"We already have very little competition."

"We can make sure you don't face any more crises like what you went through last year."

"If I'm not mistaken, those crises were largely of your making. Ivor Ramsay was your creature, and he was behind Phelan Idris. So I'm not sure how getting you involved again would be of any help to us. Now, if you need custom spell development or a discount on bulk licenses of retail spells, I'm sure we could work out a suitable arrangement. But this company will stand against the Collegium." Merlin rose, sending the signal that the meeting was coming to an end. "Was there anything else you wanted to discuss?"

Roger made no move to get up and leave. "You're making a mistake, and I don't think you understand how big a mistake you're making. We already have people positioned within your ranks. If something should happen to you, we'd have this company back under our control in a heartbeat."

"Would you?" Owen asked softly, raising an eyebrow. There was nothing that should have appeared threatening about what he'd said or how he'd said it, unless you knew him as well as I did. I wanted to dive for cover, and even Merlin began edging away. "I suspect you'd face more opposition than you expect, and I suspect your people aren't as well-placed as you think."

Roger didn't seem to read the danger, or else he was so arrogant he wasn't even looking for it. He stood and straightened his suit coat. "If that's how you feel, I won't be making that offer again. We could have worked well together, but if you're not willing to cooperate, I'll have to find other ways of getting what I need from you."

He turned and left without another word, and I jumped to my feet to hurry after him. Sam followed us, then flew ahead. As we passed under the awning on our way out of the building, I felt something fall into my hair. I glanced up and caught Sam winking at me. Acting as though I was sweeping my hair out of my coat collar, I caught the thing—a small stone, it looked like—and slid it into my pocket. My heart began racing. Had they found a way to track the car? Or was this a beacon?

I expected Roger to be in a foul mood on the way back to the office, but you'd have thought nothing was amiss, that everything had gone just the way he planned. "What did you think of that, Katie?" he asked.

"They weren't very cooperative, I guess. They can be rather stubborn. If they like the way something is, they're not too open to change."

"Owen Palmer, he's your ex, isn't he?"

I nodded.

"Is he as powerful as they say?"

"He seems to be. I've seen him win a lot of magical fights. And he knows a lot of obscure magic."

He smiled smugly. "Well, I have my own arsenal of obscure magic that he's probably never seen before."

I had to fight really hard not to smile at that, and I hoped I wasn't turning red. "He does a lot of research," was all I said. "That's what he does for fun. That's part of the reason we broke up. He wouldn't even take his nose out of an old book long enough to plan a wedding."

"He's never been up against me before."

When we returned to our headquarters, I held my breath as I entered the building from the parking garage. No alarms went off, and I forced myself not to reach into my pocket to touch the beacon. I figured the next barrier would be when we stepped off the elevator, but nothing happened. The final threshold would be when we entered the office suite, and my heart raced as I stepped through the doorway into our corridor. There were no alarms, no barrier sprang up, and no armed security men rushed toward me. Weak with relief, I started to turn off into my office, but Roger said, "Come with me. I want to pick your brain about MSI."

Here was the part I'd been dreading: having to actually betray my company. Or pretend to. I'd have to lie, and do so carefully. I wiped sweaty palms on my skirt as I took a seat across from Roger's desk. "What do you want to know?" I asked.

"What security did I miss in Merlin's office? I'm sure he's got some kind of measures in place."

"He's probably got it warded," I said. I didn't mention the gargoyle who'd been watching every moment of that meeting, but then he wasn't part of the standard security of the office. "I don't know what wards he uses because they don't work on me. There are key card kind of locks on most of the departments, like you have here. Those do work on me, because they're physical locks that just happen to be magically activated. They get updated frequently."

"What about bodyguards?"

"I don't think Merlin needs bodyguards. I've watched him take out armed robbers without breaking a sweat, and he doesn't lose magical battles."

"But he's usually alone?"

"I guess so. I don't know what he does away from the office."

"What about Palmer?"

"Well, to start with, he'd have to actually leave the office sometime. But, yeah, he's usually alone, and he lives alone." Except for a very protective cat.

Roger's smile was predatory, and his eyes were cold and hard. "Good. Good. Thank you. You've been very helpful."

Now I really wished I could call to warn them, but if they weren't on high alert after today, then another warning wasn't likely to help. I tried to focus on work, but it was hard when I was wondering what, exactly, Roger had planned. Was he going to swoop in and turn them into frogs when their guard was down?

About an hour later, I heard a furious scream. I jumped up and ran to see what was the matter. Had Roger touched a guarded book again?

When I got to his office, he was standing in the middle of a glowing circle on the floor, his fists clenched at his sides. "What happened to my spell?" he growled.

Fifteen

"What happened? Are you okay?" I asked, keeping well away from Roger. I'd never seen him look that outraged before. His evil had always been so cold and casual, but right now, he looked like he wanted to hit someone, and I had no desire for that someone to be me.

He got himself under control very quickly. "That spell should have taken me there. I left the beacon. I did everything right. Are you sure you transcribed it correctly?

Fortunately, that was one of the spells I'd given him before I got the idea to alter or hide them. "It worked for you before, didn't it?"

He calmed down even more, pausing to think. "You're right. it did."

"It is a hundred-year-old spell," I reminded him. "And MSI does like to stay on the cutting edge of magic while also researching old stuff. They're bound to have updated their security wards, or it's possible that Owen found the spell in the same source that writer did and incorporated it into the security measures."

Roger waved his hand, obliterating the glowing circle around himself. "I'll find another way in," he said with a shrug. "Or I'll catch Merlin some other time."

"My, but you've been busy," a deep male voice behind me said. I turned to see a hefty silver-haired man in a silvery gray suit. This man oozed power—both magical and personal. I thought I recognized him from the company meeting. He hadn't been at the central table, but he'd been on the first tier. I glanced back at Roger, expecting him to show deference to a man who was obviously higher on the food chain, but he hadn't changed his bearing at all. You'd never guess he'd been caught doing anything.

"I'm always busy," he said. "That's why I'm effective."

The visitor entered the office and seated himself in front of Roger's desk, crossing his legs and leaning back in the chair like he was planning to stay for a while. Roger hesitated only a fraction of a second before strolling casually over to his throne-like desk chair and taking a seat. I remained perfectly still, imagining myself to be a fly on the wall, in hopes that they'd both forget I was there.

"Funny thing is, Roger, I'm not seeing any results," the superior said. Everything about him radiated "expensive" to me, from his hand-tailored suit to a haircut so sharp that I suspected he got a trim every day. I got the sense of the kind of person who enjoyed fine food, fine wine, and fine art, and who had no taste for messes of any kind. "As busy as you seem to be, I'd expect to see big things from you. You're not freelancing, are you?"

"Let's just say that I'm in a research phase. I've recently come into some valuable information that I can use to our advantage, but deciphering it is taking some time. That's what I'm working with my assistant on." He gestured toward me, and the boss turned to notice me. I gave a meek wave. "She's a magical immune, so she can safely touch and transcribe a heavily warded document. Once I'm done, we'll have avenues into the rest of the magical world."

"Or you could do it the way we've handled things for centuries: Get our people on the inside and slowly take over without anyone noticing."

"That hasn't been particularly successful lately, has it?" Roger asked, his eyes taking on that predatory gleam that sent chills down my spine. "How many of the key companies have we lost in the past year or so? We lost Vandermeer, and we took a huge gamble on MSI that didn't pay off." I was glad neither of them was looking at me now because I wasn't sure I was able to keep all expression off my face. What would they have thought if they knew that the person who had a lot to do with both of those losses was in the same room with them? I had to wonder if Roger really knew all about my role at MSI. I'd thought I'd become famous among magical people, but maybe not so much.

And then I realized that Roger hadn't given himself credit for getting Vandermeer back. He was *definitely* working behind the back of the Collegium. If he'd wanted to move up, that would have been the first thing to mention.

"We'll get MSI," the boss said. "It's only a matter of time. Merlin is a problem, given who he is, but we'll get to him."

"I don't think Merlin's your real problem there," Roger said, his smile smug. "He's a figurehead."

"Exactly. We simply need a new figurehead, one who belongs to us, but whom they'll all trust. They'll never know they're working for us."

"And who has that kind of credibility?" Roger asked.

"You do remember that we have people on the Council. But it's not your concern. You're young, ambitious, and bright, but you're not ready yet. What I need you to do is make money for us. Stop messing around with old spells. You just about tore the connective fabric of our operation apart. You don't know how close you were to needing to buy an airplane ticket to get home tonight. If you're making money, we need to start seeing it." He stood, straightened his suit coat, and left, with a slight nod at me.

If I'd expected Roger to act in any way like a kid called onto the carpet, I'd have been disappointed. He didn't quite roll his eyes, but he didn't seem at all cowed, either. "Thank you for keeping your mouth shut," he said to me. "I never told you that you weren't to talk about what we're doing here, but you seem to have picked up on the message. That's good. You're smart."

I shrugged. "I figured that if you wanted to tell him you'd taken Vandermeer back, you would have told him yourself. It wasn't my place to do so."

His face grew uncharacteristically somber. "Do you think this was that critical decision the seer spoke of? Something pivotal was going to happen today. I just wish I knew I'd done it or not done it. I don't feel like I changed my fate today."

"I don't think you're ever aware of that sort of thing until well after the fact. I've found that it's usually the little things that end up having the biggest impact." Like deciding to take the subway to work instead of walking one morning. Would I have met Owen and learned about magic, or would they have found me, anyhow?

"Maybe it was learning that I need to get some work done to get inside. I have to bring in MSI before I go charging upstairs to make my move." His eyes were distant, and I got the feeling he was talking to himself more than he was talking to me. In fact, it seemed like he'd forgotten I was still there.

He blinked, returning to the present, and said, "I kept you away from home all night last night, so why don't you go home now? You deserve a break."

"Thank you," I said. I wondered if I should leave the beacon in his office while I had the chance. Would the MSI gang want to beam directly there, or would it be better if they entered somewhere else and then charged? I was afraid to leave it in my office; if it was found, I'd be in big trouble. That settled it—Roger's office, it was.

I made sure he was looking down at something, and on my way out, I slipped my hand into my pocket, found the beacon, and brushed against the ficus tree near the door, dropping the beacon onto the soil, where it blended in with the ornamental rocks around the tree trunk.

Now I was dying to know what Owen and the others had planned with that beacon, and I had news for them. As soon as I was home, I rushed out again, calling Marcia once I was back on the street. "I need a meeting with Owen, as soon as possible, and I'm feeling extra paranoid."

"More so than usual?"

"I met one of the higher-ups today. I don't know

how much attention he paid to me, but he's definitely suspicious of Roger. If I were him, I'd be watching me."

"Okay, I'll get back to you."

For lack of anything better to do, I went shopping. There wasn't anything I particularly needed or wanted, but I wanted to be out of Collegium control—out of my home and around more or less normal people. For about an hour, I tried on clothes and ended up buying a few brightly colored things. I wasn't sure I ever wanted to wear black again.

My phone rang, and when I answered it, Marcia said, "Go to Grand Central. I think you know what to do from there."

I was only a block or so from the subway, so I headed that way. That was when I got the impression I was being followed. I might not have magical powers, but I still felt it when someone was staring at me. Maybe it was simple situational awareness, and maybe it had nothing to do with the Collegium, but I wasn't taking any chances.

Unfortunately, since I was already at the subway entrance, I was committed. Turning back now and changing course would only show that I'd spotted them, and that would prove that I'd been looking for them in the first place.

After going through the turnstiles, I went to the middle of the platform. It was rush hour, so the station was packed. That made it a little easier for me to turn and spot my follower and then keep an eye on him without being too obvious about it. I could hide behind other people and still stare at him without him seeing me stare at him. If I hadn't been so paranoid, I might not have paid him any attention. He didn't wear all black or a trenchcoat and fedora, or anything else that made him look like someone who'd be following a person. He just looked like an average guy—an average guy who'd been maintaining a perfect distance of about twenty feet away from me since I first noticed him.

He didn't act like he thought I'd spotted him. I knew they knew I was immune to magic, so I didn't think he believed he was invisible to me. He just seemed to think I wouldn't suspect I was being tailed.

He got on the same car I did, at the opposite end. Even if he'd wanted to reach me, he wouldn't have been able to fight his way through the sardine can to get to me. I wondered if I should get off at my planned destination. I didn't want to lead him to Owen, but if I was right about what Owen had planned, that wouldn't be a problem. It would probably be easier to "accidentally" lose someone in Grand Central than at any other station along the way. If I couldn't shake the guy, I could always jump on the S train to Times Square.

I wasn't being strategic when I waited until the last second before getting off the train. It was just so crowded that it took me that long to find an open path to the door. I slipped out sideways while the recorded voice said to stand clear of the closing doors. I wasn't sure if my follower made it off the train, too, and I forced myself not to look back over my shoulder. Instead, I forged ahead, weaving through the throngs of people and making my way straight for the exit.

I headed to the mall-like area, pausing to browse in the shop windows. In the reflection, I could see that my follower was still there. He didn't look too concerned. Maybe they were just curious about me or possibly thought that I was on a mission for Roger. Being sent home right after the boss's visit with Roger must have raised suspicions. Little did they know, I'd come home to carry out my own mission, not Roger's.

I spent some time browsing in the bookstore—the sort of thing guaranteed to drive a follower crazy with boredom unless he also liked bookstore browsing. He stayed near the front, where I wouldn't be able to leave without passing him, rather than following me into the shelves.

When I reached the back corner of the store, someone grabbed me by the arm and pulled me behind the shelves. I did a double take when I found myself looking at a near twin of myself.

A longer glance revealed that it was Marcia, her blond hair covered by a brown wig. She wore jeans and sneakers like mine. "Good, you're dressed the way I guessed, and Owen was right about you hitting the bookstore," she said.

"This is part of the plan?"

"You said you were worried about being followed."

"And I was right."

"The guy by the sale books?"

"Yeah, he's been there at least since outside the Astor Place station."

"Okay, you wait here. I'll lead him out."

I eyed her up and down. The hair was close to the right color, and she was about my height, but my follower would have to be really unobservant to mistake her for me.

"Don't worry, there's a spell on me," she said, noting

my skeptical expression. "To him, I'll look like you. But we need to fix you, just in case. First, let's trade coats." Mine was khaki and hers was black, so that alone changed our appearance. She pulled a floppy knitted cap out of her bag and shoved it onto my head, then added a pair of thick-rimmed glasses. "There. You no longer look like the person he's been tailing. I suspect you know where to meet Owen."

"I have a good idea." I handed her my shopping bags, and she handed me her bag. "Okay, let's see if this works."

I lurked behind the bookcases, watching as Marcia walked right past the follower to the store exit. He let her get out the door before going after her. I looked around for any other follower I might not have noticed, but only the one guy had moved. I let them get out of sight before leaving the store and going down to the train platforms.

It was a little riskier getting to the secret passages at this time of day because there were so many people. On the other hand, that made it easier to disappear into a crowd. When I felt someone take my arm and turned to see Owen, I suspected we were going to literally disappear.

As soon as the train at the platform departed, we jumped down, ran into the tunnel, and crawled through a space in the wall. "Aren't there dragons here?" I asked. The smell of sulfur was pretty strong.

"I got them all to better homes."

"Yeah, and that's what you said the last time."

"Really, I went back and took care of it."

"No others have gotten in since then?"

"I can't entirely guarantee that, but you know I know how to deal with them."

I couldn't believe that we were wasting our precious time together bickering about dragons, but both of us were on edge. "I got your beacon. At least, that's what I think it was," I said.

"Good. I figured you'd know to play along. I take it you didn't set off any alarms."

"Not that I know of. Unless it was a silent alarm and that's why I'm being followed."

"Where did you leave it?"

"In a potted plant in Roger's office. I couldn't think of what else to do with it."

"That's perfect."

"You're not going to do something stupid like beam yourself straight into his office, are you?"

If the light in there had been better, I was sure I'd see him turning red. As it was, I imagined I could feel a little burst of heat off his face. "The combination of that and the spell for getting to the top office could let us get in and take them all down."

"You don't think he's warded against his own spell?"

"You said he was arrogant. Do you think he even suspects that we know about his spell?"

"Actually, he tried to beam himself over to MSI this afternoon, and it failed because he ran up against your wards, so he at least knows that you know enough to ward against it. I'm not sure he suspects a counterattack, but is a commando raid really the best way to handle things?"

"What else did you have in mind? Remember, we're not the FBI taking down the mob, where we have to find grounds for charges that will stand up in court. We just need to stop them."

"But we need to stop them for good. You haven't seen the size of this organization. If you take out the top, someone else will rise to fill the gap."

"Not if we also take out the ways they have power over others."

I sighed. "Maybe you're right, and I guess whatever plan you can carry out soon is your best bet, because the boss was talking about going after MSI. They want to get rid of Merlin, and they've got someone on the Council they think they can install to make MSI their company again."

"Someone on the Council? I wonder which one. I'll have to talk to James and Gloria." Owen's foster parents had once been on the magical Council and retained ties to the bigwigs.

"Meanwhile, Roger wants to get there before anyone above him does, so that when he takes over, he'll already have the power base in place. I'm not entirely sure what his plan is. I get the feeling that while the Collegium has been mostly secret so far, he wants to go for more obvious world domination."

"Minerva said we have to stop him. She saw some frightening things if he succeeds. Fortunately, so far he seems to be making all the right choices—for us, not for him. That's why we need to act soon. We have to stop him before he goes further, and then we'll stop the Collegium."

"You know, it might undermine them if they couldn't operate in secrecy anymore. We could bring them down by sharing evidence of what they've done. They have a massive library, but I've only been there once, so I don't know what's in there, just that it goes way back in time. I'd need you to translate most of it, but I'm sure there's something we could use in there."

"I think we'd need something current. What about concentrating on the people in charge? What do you know about them?"

"Today was the first time I saw one of the bosses up close. I got the feeling Roger's been hiding me. He didn't even introduce me other than as his assistant. And I can't use that spell of yours to get to the top, thanks to the magical immunity."

"But we do already have magical people inside."

"I thought I was the first one to infiltrate them." And then it dawned on me. "Yeah, we've got a whole frog pond full of people who aren't happy with the Collegium."

"You know what to do about that."

I shuddered at the thought. "I don't seem to have to go through any kind of security screening to go down to the frog pond, so I might be able to reach them and kiss a frog or two. I'd need to transcribe a copy of the spell to get to the top for them to use."

"We should coordinate. Do you think Roger's likely to be in his office tomorrow afternoon?"

"I have no idea. He doesn't keep to a strict schedule. For all I know, he'll be off meeting with harpies or threatening little old ladies who run magical bakeries."

"I just wish there were a way you could signal us from in there."

"I have some access to the outside world now, but I suspect it's still pretty restricted. I might be able to reach Minerva if I need to get a message to you." I shook my head. "I still don't like it. You know how dangerous these people are."

"That's why we're trying to stop them. And how do you think I've been feeling all this time while you've been working with them?"

I slid my arms around his waist and snuggled up against him. "Aww, you care."

He returned my embrace. "Of course I care. It's been awful, knowing you're spending your days with that psycho—especially now that I've met him."

"That's probably the worst I've seen him. Well, other than when he flipped out when he couldn't just pop into MSI. Most of the time, he's actually kind of nice. He'd be a great boss if you didn't know about the world domination and frog stuff."

"You aren't going to have a problem taking him down, are you?"

"Heck, no. I know about the world domination and frog stuff."

"So, how's this for a plan? We pop in, take down Roger, then you and maybe some others go down and save the frogs, and we all use the spell to get to the top and take them down."

"You make it sound so easy. It can't possibly be that smooth."

"There might be a few complications."

"Does the beacon let you know where the building actually is? Can't you just storm the castle that way?"

"Believe it or not, the office building is really just a parking garage and one level here in Manhattan. We tracked it, and that's all we found. Everything else is distributed around the world through various portals. Your office—assuming that's where you went when you went back to the office—is in London. That makes it really hard to get to them through conventional means. Raiding the entrance here in the city does no good. If we found a location we could raid, they could run to another one before we got to them. That's why we needed that beacon, to be able to jump straight to them."

"We're only going to have one shot at this, you know."

"That's why we're taking it. If anything goes wrong, get out of there, immediately. Get to the parking garage as soon as you can, and from there someone can get you to safety. We've got gargoyles watching it now."

I nodded. This was starting to sound serious.

He caught my chin and tilted my head up. "Hey, it's gonna be okay. Have you ever seen me lose a fight?"

"Not a magical one, no."

"We're prepared. We have a counterspell for any spell he might possibly use. I'm more worried about you getting caught in the crossfire."

He gave me a gentle kiss that lingered. "And now we'd better get out of here. Before long, they'll realize they're following the wrong person. You need to meet up with Marcia in the ladies room in the dining concourse."

We indulged in one last kiss before sneaking out of the hiding place. We had to wait for a train to leave, and then we returned to the platform. He blended into the crowd of people getting off the adjacent train, and I headed for the bathroom. I spotted the tail lurking nearby, watching the doorway, so I guessed Marcia was inside. He didn't give me a second glance when I passed him on my way in.

I didn't see Marcia right away, but when I called out her name, she popped out of a stall. "Is he still out there?" she asked.

"Yeah."

"Then it looks like it worked." We traded coats again, and I gave her the hat and glasses. She gave me my shopping bags. "Did you get what you needed?"

"Yeah."

"You don't sound very enthusiastic."

"He's got a crazy plan, and my warnings only made it worse."

"If he wasn't coming up with crazy plans, he wouldn't be the guy you fell in love with. Now, fix your hair. You've got hat hair."

She took off her wig and smoothed her hair before heading out, and I checked myself in the mirror. She was right. I did look rather frightful. I fixed my hair as well as I could and touched up my lipstick, then took a few breaths before leaving the bathroom. The shopping bags felt heavier than they had before, and I noticed that there were a couple of new ones. She'd really done her job in covering for me. I figured that was enough shopping to have validated my visit to Grand Central, so I headed for the subway, feeling my tail fall in behind me.

I changed trains at Union Square to go across town and walked the rest of the way home. I noticed my follower reflected in the glass of the front door as I unlocked it, and I wondered how long he'd wait out there before he realized I wasn't going anywhere.

With the big MSI operation planned for the next day, I didn't dare do anything that might make the Collegium suspicious while they were watching me, even if they were just keeping an eye on me because they thought Roger was up to something. What were they even looking for, anyway? Clandestine meetings with his secret army?

My personal phone rang, and I saw on the caller ID that it was Marcia. "Hey, just checking to see if you made it home okay."

"Yeah, I'm home. But the subway was super crowded, and there were more people than I'm used to on the sidewalk on the way home." I hoped she got my meaning. I went to the French doors, hiding behind the curtains to watch the guy still standing across the street. Him lurking out there was obvious enough that I thought I'd look pretty dense if I didn't notice it, so I added, "I think I'm being stalked."

"Ooh, creepy," she said. "Are you sure?"

"It's hard to tell. But there's a guy who's been lurking on my street for long enough that I'm starting to think I should bring him some cocoa."

"Maybe you should call the police."

"Maybe I should, just to report the lurking. I don't know if he's actually following me." If he'd suddenly moved out of sight, I'd have known for sure that they were listening to me, but he stayed where he was.

"Can you hang on a sec? I've got a call coming through on my other line."

While she was away, I stood watching the lurker. In a way, it was nice to have my paranoia validated. It would have been a total waste if I'd taken all those precautions all this time and nobody had been watching me at all.

"You still there?" Marcia asked, and there was something different about her voice.

"Yeah. Is something wrong?"

"Did your friend you ran into this evening say anything about his plans for the rest of the day?"

"No, nothing in particular. Why?"

"I just heard from Rod, and he hasn't been able to get in touch with him."

My whole body seemed to turn to ice. "What?"

Sixteen

"Whoa, calm down!" Marcia said, but I noticed that she didn't sound very calm. "I didn't say that, just that Rod hasn't been able to get in touch with him. He's probably just working late and not answering his phone."

Forcing myself to stop hyperventilating, I said, "Yeah, and it wouldn't be the first time. When he gets in the zone, you could set off dynamite next to him, and he'd just think he needed to tweak an element in the spell he's working on." I took a long, deep breath and let it out slowly. "Though it might not hurt to have someone go to the office to check on him."

"Rod's on his way over there. He didn't say anything to you about where he was going next?"

"No. He was talking about plans for tomorrow. I'd guess he'd be setting up for that tonight. Maybe he's talking to his boss about that? He might not have taken his phone to the meeting." Already, I felt a bit better. That explanation made perfect sense. It wasn't even grasping at straws.

"Gemma and I will run over to his place to check, just in case."

I was already reaching for my coat. "I'll join you."

"No! Remember? You've got other stuff you're working on."

I forced myself not to groan out loud. "Yeah, you're right." It would be a pity to blow the entire operation when we were on the verge of a breakthrough. I told myself that Owen was just meeting with Merlin and Sam to plan their battle strategy. We were panicking over nothing because we were all on edge right now. "But keep me posted and let me know if you hear anything."

"Will do."

After I ended the call, I went back to the window and peered out between the blinds. There was a different person standing in the same place as my previous follower, so I must have missed a shift change. His posture looked more bored than alert. The gargoyle on the roof hadn't moved, but then that was what gargoyles were best at.

I resisted the urge to pace, mostly because I didn't have the room for it and just one lap around the small apartment had left me with bruises. Instead, I sat on the sofa, the TV remote in one hand and my phone in the other. I was too restless to actually watch anything, so I flipped up and down the dial. The Collegium had sprung for the full cable package, so I had every channel that was available. I didn't even realize that there were so many channels.

I wasn't sure how much time passed before my phone rang again because I was forcing myself not to look at the clock. It was Marcia again. "He's not at home, it doesn't seem. At least, he's not answering the door. Does he ever do that?"

"He has, but only when he was really, really upset about something. He seemed to be in a pretty good mood when I saw him, so I doubt he's barricaded himself in to pout. Any word from Rod?"

"Not yet. That will take longer than us only going a few blocks."

"Right, right. Of course."

"I'm sure it's just Rod worrying. You know what he's like."

Actually, I hadn't thought of Rod as being the mother hen type, but then Owen was like a little brother to him, and he'd been charged since childhood with looking after Owen. "Let me know the moment you hear anything."

More waiting ensued. I made it all the way around the channel dial, even through all the music channels. It was getting late, and I thought I ought to be getting ready for bed, but I wanted to be fully dressed in case I had to go out. Not that I was sure what I could do if I went out. The Collegium and Roger believed I'd broken up with Owen. I'd give myself away if I went running off to wait in an emergency room or to search for him, and there were people better at searching than I was.

One thing I worried was that he'd done something really crazy, like testing that beacon in the evening after Roger was gone, making sure it worked before they did the actual raid. What if he'd done that and was caught or got stuck? I imagined finding him hiding under my desk the next morning. It was a better mental image than all the worst-case scenarios that were flooding my brain.

Finally, my phone rang again, and this time it was Rod. "He didn't say anything to you about what he planned?" he asked, skipping all pleasantries.

"No, just that he had big plans for tomorrow."

"Yeah, we'd discussed that."

"You didn't have any prep work planned for tonight?"

"Not that he mentioned to me."

"So, you didn't find him at the office?"

"Nope. Sorry."

"Have you checked at his folks' place? He mentioned having something he wanted to talk to them about."

I could practically hear the relief coming through my phone. "That didn't even cross my mind. It's a bit late to call there, but I'll check in with them first thing in the morning."

I tried to feel the same kind of relief, but I found too many holes in that explanation. I had a feeling I'd learn exactly what happened the next day, and the news wouldn't be good.

I hadn't heard from Rod by the time the car came to pick me up for work in the morning, and that meant I wouldn't hear anything until the end of the day—unless I heard it from Roger. I'd be cut off from the rest of the world while I worked in London without actually being able to visit the city.

I hurried through changing clothes and got to my office. Everything seemed strikingly normal. There were no signs of a battle having been fought there overnight, and there were no wizards lurking under my desk. Roger wasn't in yet, but when I stopped by his office, I saw that the beacon was still in the potted plant.

I was heading back to my office when I saw Trish approaching. I hadn't seen her since I'd been given the job as Roger's assistant, so I'd assumed that she'd been either booted or reassigned. Since she was still in the company uniform, I supposed that meant she'd been reassigned. "Wow, you're still around," she said. "I was starting to wonder if you'd vanished and if I should try to look you up."

I felt a pang of guilt that I hadn't thought of checking on her. "No, I'm still around," I said. "I just got moved." Actually, I was kind of surprised that she didn't know that. Had she not been told that she didn't get the assistant job?

"Closer to the boss, I see."

"Yeah. The better to cater to his every whim."

She glanced around furtively, then whispered, "I've got to drop something off, but then can we talk?"

"Sure."

She ran to Roger's office, returning a moment later. "This way. I think I know a place that's safe." She led me to the women's restroom at the other end of the hall and turned on a water tap. "Okay, we knew this place isn't on the up and up, but how bad is it? There's something brewing, and it's giving me really bad vibes." she said.

"Well, it's magic, which makes it a little weird," I said.

"You've got more experience with magic than I do, so I guess you'd know, but isn't it weird even for a magic place? It's not the magic that's strange. It's like working for The Firm, or something. People keep vanishing, and there's all this security. We aren't even allowed to know where we're working. Yeah, I knew all that from the start, but it's been getting really strange. He's had me reading some wacked-out books that sound like a how-to in medieval torture. Somehow, I don't think this is just a hobby for him."

I hesitated, unsure how I could answer her. Could it be a trap? This would be a great way to get me to admit my suspicions and what I was up to, and that would help her earn points with the management. The timing was awfully suspicious. What were the odds that she'd approach me with concerns the day after someone started following me?

But I figured even a person who was totally on board and not spying for the enemy would think some things were weird. "It is different from my last company," I admitted. "The security is a bit strict. I don't think you'd have to go through so much even to work for the CIA."

"I know, right?" She turned the tap up even louder and leaned closer to me to whisper, "And have you seen them turn people into frogs? What's up with that?"

"Well, I suppose it's better than killing them."

She gave me a suspicious look, like she was starting to fit me in the same category as Roger. "I don't know about that."

"It's reversible. You know, like in the fairy tales."

Her face screwed up in distaste. "Kissing them? Ew!"

"But it does work."

"And then there was a guy he met with. A few days later, he sent me to that office, and there was a picture of him on the wall in that room, but he wasn't anywhere around. I felt like the picture was watching me, like it might even move when I wasn't looking."

I couldn't help but shudder. With Owen missing, I had to wonder if that's what had happened to him. I knew how to save him if he was a frog, but I didn't know if they'd found a way to break the picture spell. "I've heard something about that spell," I said vaguely.

"So, I'm not going crazy?"

"No, afraid not."

"Damn. I mean, it's a cool job and all, but I'm not sure I'm down with this. There have got to be other companies that could use a magical immune."

"That's a talk we should have elsewhere." I didn't think I'd said anything that would get me in trouble if she was a plant, but I got the feeling her concerns were genuine.

I picked up some coffee at the nearby break room before heading back to my office, so I'd have a reason for having been away from my desk. There still wasn't any sign of Roger. Him and Owen both being missing at the same time set off all my mental alarm bells.

While he was out, I took advantage of the opportunity to make a couple of copies of the spell that would take us to the top of the Collegium and hid them in my desk drawers, so I'd be ready for when the raid happened. I just wished I knew approximately when that would be so I could brace myself.

I was back at work transcribing the final pages of the book when I heard cheerful whistling coming down the hall. I looked up to see Roger leaning nonchalantly against the door frame. "You can thank me later," he said with a smile.

"For what?" I asked, unable to keep the suspicion out of my voice, and probably also off my face.

"I took care of a little problem for you, and also a problem for me. Let's just call it a win-win. Two birds with one stone."

"Oh?" I could feel a ball of dread forming in my throat, cutting off my breathing and making me want to gulp.

"You'll find out later. It's a surprise. But for now, we've got business to attend to. Come on."

He led me not to his office, but to the elevators. I hoped we weren't going to be out long because it would ruin the plans for the attack if he wasn't in his office. That was, if the attack was still on with Owen missing. If he was still missing. I hated being cut off from outside communication like this.

We seemed to be in the car far longer than usual, and when we stopped, we were at the mansion I recognized as the magical Council headquarters. It had been miraculously rebuilt after being almost totaled in the previous summer's epic showdown. "The Council?" I asked.

"Oh, you know it? I'm getting to them before my boss can. I'm sure a clever person like yourself has already figured out that I have my own agenda. I'm not waiting on them to act. And if there's someone they've got on their payroll, I'm going to turn them to me. Now, keep your eyes peeled and let me know if they've got anything I can't see."

We seemed to be expected, for we were waved right in. I didn't recognize the person who greeted us from my interactions with the Council, and I got the impression she was a staffer for one of the members. She was young, brisk, efficient, and eager, and she melted under the force of Roger's best smile. "I'm so glad you called," she said, pushing her hair back behind her ear. "I'm Lynnae

Greene, Mr. Burke's assistant. He's interested in your proposal, but can't meet with you about it now. I do have some questions for you, though."

She ushered us into an office, where the discussion sounded like just about any business meeting between people who were trying to sound each other out without giving away any specifics. I couldn't quite tell if she knew exactly who she was dealing with or if she was entirely unaware that she was selling her boss to the Collegium. I really missed being around people who said exactly what they meant rather than talking around it in vague terms. Heck, I missed being able to be blunt and direct.

"I am curious to know how you have an influence over hiring at MSI, though," she said, and I perked up, returning my attention to the immediate present.

"Let's just say that there are changes in the works. I represent a group of investors who are exerting our influence. The current leadership was something of an experiment, and you know it wasn't actually planned. It was part of a scheme. I don't know why we should be tied to that situation when it's no longer relevant. Don't get me wrong, he's a great wizard, but is he really the person who can best lead us in the current century?"

Her easy acceptance of the blatant lie about representing investors told me that she didn't know what was really going on. She was still willing to undermine MSI, but she didn't know she was selling them out to the Collegium. I took note of who she was and who her boss was so I could warn Merlin.

That was, if I got a chance to. Were the plans still on without Owen? Assuming Owen was still missing.

Roger looked positively gleeful in the car on the way back to the office. "They really aren't prepared for someone like me, are they?" he asked—rhetorically, I was sure. "Even the Collegium has become stale and corporate. The slightest bit of innovation, and they don't see you coming."

I successfully refrained from mentioning that it was hardly innovation to use a century-old playbook, but it was a struggle. I don't think he would have even heard me, though. He was caught up in his own little world that he ruled, and I wasn't sure he was aware of my presence. He was in full villain monologue mode.

"I know it's ironic that the person this man took down was my great-grandfather, and now I'm using his methods against his successors, but that just makes it better," he said. He gestured, and a glass of champagne appeared in his hand. "Would you like one?" he asked me.

"No, thanks."

"But I have big plans. Why do we lurk in the shadows? Why are we such a secret? We should be known and feared. We have magic. We should be ruling the world."

When the car stopped after a fairly long drive, I was surprised when we didn't emerge in the parking garage. Instead, we were outside a row of old houses in a neighborhood perhaps best described as "questionable." Except one of the houses seemed to have been lavishly restored so that it looked the way it must have back in the day when this was a nice neighborhood and these were single-family homes instead of being carved up into apartments.

"He's supposed to live around here..." Roger said, frowning at the row of houses.

"You're looking for a wizard?" I asked, wondering if I should tell him what I saw.

"Yes. You see something?"

"One of these houses is really nice."

He grinned. "Of course. He's got it veiled. You wouldn't want to advertise that to the neighbors. Lead the way."

Hoping I wasn't leading Roger to a new victim, I went up the front steps of the nice house and rang the doorbell. A harried-looking man, his hair sticking out in every direction and his clothes askew, answered it after a few minutes. He tried to slam the door when he saw Roger standing behind me, where he hadn't been visible through the peephole, but Roger held out a hand, pushing the door open, and shoved past the man into the house. "You're late," he said.

"You can't rush this kind of work," the man said, sounding less frazzled than he looked.

"I'm not rushing you. I'm asking you to stick to the deadline you agreed upon. My plans hinge on this spell, and my other efforts to get help with it have been somewhat less than fruitful. Now, what do you have?"

"It's not ready. My last few tests haven't worked." He gestured to his hair and clothes. "And this is in controlled laboratory conditions. Worse could happen in the real world."

I figured that looking that messy would be Roger's worst nightmare. "What kind of worse?" he asked, eyeing the man's appearance with distaste.

"This could happen with your skin and organs. I have failsafes to shut it down if it's not working. If you tried this against a real block and it didn't work, it could kill you."

"Oh, is that all? Would the first one being killed break it down?"

The man blinked at Roger, like he wasn't quite sure what Roger was asking. "Excuse me?" he finally said.

"If I sent one person through and this happened, would it be safer for the rest?"

"Maybe. I haven't tested it that way, since it would involve my own death, and that would make it difficult for me to report the results."

"What if I found a subject for you?"

The man and I exchanged a horrified glance, but Roger was already on his way out the door. Who was he going to sacrifice to test it? I hoped not one of his frogs. I started to run after him, thinking he was heading back to the office, but he just stood on the sidewalk, watching the street with his hands on his hips, like he was evaluating what he saw.

Two teenagers came by. They probably should have been in school, and when they saw Roger, they took on the furtive appearance of people trying not to be caught doing something they weren't supposed to do. He did look like he could be some kind of official.

He smiled at them, and it might even have looked like a friendly smile if I hadn't known him. "Hey, kids, how'd you like to earn some money?" he said. I thought he couldn't have sounded fishier if he'd invited them into his plain white van with promises of candy, but their eyes lit up.

From behind Roger, I shook my head at them and gave them a warding-off signal, hoping they'd pick up on the danger, but he'd said the magic word, "money," and they were hooked. "What do you need?" one of them asked.

"I need you to help me with something, both of you, inside this house."

They were apparently street-savvy enough to question this, for they exchanged a glance with each other. "You can't do it out here?" the kid responded.

"No, sorry."

The kids resumed walking. "Sorry, nope."

But by walking on, they moved closer to Roger, and he waved his hand when they neared him. Both of them froze, and their eyes went blank. A twitch of his finger made them follow him up the steps and into the house.

"You can't do that!" I protested. "They're just kids!" I could stand by and watch people be turned into frogs, since I knew that the spell could be reversed, but this could kill them, and I didn't care if I was breaking cover. Any reasonable human being who wasn't a sociopath would protest.

He whirled on me. "I can't? It's not up to you to tell me what I can't do. Why should they matter to you? They're nobody, and they're not even magical. They'll never know what happened to them."

The magical scientist, or whatever he was, was equally appalled. "I can't test this on people," he said.

"You'll do what I say," Roger snarled. "Now, here are your subjects. Send the first one through, then see what happens to the second one."

The scientist led us to a back room that looked a lot like Owen's lab might if it were in someone's house. It was full of old books and arcane equipment. Twitching like he was distinctly unhappy, the man fiddled with some things on one piece of equipment. I could tell that the use of magic in the room was surging, even though it didn't affect me.

I realized that they were testing a new version of the beaming spell, designed to get past the MSI defenses. Roger grabbed one of the entranced kids by the shoulders, and I called out, "Wait! Will it work the same way if he's not casting the spell?"

"She has a good point," the scientist said. "Whoever goes through has to cast the spell for himself." The look he gave me told me that it wasn't necessarily true, but that he'd jump at the excuse.

"Fine," Roger snarled. At a gesture from him, the kids walked, zombielike, toward the front door.

I followed to make sure they were okay. When they hit the sidewalk, they went back to going on their way, seemingly unaffected. I allowed myself a sigh of relief. And then the harpy appeared.

When she swooped down out of the sky, my instinct was to duck for cover, but she ignored me. She landed on the sidewalk and went up the steps, just as a second harpy joined her. It seemed that Roger had called in other test subjects. These didn't count as innocents, but I still wasn't comfortable with the situation.

"He's going to use you to carry out a dangerous test," I hissed to them as I followed them to the back room. I couldn't tell if they heard me or if they were ignoring me.

"You summoned us," one of the harpies said to Roger in a voice like nails on a chalkboard.

"Yes, I have a duty for you." He handed her a sheet of paper and a small pebble. "Do this spell."

She didn't even question him. She read the spell, apparently internalizing it, handed the page back to him, clutched the pebble, closed her eyes, and murmured a few words. I instinctively flinched when she disappeared in a burst of light, then I was afraid to look at the results. She lay on the other side of the room, more or less in one piece. I couldn't tell whether or not she was alive, and she'd been such a mess to begin with that it was hard to tell how much she'd been altered. She didn't get up. I wanted to run to her to make sure she was okay, since the barrier wouldn't affect me, but I wasn't sure what I could do for her, and I wasn't sure she'd be grateful for the help. Right now, I was safer on this side of the magical test barrier.

Roger turned to the other harpy. "Now you. It should be easier for you if my theory is correct."

She looked at him like he was crazy—if you can shock a harpy, you're really bad news—and moved as though to run for it, but he held up a hand, using magic to hold her still.

"If you won't do the job, you won't get paid," he said, his tone perfectly polite, like he was only asking her to rinse out her coffee mug.

With a snarl, she took the spell and a pebble from him, then read the spell. She, too, disappeared in a flash of light, reappearing on the other side of the room. She, at least, was vertical, though she looked a little fried. With a death glare at Roger, she bent to check on the other harpy.

"Ah, excellent," Roger said, rubbing his hands together. "That should work. I'll just send a few shock troops through first to soften the barriers before going through with the valuable people. Thank you," he said to the scientist.

"Here's the modified spell. You have the mates to the beacon?" the scientist said, looking a little less nervous.

"Yes, I have plenty." He reached into his breast pocket, pulled out a wad of cash, and peeled off a few bills to hand to the scientist. "Good work, even if it was a little slow."

The scientist went back to one of his devices, and I felt the magic ebb as he brought down the wards they were testing. Roger walked over to the harpies and threw a few bills at them. "This should cover your time, and this activity falls under your retainer," he said. I was relieved to see that the first harpy was starting to stir, then realized how odd that feeling was when I was used to thinking of them as an enemy.

"We said we would fight for you. We did not agree to be test subjects," the vertical harpy snarled.

"You're working for me to do whatever I need you to do," he replied. "And I'll need all of you this afternoon. We'll meet at the usual place at four thirty. Come along, Katie."

When we were back in the car, he fixed me with a stern glare and said, "In the future, you are not to contradict me in front of other people. When I ask for your input, I want you to be candid, but when I don't ask for it, I don't want to hear it."

I was only able to say a humble, "Yes, sir," because I knew that this was all going to be over with very soon.

All smiles once again, he settled back in his seat and said, "That went well, in spite of your ex's lack of cooperation."

"Ex-excuse me?" I stammered.

"I thought I might as well go to the source in figuring

out how to break through the new wards, but he wasn't very helpful. I suppose that was to be expected. On the bright side, you won't have to worry about him anymore."

"I wasn't worried about him," I said, trying to sound carefree, even as my stomach went into freefall. "I haven't even thought about him in ages."

His smile slipped ever so slightly. "Oh? Well, you'll have to think about him even less now. I took care of him for you. Well, really, mostly for me, since I needed him out of my way, but I thought you'd also be pleased."

"What did you do to him?" I asked, trying to sound only mildly interested rather than panic-stricken. I couldn't believe that I was actually praying he meant the frog pond and not something worse. He'd mentioned Owen refusing to cooperate. What torture had he used?

"Don't worry, he's comfortable. Let's just say that he's found a new pad."

I vowed to myself that I'd save Owen if I had to kiss every frog in the city.

Seventeen

It took every ounce of will I had, but I made myself follow Roger back to our offices. I didn't care what it took; that man was going down today.

But for that to happen, the MSI gang needed to attack before Roger went to meet up with his evil army. I didn't know if the MSI team was still planning whatever they were going to do with Owen missing, but they needed to do it—and soon.

I just wished I had a way to warn them. How could I get a message out when I was cut off from the outside world?

The beacon, I realized. They had to be able to see where it was, and if it moved, maybe they'd see that as a signal. I gathered up the pages I'd transcribed so far that day and took them to Roger's office. On my way out, I "accidentally" dropped my pen, and when I bent to pick it up, I snagged the beacon from the potted plant and put it in my pocket.

I wondered where the portal that took me to London

was. I had a feeling it was somewhere in the hallway between the entrance and the suite of offices around Roger. I headed down the hallway to the break room for coffee, then farther down the hall to find Trish.

"You're right, something's fishy," I whispered to her. "I may need you later." Out loud, I said, "Have you checked out the spa downstairs? I was thinking about a spa day later this afternoon. My nails are a mess, and I could use a back massage."

She nodded and gave me a thumbs-up. "Ooh, sounds wonderful. I bet I can get away a little early today."

I returned to my office. I figured by now I'd got the attention of anyone who was watching the beacon. Just in case, I paced the perimeter of my office, drawing a circle. I didn't know how high the resolution was, but it was the only way I could think of to convey urgency.

Satisfied that I'd done what I could do, I picked up a sheet of transcription that I'd deliberately left behind and headed back to Roger's office. On my way in, I dropped the beacon back in the potted plant. "Sorry, I forgot this page," I said, placing it on his desk.

"Thank you," he said, so graciously that it was hard to reconcile him with the man I'd watched earlier that day be willing to send innocent kids to their deaths just to test a spell. "Why don't you take off early today? I've got some stuff going on, and I won't need you."

"I was just thinking about booking some spa time," I said. "All this bending over an old book is killing my back."

"Yes, you should definitely do that. I wouldn't want you to end up with back problems. You're too valuable to me."

I felt sick smiling at him, and even sicker at the thought that I'd facilitated any of his evil, even if it had been in the service of stopping him for good.

I hurried back to my office because I didn't want to be there when the raid happened. *Would* the raid happen? Had I done enough? The only other thing I could think of was calling Minerva or Rod. If they were supposedly working for the Collegium—or for Roger—then I might have a legitimate reason to call them from the office, and the call might get through.

I scrolled through the menu of recent calls on my phone, looking for the time I'd called Minerva to arrange the session with Roger. Finding it, I hit the "recall" button and held my breath, hoping it would go through.

It seemed to take forever, perhaps because the call was traveling such a distance, or perhaps because of perception. Every second was stretching out to hours for me today. I couldn't help but gasp when I heard ringing. It was going through.

Or was it? I didn't recognize the voice that answered. "Please state the purpose of your unscheduled call," it said.

"Setting an appointment with an outside consultant," I said briskly, hoping my voice didn't tremble too badly.

"One moment."

I silently prayed that the "one moment" meant the call was being put through, not that it was being checked with my supervisor. After another seemingly eternal wait, I heard ringing again.

"Why, Katie, this is a surprise," Minerva's voice said, and I sagged with relief when I heard it. "Let me guess, your friend needs another consultation. I don't think it's going to help much."

"It could make a big difference if it happens *NOW*," I said, putting all the emphasis I could on the word. She was a psychic, so I hoped she detected all the vibes around it.

"I'll have to check my schedule and get back to you," she said, and her voice sounded so light and casual that I wasn't sure if she'd picked up on the message or if she was just doing a really good job of playing it so cool that nobody listening in would suspect a thing. "Would sometime in the next half hour be good?"

Okay, that sounded like she'd picked up on it. "That would be fine, but much later than that would be too late because there are other plans."

"Just hang tight, and I'll get back to you."

I disconnected the call, put the phone down, and rubbed my sweaty palms against my skirt. Now, should I stay up here and wait for the raid, or should I go down and revive some frogs to give us more troops on the inside? If I timed this wrong, it could go very badly.

My phone rang, making me jump, and I saw Minerva's number. "This afternoon is good, probably in about ten minutes," she said.

That meant it was time. I found the copies I'd made of the internal key spell and put them in my jacket pocket, then opened my desk drawer to find the small case of toiletries the company provided, since we weren't allowed to bring in anything of our own. I pocketed the tube of lip balm—I wasn't kissing frogs bare-lipped—and headed straight to Trish's office. "Grab your lip balm, it's frog-kissing time," I told her softly.

She opened her drawer and pulled out her tube, which she brandished defiantly. Together, we headed for the elevators down to the spa. As we rode in the glass elevator, I couldn't help but look up in the atrium toward the level where our offices were. How would I know that the raid had happened or that it was successful?

We reached the frog pond, and Trish eyed the frogs warily. "So, we just, um, kiss them?"

"It doesn't have to be on the lips," I said, popping open my lip balm and giving myself a couple of coats.

With a shrug, she did the same. I bent to pick up the first frog that came to me, hoping that, even in frog form, Owen would recognize me and come straight to me. I bent to kiss it on the head, squeezing my eyes shut so I wouldn't have to look at what I was kissing.

Actually, it didn't feel too bad—at least, not until the magic kicked in and the frog began to vibrate. I dropped it quickly, and it hung in mid-air, a glowing nimbus surrounding it.

"Oh, my God," Trish breathed.

"Yes, it works, now hurry, because someone's bound to notice it soon."

With a shrug, she picked up a frog and, grimacing, gave it a quick peck, with a similar result.

I grabbed the next frog and kissed it. As I released it, I saw that the first former frog had solidified into human form. It was Philip. "Katie! How can I thank you?" he said, coming toward me with his arms extended.

"You can grab a frog and get to kissing. I want to get as many freed as possible before they catch us." He blinked in surprise, then seemed to notice his surroundings. Upon realizing that he wasn't in friendly territory, he went to work.

As each frog returned to human form, we put him to work with us—and most of them were men, though Sylvia Meredith was among the first wave of frogs. A couple of frogs turned out to apparently be genuine frogs. They just squirmed out of our hands after being kissed.

But still, there was no sign of Owen. He should have been the newest frog, the one retaining the most of his human instincts. I'd have thought that he'd have come straight to me, especially once there was all the magic in the air from so many spells breaking, all at once.

When we had a critical mass of former frogs helping save the others, I took charge of setting up a defensive perimeter with some of the people. "They'll come after us," I warned. "Be prepared to shield yourself and fight back." They didn't need a lot of urging, not after what had happened to them. I didn't know who these people were and whether I would have sided with them or even associated with them in other circumstances, but for now, we were all allies.

The first attack came from the spa. A white-coated technician came running out. "What do you think you're doing?" she demanded.

"Liberation!" Trish shouted defiantly, pumping her fist in the air. The former frogs joined in the cry. The technician ran back toward the spa, presumably to call for help, but one of the frog people froze her with a burst of magic. I suspected it wouldn't be too long before someone else noticed and came with reinforcements, but the more time we could buy, the better.

Now it was getting hard to find frogs, as most of them had been disenchanted. The only ones left seemed to be the real frogs, most of whom had hidden under lily pads after being kissed a few too many times.

But where was Owen? Was he back at the office, perfectly safe, and I just didn't know because I'd been out of contact?

No, the coincidence was too unlikely. I couldn't believe that Owen had gone missing and that Roger had at the same time taunted me about him. But hadn't he also said something about Owen not cooperating? That must have meant that he hadn't turned Owen into a frog right away. He must have questioned him first, and if that was the case...

I felt sick at the thought that Owen might have been tortured. Even if he wasn't currently a frog, he might still be a prisoner somewhere in this building—or the buildings all over the world it connected to. I wouldn't have been at all surprised to learn that there was a real dungeon, in addition to the frog pond.

But I couldn't give up on the frogs yet, not when they were still my best lead.

By this time, security forces were arriving to check out the massive frog rebellion. I let the former frogs handle it, since most of them appeared to be magical people. I felt magic flying all over the place, but I ignored it, as none of it would affect me.

I kicked off my shoes and stepped into the frog pond. It was only about knee-deep, even in the middle. "Owen, where are you?" I muttered as I waded, searching for any frogs that might still be left.

I heard a faint "ribbit" from the other side of the pond and waded in that direction. There was a waterfall that spilled into the pond from over a rock formation, with some greenery and flowers on the shore line.

All that greenery made it hard to find a frog that wasn't coming to me. "Owen, are you here?" I called out, feeling a bit strange about talking to frogs, but then these were desperate times.

There was another faint "ribbit," followed by a croak, and soon I spotted one lonely little frog on the shore that appeared to have been trapped with one foot caught in a grating. I wasn't sure if it had been an accident or if this was something that had been done to him.

I bent over it, murmuring soothingly, "It's okay, let me help." I couldn't seem to free the foot without hurting him, and I had a feeling it would hurt even worse if I broke the spell while his foot was still trapped.

"Philip!" I shouted across the pond, but he didn't seem to hear me in the melee. "Okay, time for plan B," I muttered. I tugged on the grating, lifting it to carry it and the frog with me. It was heavy, but I managed to balance it carefully on my hip. "Don't worry, we'll take care of you," I told the frog, but it didn't seem all that agitated. In fact, it seemed weak and tired. It must have been struggling to free itself all this time, and I wondered if it had been able to find food while it was trapped.

It was difficult to wade across the pond while carrying the grating, and it got harder when I came close to the bank where the former frogs were holding off the Collegium security people. I wasn't worried about what any stray spells might do to me, but there was some risk in what they might do to the frog I both hoped and feared might be Owen. If it was Owen, he was hurt and weak. If it wasn't, I didn't know where he was.

When I was close enough that I thought he might be able to hear me, I tried calling for Philip again. He whirled and rushed to gallantly take the grate from me and help me out of the pond. "Thanks," I said. "Can you do something to free this frog? I don't think we want to turn him back into a human while he's trapped like this."

Philip waved his hand over the grating, and next thing I knew, I had a frog sitting in my hand. "Okay, let's see if I can get you back to normal," I murmured as I bent to kiss it.

The glowing that ensued told me that it had, indeed, been an enchanted frog. I held my breath, watching the nimbus around it grow and take human form, but my anticipation quickly turned into disappointment when I saw that the frog wasn't Owen. I didn't even recognize this man, but judging by his clothes, I got the impression that he'd been a frog for a long time. Apparently not all the enchanted frogs were set free in ponds. He held his left wrist gingerly, like he was in some pain, as he blinked at his surroundings.

Though I was disappointed, Philip's face lit up. "Kenneth?" he said. "I don't believe it!"

"Philip? What happened? Where are we?" the former frog said.

"That is a very long story, brother. But for the moment, we must defend ourselves."

While it was lovely that Philip had apparently been reunited with his long-lost brother, I wanted to cry because it wasn't Owen, but I didn't have time for that. I had to find out what Roger had done with Owen, and doing that would require getting out of the atrium. At the moment, we were penned in. The Collegium security goons had all the exits surrounded, and while the former frogs were holding them off, it didn't look like we could get past them. We were in a standoff.

Then, quite abruptly, the security guards turned and ran the other way, leaving only a token force. The MSI raid must have started. "Come on!" I shouted and charged at the lone guard left blocking the way to the elevators. He blinked in disbelief when he saw me coming, and then his expression turned to one of alarm when he saw the rest of the former frogs coming at him.

His shock gave one of the frogs the opening to stun him with a spell. As we congregated in front of the elevators, I passed the copies of the spell out to the frog people, saying, "Do this spell in about five minutes, and be ready to fight. It'll take you to the head of this outfit."

I gathered Philip, Kenneth—who wouldn't be of much help in his condition but who wouldn't leave Philip's side—Sylvia, Trish, and a few who looked like good fighters into the next elevator that arrived and hoped they hadn't gone into lockdown mode.

The elevator took us where I expected it would, and we ran toward Roger's office. Fortunately, they hadn't shut down the portals, presumably because they wanted to be able to get help to him rather than isolating him in London.

The scene in Roger's office was rather chaotic when we arrived. He was hunkered behind his desk, popping up every so often to shoot a burst of magic at the intruders. A few security forces were ranged outside the office, but didn't seem able to get in. I figured Merlin must have warded the room.

But the wards wouldn't stop me. "Can you distract the security guys?" I asked my frog army.

A couple of the men looked at each other, nodded, and ran down the hall. Soon, explosions echoed from that direction, sounding like an invading force arriving. The security guards ran to deal with it, and I dropped to my hands and knees to crawl into the office.

They were all too busy to pay much attention to me, and I didn't think Roger could see me from this angle. I made it to the shelter of his desk, where I turned to face the MSI team. Rod saw me first, and I gave him a thumbs-up and gestured toward the door. He glanced over, saw reinforcements, and motioned to Merlin, who waved at the door. I beckoned for the frog team to join us. As soon as they were inside, Merlin waved his hand at the doorway again.

The MSI team was motivated and the frogs were angry, so Roger was rather outgunned and outclassed. Even so, he seemed remarkably calm, and not even with the kind of icy stillness Owen got in a crisis. At least that was an emotional reaction. This was the absence of emotion, like he wasn't at all alarmed that he was in danger and his plans might be destroyed. That was probably what made him so hard to fight. He wasn't dismayed enough to give up. He just kept going.

He wasn't fighting so much as defending, it seemed. He'd put up a pretty good magical shield around himself, so he just needed to wait them out. They didn't dare stop attacking him, though, lest he be able to come back at them. What they needed was a spell to break up his shields or enough combined power to crack them.

That was when I noticed the terrarium in the back of his office. I'd never bothered to study it before. I'd assumed it was part of the office decor. Now I wondered if it was where he kept his most valuable prisoners. I inched my way around the desk until I was barely behind the corner adjacent to the side where Roger was. If I moved any farther, he'd see me.

There was a particularly violent burst of magic from the other side of the room, one that required Roger to do something to counter it, and I took advantage of the distraction to dive across the floor, coming up right in front of the terrarium.

There was a frog in there, one that sat staring at the view outside, with a very non-froggy look of consternation on its face. I lifted the terrarium lid and reached inside to pick up the frog.

"Hey, stop that!" Roger called out. I ignored him, knowing he'd have to resort to physical violence to hurt me, and kept the frog shielded with my body. "No, don't!" Roger shouted, and I could hear his footsteps moving toward me.

Knowing I didn't have much time, I gave the frog a quick kiss. Nothing happened. It was just a frog. "Damn," I muttered, dropping the frog back in the tank. It must have been wishful thinking that made me see expression on its face.

Was there another frog in that tank? I didn't have time

to look because Roger was already upon me, grabbing my shoulders and yanking me back, away from the terrarium. I kicked at his shins, but that wasn't very effective, since I'd left my shoes downstairs at the frog pond. I elbowed him in the gut, which got him to loosen his grip on me enough for me to worm my way free.

Meanwhile, his focus on me had given the MSI gang and the frog army an opening. I couldn't see what they were doing because my back was to them, but I felt the tingle of strong magic being used very close by, and Roger didn't grab me again.

I had other things to worry about, so I didn't turn around to see what was happening, figuring that Merlin had it under control. I stood on my tiptoes so I could reach all the way into the terrarium and dig around. There had to be another frog in there.

Finally, my fingers encountered something cool and smooth at the back of the tank, under some leaves. When I touched it, it didn't respond the way I'd have expected a frog to. It didn't jump away or twitch. But still, it felt like a frog.

I got my fingers under it and moved my hand until the frog was resting in my open palm. It seemed awfully limp, but I was pretty sure it was still alive. When it moved one leg ever so slightly as I lifted it out of the terrarium, I heaved a huge sigh of relief.

I was afraid of what the frog's lethargy meant if this was Owen, but I was even more afraid that it might not be him. If it wasn't, I was out of ideas. He wasn't in the frog pond, and if he wasn't in Roger's office, then where would he be?

"I swear, this is the last frog I ever want to kiss," I muttered as I bent to brush my lips across the top of its head.

This one was definitely enchanted. It began to glow, and when I released it, it hung there in midair. I turned to see Rod, Trish, and some of the others standing by my side. "Is this...?" Rod asked, the rest of his question trailing off.

"I don't know. I hope so," I said, my voice plaintive. I didn't know what I'd do if it wasn't Owen. Almost afraid to look at the frog for fear of being disappointed again, I checked on what was happening around me. Merlin seemed to have subdued Roger, who now lay immobilized with silver chains wrapped cocoon-like around his body. The rest of the team was watching the warded doorway, where Collegium forces had the exit blocked.

With a lump in my throat, I turned back to see that the frog's nimbus had taken the shape of a man who seemed like he could possibly be Owen—just a bit below average height and a slim frame that was solidly packed with muscle.

Finally, the glow around him faded so that we could see that it was, indeed, Owen. I cried out in joy, but my joy quickly turned to dismay when he slumped to the ground.

Eighteen

Rod reacted while I was still in shock, jumping to catch Owen before he hit the ground. He lowered him gently to the floor, and I knelt beside Owen, reaching to hold his hand. He was awfully pale, but I couldn't see where he'd been hurt. His clothes looked fine, with no tears or blood showing, and his limbs seemed to be in the right places at the proper angles. There weren't any bruises on his face. I placed my hand against his cheek, and his skin was clammy—not too different from the way the frog had felt. Had something gone wrong with breaking the enchantment?

I brushed his hair off his forehead and glanced at Rod. "What do you think is wrong?" I asked.

"I don't know." He gave Owen a light slap on the cheek. "Hey, buddy, snap out of it. Come on, we're counting on you." Owen stirred slightly, but didn't wake up.

"You know, if that frog prince stuff is true, then maybe Sleeping Beauty is, too," Trish said.

"A sleeping spell would explain how Roger was able to overpower Owen," Merlin said.

It was worth a shot, and kissing an unconscious Owen was way more pleasant than kissing a frog, so it wasn't as though there was a downside. I bent and brushed my lips against his, thinking very hard about how much I loved him as I did so, in case there was something to that True Love's Kiss idea.

His eyes opened immediately, and he sat straight up with a gasp. "What happened?" he asked. Then he glanced around the room, noticing the MSI gang, me, the frog army, and a thoroughly trussed-up Roger. "Where am I?" he asked, frowning.

"Roger's office," I said. "The attack's under way. Are you ready to fight?"

"Well, um, yeah, I guess." Rod extended a hand to help him to his feet. "How did I get here?"

"Very long story," Rod said, patting him on the shoulder, "and it's probably for the best that you don't remember it."

"Now, I believe we should take this fight to the next level," Merlin said. "I'll need a couple of volunteers to remain here with Roger."

A couple of former frogs stepped forward, grinning like they knew they were going to enjoy this. "Perhaps you should stay, as well," Philip said to Kenneth.

Kenneth shook his head. "No. If you're engaging in a final confrontation with these people, I want to be a part of it."

"Do you think you'll be able to take me with you?" I asked. "I might be useful."

"There will be enough of us using the spell that I believe we can carry you," Merlin said, "though I'm afraid we won't have enough power to take a second immune."

Trish held a hand up in a warding-off gesture. "I'm totally good with that. I'll hang here. I might be useful on this front. And if I happen to accidentally kick this guy a time or two while he's down, well, some things just can't be helped."

"We'd better hurry. I already sent some of the former frogs to the top," I said.

Owen and Rod got me between them, each holding one of my hands. I was relieved to see that Owen already looked a lot more like his usual self, though more casually dressed than he usually was on a workday.

The magical people recited the spell in unison, and then I felt my stomach drop away as Roger's office vanished. A blink of an eye and another jerking sensation later and we were in a place that looked a lot less like a modern office building and more like a supervillain's lair might have looked in the Middle Ages.

The walls were rough stone, giving the impression that this space had been carved into a mountain rather than built. Torches set into the walls cast flickering shadows. I couldn't tell if there were any other light sources, but it did seem to me like the room was a little lighter than it should have been in the middle, even as the torches left deep shadows along the walls.

The middle of this room was filled with a large round table—magical people loved their Camelot imagery—only instead of being a gathering of equals with no one person at the head, which was supposed to be the point of the

Round Table, there was a very obvious throne at the table, with all the other chairs being lesser.

The man who'd run the big meeting sat in that throne, and I'd have said he looked unhappy, but that was only because he wasn't exactly smiling. Really, it was hard to read his face. Possibly smug, if he knew something we didn't know and we'd actually walked into a trap. Someone in his situation—surrounded by his former prisoners and with the most powerful wizard ever invading—should have looked more afraid. He merely looked like we were going to make him late for his tee time.

"Merlin," the man said. "I had a feeling you'd be here eventually."

Merlin walked toward him, frowning like he was trying to place the face of someone who seemed vaguely familiar, though out of context. He finally said, "Mordred? I see you've grown up."

Mordred—*Really? Mordred?* I couldn't help but think—laughed. "Up and old, I'm afraid. You don't seem to have aged a moment. Hibernation must have been good for you. You owe me a favor."

"And you're looking remarkably good for your age. I should have known you were behind all this. It does seem to be your style."

One of the former frogs rushed forward. He was dressed in clothing that fit the room pretty well, which meant he had to have been a frog for a very long time. "Mordred! But you're dead!"

Mordred smiled. "Rumors of my death have been greatly exaggerated—I've always wanted to say that. Yes, I fell on the battlefield, no thanks to Arthur, but I wasn't quite dead, and I had friends who came to my aid and brought me here." He gestured at the room around us. "It's a magical place of healing and life, and as long as I stay here, I don't age. What you see here"—he indicated his face and silver hair—"is the result of short forays into the outside world over the centuries. Those minutes do add up over time, alas."

"You betrayed us!" the medieval frog shouted.

"But I didn't kill you. I deserve some credit for that. Unlike some people, I deal humanely with my enemies. I'm sure we lost a frog or two who escaped at a bad time and didn't cope well with the outside world, but otherwise, we took good care of our captives."

"I'm not sure I consider being made to spend a century as a frog to be humane treatment," Philip muttered.

Mordred must have heard him, for he smiled and said, "But look at you now. The spell could have been broken at any time. It's not my fault that you weren't able to persuade a young lady to kiss you until recently."

"You're the one who's been pulling the strings of the Collegium all along," Merlin said, getting the conversation back on track.

"It's gone by many names over the centuries, starting with the Knights of the Round Table. I merely twisted it to serve my own ends. But enough about the past. The present is what's important. I take it you've already dealt with that fool Roger."

"That fool was on the verge of ousting you and taking over your organization."

"He merely thought he was. That book is a trap. It allows me to eliminate those who are too ambitious by ultimately bringing them straight to me, after they do quite a bit of work that benefits my organization. He was right on schedule." Now he finally frowned, looking truly displeased rather than mildly amused. "But it seems that he also opened the door for you. That wasn't planned, but I may let him live, depending on today's outcome, of course. How did you manage to use his work to get to me?"

I hid behind Owen, not wanting the credit right now. "Oh, we have our sources," Merlin said. "You're not the only person who can get people on the inside or turn people. Now, what's this about trying to get rid of me? Again?"

"You've been a thorn in my side from the day we met," Mordred said.

"I spent quite a long time well out of your way."

Mordred sighed. "Yes, I know. Who do you think arranged that? It was so much easier to take down Arthur when he didn't have your help. But you were there. I *knew* you were there. At any moment, you might have come back, and I was never sure I was ready for it." Mordred looked like he was maybe about sixty, but right now he sounded like a petulant kid complaining that he knew his brother was looking at him. "And then I felt I was ready for it, and I wanted to sleep at night without dreaming about you returning and taking everything away from me."

"And so you arranged for me to come back, hoping your proxy could defeat me and get me out of your way for good."

"I may have miscalculated somewhat. But here you are now."

"I'm not alone." Merlin gestured at his people and the army of former frogs.

"Neither am I," Mordred said, now with that smug "you're caught in my trap" smile I'd been expecting from the start. "I set it for Roger, but it will work just as well for you."

Apparently, the torches had just been for effect, to create deep, dark shadows, for out of those shadows stepped knights in somewhat dented armor. I wasn't sure I wanted to see what was inside those suits. I knew they couldn't have really been from the Camelot era, since armor like that didn't come along until much later (I'd once been chased by a museum display, and you don't forget that sort of detail), but they still fit the aesthetic of the room. And they were scary—menacing automatons unlikely to show mercy.

The knights clanked toward us, surrounding us and closing the circle, pressing us closer to the table. I edged nearer to Owen and wished I had something I could have used as a weapon, though I wasn't sure what good it would have done against that armor, and probably also against magic. I regretted once more leaving my shoes behind. Heels made a decent weapon, in a pinch. On the upside, I was probably more mobile this way if I had a chance to run for it.

Owen and Merlin exchanged a glance, then acted simultaneously, throwing up a shield around us all that slowly pushed the knights back away from us. Meanwhile, Sam took to the air, flying to near the top of the room with a few other gargoyles. They threw magical firebombs at the knights, who did nothing to dodge them. The livery over the armor went up in flames without the knights moving. If they weren't already dead inside those suits, they would be soon.

Mordred laughed and clapped his hands. "Nice work. Yes, the knights are just for show, but you have to admit that they're a *good* show. That usually has the would-be usurpers begging for mercy. Not that they get it."

"I'm quite familiar with your tricks, Mordred," Merlin said, "though the more advanced armor does make that one more effective. It's not quite the same with just leather, though that did create a stir on the battlefield." He pulled out one of the chairs and took a seat. "So, you've achieved your goal of power, and what are you doing with it? You're shaking down small businesses and taking over larger ones. That must not be very satisfying. What were you going to do after disposing of me?"

This seemed like rather an odd time to sit down and have a little chat. I glanced at Owen to see if he knew what Merlin was up to, but he shook his head slightly. He still seemed a little disoriented, and I could hardly blame him. One minute he must have been on his way home, and then something had knocked him out, he must have been questioned or threatened, was knocked out again, then he woke up in a strange office in the middle of a fight, and now he'd been transported to a dungeon-like space, only to be confronted with Mordred.

Come to think of it, *I* was a little disoriented, and I hadn't even gone through the sleeping spell and frog experience.

"Can we get out of here?" I whispered to Owen.

"Why? We can't just let him go. We'll have to deal with him sooner or later, and it might as well be now."

"But I think we'll have a better chance of dealing with him on our turf. He's bound to have this place booby-trapped, and if it's the magic here that's keeping him alive, getting him out of here may make him weaker."

"But if we can't overpower him, how will we get him out of here?"

"We've got the beacon for Roger's office, right? We could go back there to start." My mind raced furiously. There were a lot of moving parts involved here, and I was trying to put them all together.

For one thing, I wondered how much of the Collegium knew who they were really working for and what he was up to. Then there was Roger's plan. He definitely didn't know who his boss was or that he'd been set up. We might be able to use that. Meanwhile, Roger had all those harpies and skeletons gathering, ready for an assault on MSI. There was a potential plan in there, but I couldn't quite manage to fit it all together. I just felt like if we somehow got all the players into one spot, something was bound to happen.

"Merlin's buying us time, so we need to do something," I whispered.

"Okay, it's worth a shot," Owen said. He edged over to Rod and whispered, "Do you have one of the beacon stones?"

"Yes, why?"

"Do you think you can get us out of here and back to Roger's office?"

"All of us, or just some of us?"

"Katie thinks it might be a good idea to get Mordred out of here."

Rod raised an eyebrow. "Oh, good idea. The boss has one, too. It would probably help if we could coordinate."

He moved around the table until he was standing right behind Merlin. Owen hurried in his wake, but I hung back. I knew it would take extra power to take me out with them, and if Mordred put up a fight, they'd need all the power they had.

Merlin gave a slight glance to Rod, then leaned back in his chair, casually easing his hand into his pocket. A second later, I felt a burst of magic that immediately dissipated.

Mordred laughed. "Did you really think you could get me out of here that way, using my spell? That will never happen, and you won't be able to get out that way, either, not unless I let you." He glanced at his watch. "But you might want to start thinking of how to do it. I understand that Roger contracted with some friends to raid your little company. I would have hated to disappoint his friends, so I made sure they got paid and got their assignment, as well as what they need to get in. You've got about an hour before your company comes under attack, and it looks like your best people are all here."

Owen backed slowly toward me. Mordred was so focused on Merlin that he didn't notice. "What's he talking about?" Owen whispered when he reached me.

"Roger found a way through your protection against his beacon spell—well, for the second wave of attackers. He's got a bunch of harpies about to attack MSI."

"Then we've got about an hour to resolve this."

"Maybe there's some other way out, and they wouldn't be able to stop me."

I moved around to the other side of the table. The knights had stopped moving after the gargoyles' firebombs, and I tried walking up to one of them. He didn't react, so I slipped past him. Owen moved as though to follow me, but he came up short—probably stopped by a magical barrier behind the knights. "Be careful!" he urged softly.

I waved an acknowledgment and hurried toward the edge of the room. It took me a while to find a door. For a moment, I even thought that there might not be a door, that the only way in or out was to use the spell. That gave me a bout of panic because it was very difficult to move me magically, even without someone fighting against us. Fortunately, I found a door in a shadowy area between torches, a heavy wooden one braced with iron.

I could tell that the door was magically warded from the tingle I got when I touched it, but it didn't seem to have been physically locked, for I was able to pull it open. I had to put my full body weight behind it to get it to budge, and it was hard to get any leverage in my stockinged feet that slipped on the stone floor, but I eventually opened it enough to peer through.

I was surprised to see light coming from above— far above. It was a cold light that was either artificial or moonlight. According to my watch, it was only about four in the afternoon, but I had no idea where in the world I was. If it was moonlight, then we were too far away to get back to MSI in time physically. But I hoped I might find something out here that would give us a clue of something we could do.

The door led into a chamber even rougher than the room I'd left. It was like a chimney; tall, hollow, roughly cylindrical, and open at the top. It looked like there had been steps carved into the wall, leading up to where the light was. I hesitated, unsure what good it would do to go up there. On the one hand, it would be nice to find out where we were, but there was also the risk of something waiting up there for me.

It was a good thing I hadn't charged ahead because I heard a soft rustling sound from above and thought I saw a hint of motion. Soon I saw someone coming down those steps.

I felt momentarily weak with the relief of a near-miss. If I'd started climbing as soon as I saw the steps, I'd have run smack into the newcomer where there was no place to hide, and with no protective railing it would have been very easy for one of us to end up knocked over the edge. I flattened myself into a slight recess in the stone wall just below the bottom section of steps, where I thought I'd be hidden by shadows, unless the person coming down the stairs brought a light and was really curious and perceptive.

For once, I was grateful for the all-black Collegium wardrobe. I was even wearing black tights. The only thing that might stand out was my face, and I pulled my hair forward to cover myself as much as possible. It wasn't really dark, but it was darker than my skin.

I was actually rather surprised that the figure descending the stairs wasn't using a light. I'd have been quite uneasy on those uneven, worn steps without being able to see where I was going and with nothing to hold on to. It suggested to me that this person was quite familiar with this staircase. Or had excellent night vision. Or didn't want anyone to see him coming. Or possibly all of the above.

When the person reached the final turn of the stairs, just before the steps over my head, I finally got a good view and realized that it was a woman. At least, she had long hair, narrow shoulders, and a coat that belted at the waist, creating an hourglass silhouette. At the bottom of the stairs, she paused, and I could hear her breathing heavily—not panting and gasping for breath, but sounding like she'd been through some exertion and perhaps was a little nervous.

She gave a cursory glance around the small chamber, but if she saw me, she showed no sign of it. She then stepped toward the door and stood facing it. She laced her fingers together and stretched her arms out in front of her, like a concert pianist limbering up before a concert. Then she held her hands out and began chanting softly.

I couldn't hear her exact words, but I recognized a spell when I heard one, and I felt magic building to rather intense levels. I wondered if I should stop her or wait to see what she did. Was she possibly an ally of Mordred's, come to help him, or was she an enemy, coming to confront him?

I figured she was most likely not an ally, or she wouldn't have needed to use a spell on the door. That was confirmed when she touched the door and was knocked backward. "Damn!" she muttered, making a sound for the first time.

That voice seemed rather familiar, but I couldn't place it until she rolled over and pulled herself to her feet, and then I saw her face, lit by the moonlight above. It was Evelyn. She looked very different with her hair loose and without the mildly pleasant expression she usually wore.

288 · Shanna Swendson

I weighed my options. I could remain hidden and hope she went away, or I could confront her and see what she was up to. I figured that my cover was already blown, plus she couldn't use magic against me, so there wasn't much of a downside to letting her know I was there, and I might learn something.

"Evelyn!" I said, stepping out of my hiding place.

She looked less surprised than I expected when she saw me. "Oh, so you're here. I hope not alone."

"No, not alone. But you don't seem that surprised."

"I figured you were a plant of some sort all along. I suppose it takes one to know one."

"You were undercover, too? For whom?"

"Myself. The Collegium ruined my family, though I'm not sure anyone in the family knew what had really happened. I did the research and learned about the threats, learned what probably happened to my great-grandfather that caused our business to be taken away so that my family lost everything. That's when I started working to find my way in."

"But you said you were from one of the minor families."

"I am, in a sense, through my mother's side of the family, but I may have amplified that connection somewhat as a way to get in."

"It must have taken years to reach the position you did."

"I'm very patient. And then, wouldn't you know, I ended up working for the guy who had his own delusions of grandeur, which kept me away from the hierarchy. But I learned as much as I could, and today, thanks to all the excitement, I managed to get away from the office in its local site, and I made it here."

"What were you planning to do?"

She took an object out of her coat pocket. I couldn't see much of what it was in the faint light, but it had an eerie gleam that came from within. "I can destroy the magic in that chamber that keeps him alive. Without its head, the organization should shrivel. He put so much effort into keeping everything secret and isolated that without him, it probably won't function anymore."

"There's just one problem."

She sighed. "I know, I can't get in. How did you get here?"

"I came with the group that teleported over, using the spell that turned out to have been a trap for Roger."

"And you were able to get out because you're immune to magic."

"Maybe I could take your gizmo in there."

She held it against her chest and shook her head. "No. I have to be there to see it happen. I want to look him in the eye and make sure he knows exactly who ruined him."

"Would you rather take him down or cling to your revenge fantasies?"

I could see her wrestling with the decision. At last, she said, "Let's try it with you opening the door, first. Then we'll see if I can get through."

It was easier to open the door from the outside because I could lean my weight against it instead of having to pull. I stepped through the opening but didn't feel anything. Maybe all the magic was on the door itself. If it blasted you across the room when you touched it, that was probably good enough security. I did feel some magic on the threshold, but it was different—possibly the anti-aging field keeping Mordred alive.

"Okay, give it a try," I whispered.

She squeezed her eyes shut and clutched her device before stepping decisively through the doorway. When she opened her eyes and found herself inside the chamber, she let out the breath she'd been holding in a big whoosh of relief.

The situation inside didn't seem to have changed in the few minutes I was gone. Mordred was still holding court, monologuing like a Bond villain. The knights still held a perimeter around the Round Table, holding in the MSI people and former frogs.

"What do you need to do to set it off?" I asked.

"Get it across the threshold," she replied. "It's already working. That is, if it works."

I glanced back to the table. "How will you know it's working?"

"I don't know. I'll admit, I was hoping he'd revert instantly to his real age, but it seems that it will just stop protecting him."

"Then, depending on how healthy he is, we only have to wait ten to twenty or so years to defeat him decisively."

And we only had about forty-five minutes if we were going to save or even warn MSI.

Nineteen

"Can you deactivate that thing and send the room back to normal?" I asked Evelyn.

"I'm not sure. But why would I want to do that?"

"The best hostage against someone with an ego that size is himself. I bet we'll get what we want if we tell him we'll cut off his youth magic if he doesn't cooperate."

"But what I want is to make him suffer."

I tried not to sigh in exasperation and thought of a way to get her cooperation. "I'm sure we'll get to that eventually. But since at the moment you seem to be giving him a gradual, ordinary aging and death, you're not really bringing him down. My way, he suffers more."

That got her interest. "Really? Okay, then we'll try it your way. What do I need to do?"

"Hold that thing and look threatening. Now, come on."

Keeping to the shadows along the wall, we worked our way around the room. With a magical barrier surrounding the knights, I wasn't sure Evelyn could get through it to approach Mordred directly, and even if the barrier was one-way, I didn't want to trap Evelyn in there, in case this didn't work. Instead, I aimed for Mordred's end of the table, where we might get close to him without being inside the circle.

The MSI folks and the former frogs looked pretty glazed. Mordred's villain monologue must have been somewhat less than enthralling. Even Merlin looked bored. Owen perked up, and I realized he'd noticed me. He immediately went still again after that initial reaction, so no one else picked up on it.

When we were behind and just to the right of Mordred's throne, I stepped forward through the gap between two of the knights, cleared my throat, and said, "Excuse me. I hate to interrupt, but there's something you should know."

Every eye in the room—except for the frozen knights— turned to stare at me. "What is it, Miss Chandler?" Merlin asked before Mordred had a chance to.

"I just thought you'd be interested in knowing that the protective magic on this room isn't working anymore." I gestured at Evelyn, who'd come to stand beside me. She held up her magical gizmo. "You're going to age like everyone else. It might even be accelerated, come to think of it. I don't believe that wrinkle was there before, and was your hairline like that ten minutes ago?" That was a lie, but I needed to sell this if it was going to work.

Mordred came off his throne and spun to face us. "What?" he asked, his voice shrill with panic.

"It might not be permanent," Evelyn said. "I can restore it if you cooperate."

I was surprised when Mordred recognized her. "Don't

you work for me?" he asked. "Why are you doing this? Do you know what I do to traitors?"

"It's no worse than what you do to people who think they're your friends," she said with some bitterness. "You only thought I was working for you. I've really been working for myself all along. And if you don't want to die, old man, you'll do what she says."

"All you have to do is let us go from here," I said.

I could see the dilemma in Mordred's eyes. Should he give up some power now or take the risk of dying like a normal person? He let his breath out, his body sagging slightly, so that he looked years older, then he gestured. I felt the magical barrier drop, and the knights moved back to their places by the wall. "You may leave," he said. "Now restore my magic."

"Not until we're sure that when we leave, we end up where we want to go," Evelyn said.

Merlin rose from his seat. "Everyone gather 'round, now."

The others all clustered around him, but Kenneth cried out, "You're going to just let him go?" He looked stronger than he had before, and he was no longer cradling an injured arm—apparently the room's magic had worked on him, as well as Mordred.

He and Philip both shot magic at Mordred, who disappeared. A frog appeared on the floor where he'd been. It tried to hop away, but I'd had a fair amount of practice in catching frogs already that day, so I was able to scoop him up and hand him to Merlin, who dropped him into his pocket.

Evelyn stared open-mouthed at Kenneth. "Granddad?

Well, Great-great-granddad? Kenneth Vandermeer? I've seen pictures of you, and you look just like that."

"Great-great-granddad?" Kenneth asked, his eyes growing wide.

Philip clapped him on the shoulder. "A long time has passed. You have a lot to catch up on."

"I didn't even know I was a father," Kenneth said, sounding stunned.

Evelyn gasped. "And you're my great-great-uncle Philip."

"We can have the family reunion later," I said. "For now, we've got a company to warn and save."

The magical folks did the spell, and I was relieved when it took me along with them. We found ourselves back in Roger's office, but there was no sign of the trussed-up Roger. A couple of frogs hopped along the floor, and Trish lay in the corner, her wrists bound with a printer cable and packing tape over her mouth.

While the others set about restoring the frogs to their human selves, I removed the tape from Trish's mouth and unwrapped the cable from her wrists. "What happened?" I asked.

"The security forces got in, and they were just too much. Roger said something about an appointment to keep."

"He's attacking MSI," I said.

"Your old place? I guess you still work for them, huh?"

"I have been all along. Are you okay?"

"I'm fine. Just spitting mad."

"Then let's go deal with them." I stood and helped her to her feet, then turned to Owen. "Surely you didn't leave Roger's beacon in Merlin's office."

"No, I brought it to my lab to study it," he said, then

he went pale. "Oh no, that's where he'd arrive if he gets through. We've got to get back there, or get it away, or something."

"Then let's get back," Rod said. "We can retrace our own spell. The MSI people can get through our shields, but the rest of you will have to take the long way."

"I'll take care of getting them out," I said. When the MSI gang had vanished in a blink, I gave a "follow me" gesture to the frog people, Trish, and Evelyn. "This way." I hoped they hadn't shut down the portals so that we were stuck in London because that would be a long trip back, and I didn't have a passport.

Out in the hallway, the scene was chaotic as employees rushed for the exits. Alarm sirens sounded throughout the building. There was a ripple effect in the hallway, like the portal was breaking down. I didn't know what would happen to us if we were in the middle when it failed, but we didn't have much choice. We all made a run for it, sprinting down the hallway. I felt a bit disoriented for a second, like my body was in a suspended state, but then I stepped out on the other side. The others all seemed to be with me. I hadn't taken a head count, but it didn't look like anyone was missing. Where the portal had been was now a blank wall.

I wasn't sure if we had to go through more portals, only that the garage where the car went every day was in Manhattan. We needed to get out before any other portals between us and the exit failed.

The scene in the galleries around the atrium was even more hectic, as all the employees rushed to their changing rooms so they could get their stuff back and get out before the magic holding this enterprise together gave out entirely. Had breaking the magic on Mordred's lair done this, or did it have something to do with Mordred being taken out of the building?

I led the group to my changing room, fighting my way through the sea of panicked people, so I could at least get my purse. I didn't know if I'd have a chance to get back here once we left, and I wasn't leaving my credit cards and keys behind. I also took the opportunity to put on some shoes and grab my coat while Trish and Evelyn ushered everyone through the room and out the door.

The alarm on the wards went off when I tried to leave while still wearing my Collegium gear, but by this time, it didn't make much difference. The whole place was already in chaos. My group followed me through the room and to the elevators.

There were a couple of limos waiting in the garage. We ran up to one, and the driver rolled the window down. "Out of the car," I ordered.

"Excuse me?" he asked. A second later, he was a frog. I looked back to see Philip smiling grimly.

"We can restore him later," he said.

"Can you drive?" I asked him.

"I haven't yet learned that skill."

"Trish?"

"I've got it. But where are we going?"

"Philip, direct her to MSI. As many of you as can fit, get in." We proceeded to learn how many former frogs you could fit in the back of a limo. When the car was full, it took off. "The rest of you, with me," I said.

The driver of the next car I approached was already

out of the car and standing with his hands up. "The key's in the ignition," he said.

"Thanks!" I replied. "Now, go see to your colleague over there, and you might want to look into other job opportunities."

I got that car loaded, then slid into the driver's seat to find Evelyn already sitting in the front passenger seat. "I'm coming with you," she said.

"Okay. You can be lookout." I adjusted the seat so that I could reach the pedals and turned the key, starting the car. I could drive, but I'd never driven in New York, so this was going to be a new experience for me. Fortunately, what I drove back home was a pickup truck with a long bed, so maneuvering a limo wouldn't be that different. I hoped.

We came out of the garage and into something that looked like a service alley, which opened onto a busy street. I paused to check my bearings. Judging by the positions of the Empire State Building and the Chrysler Building, I guessed we were probably not too far from Madison Square. I pulled out into traffic, made it to the next street heading across town, and then turned onto Second Avenue heading downtown. That may not have been the fastest way to go, but it was the way I was more sure of, and the last thing I needed was to get stuck on a highway, unable to get off when I needed to.

It was some of the most nervewracking driving I'd ever done. I was used to driving in the country or in a small town. I might have occasionally braved Austin traffic, which wasn't pleasant, but that tended to be gridlock on freeways rather than a grid of streets with stoplights on each block, not to mention all the crazed taxi drivers, suicidal bike messengers, and oblivious pedestrians. It was particularly interesting barely moving a block at a time when driving a vehicle that seemed to take up a whole block.

I glanced in the side mirror and saw another black car following me. In this city, that wasn't unusual. In fact, it seemed like half the cars on the streets were either yellow cabs or black car-service vehicles. But I had a funny feeling about this black car.

I thought for a second about trying evasive maneuvers, but decided not to bother. For one thing, there wasn't a lot of evading you could do when crawling along in city traffic and stopping at lights. For another, they probably already knew where I was going, so it didn't matter whether or not I lost them. My only real concern was that they might try to stop me before I could get to the MSI building.

Without taking my eyes off the road, I said to Evelyn, "See if you can find an intercom button or some other way to talk to the back." Out of the corner of my eye, I saw her lean forward and examine the dashboard.

"Got it," she said after a couple of minutes. "What do you want me to say?"

"They're all magical people, right? See if they can do anything to shield us against the car that's following us."

She hit the speaker button and relayed that request. "We've got it," came the reply, "but it would help if you could give us visibility in here."

Evelyn searched the dashboard again and hit a button. "How's that?" she asked.

"Great. Now, what about the moon roof?"

She found another button, and I could only imagine the attention we'd get with a person in old-fashioned clothes popping up through the roof of a stretch limo in the middle of city traffic. But hey, as long as it worked. And this was New York, so maybe no one would notice or care.

My hands were white-knuckled on the steering wheel as I tried to maneuver around slower traffic and insert some other cars between us and our follower. I felt a little sorry for all the people in the back of the limo, who probably hadn't put on seatbelts. Some of them may never have even been in a car before, and this wasn't the best introduction to the modern world.

I glanced in the mirror again and couldn't see our tail. "Do you see another black car behind us?" I asked Evelyn. She leaned to check her mirror.

"There are black cars, but I can't tell if one is right on us. I'll ask the people in back." She triggered the intercom again and asked about our follower.

"They're still there, but farther back, and they shouldn't be able to see us," came the reply.

"You didn't make us entirely invisible, did you?" I asked in a panic. Looking like a huge, blank space of pavement in Manhattan would be very dangerous. Any huge, blank space of pavement would immediately be filled, and physics said that two things couldn't occupy the same space at the same time.

"No. We just look silver instead of black."

I actually said, "Whew," out loud and tried to relax a little while maneuvering an ocean liner through city streets full of smaller cars that kept darting in and out when they found an opening.

By the time I crossed Houston, I was feeling a little more comfortable, but soon I found myself in the more confusing layout of lower Manhattan, where the simple grid pattern dissolved. I navigated on instinct from that point, turning onto streets headed in the direction I needed. I whooped in triumph when I saw the building ahead of us and pulled up in front, behind the other limo that was already parked there. It wasn't a legal parking place, but the car wasn't registered to me. I figured the Collegium could pay the parking ticket or impound fee.

I jumped out, ran around the car, and opened the passenger door. "Okay, everybody out," I said.

While the former frogs did their impression of a circus clown car act, with one after another emerging, I glanced up at the building's turrets. I didn't see any sign of a fight going on. It looked perfectly ordinary.

The black Collegium car pulled up just as the last person made it out of the limo. "Hurry, get inside," I shouted. I ran in at the tail of the group before the car's driver opened his door. Inside, I found Trish, Philip, and their group waiting in the lobby. "We weren't sure where to go," Trish said.

"I guess we could listen for the sound of battle," I said, but everything seemed awfully peaceful.

Just then, Owen came running down the lobby stairs, Rod and Jake in his wake, holding a small, glowing object. "I think I've got it shielded, but I don't know if it will work against his countermeasures," he said, panting, as he sprinted through the lobby toward the door. We all scrambled to get out of his way.

"How long did it take you to get here?" I asked Rod. "I'd have thought you had plenty of time to move it."

"Sorry, my fault," Jake said, wincing. "I put it away, and it took us awhile to find it."

Owen had almost reached the door when I heard a sizzling sound. There were a couple of pops, and several harpies fell out of the sky, crashing to the floor to lie motionless. A second later, another group appeared, along with a few of the skeletal creatures, and they surrounded Owen. More harpies and monsters arrived, and then, finally, Roger stepped out of thin air.

He paused to straighten his tie before glancing around at his surroundings. "Interesting. You moved the beacon. Obviously."

Merlin came walking down the steps into the lobby. "You may as well give up now," he said. "You won't get any farther into the building, and your organization is on the verge of collapse. You were playing into your boss's trap, all along."

"Yeah, you should thank us," I said. "He was setting you up, giving you enough rope to hang yourself. You'd never have taken over."

"It's been done before." He was as calm as ever. I had to wonder if this guy was maybe a robot. Nothing seemed to rattle him.

"The book was a fake," I said. "It's been the same boss all along, for the past thousand or so years. He was getting you to do his dirty work, and then he'd have trapped you and got you out of the way."

"Where is he now?"

Merlin pulled the frog out of his jacket pocket and smiled. "I'll find a good home for him."

Roger laughed. It was an eerie sound, more like an evil "mwa ha ha" than true mirth. "Then the way is clear for me."

"Not so fast," Sam the gargoyle said, swooping down from the ceiling. "Now what say you take your ladies and your skeletons out of here. Go try to take over what's left of your company."

"You won't find much left," I said. "And you'll need an airplane to get to your office. Things are kind of falling apart."

"It's only a building," he said with a shrug. "It's the organization that matters."

"I believe you'll find that's gone, too," Evelyn said.

He turned to her, raising an eyebrow. "Really—you, too, Evelyn? *Et tu, Brute.*"

"Obviously, you're not as sharp as you think you are, since you had two plants working closely with you," she said with some relish.

"But why? Didn't I treat you well? I was a good boss, to both of you."

Out of the corner of my eye, I saw the security forces converging on the lobby. Gargoyles circled above, keeping the harpies in check, and other people and creatures emerged from various passageways. I knew we needed to buy time to have all our people in place.

"It wasn't really about you, Roger," I said, walking toward him. I hoped he'd be distracted by following my movement and not notice the other motion around him. "I was on a mission. It wasn't personal at all. Actually, you were the best boss I ever had. That is, until you started turning my friends into frogs. That's not exactly something I can overlook. Mostly, though, I was using you to get to your boss, and it worked, so thanks!"

Evelyn apparently picked up on what I was doing, or else she just wanted to give him a piece of her mind, because she followed my lead. She walked straight up to him. "I was also using you to get to your boss, but for me it was all about revenge for what the Collegium did to my family."

"You worked for me for years!"

"I'm very patient," she said with a shrug. "And you did help me achieve what I wanted, so I owe you thanks for that."

By this time, all our forces were in place. Merlin stepped forward and said, "Enough talk. Stop this foolishness, call off your monsters, and surrender. We have you surrounded."

Roger glanced around, seeing that he was, indeed, surrounded by angry former frogs and the entire might of MSI. But he didn't look the way you'd expect someone who was cornered like that to look. There was no tension in his body language, no fear in his eyes. He merely smiled, his eyes remaining cold and hard. "I'm not the only one who's surrounded," he said.

I followed his glance to where Owen still stood in the middle of a bunch of skeleton men while harpies circled him overhead. They'd homed in on him because he was holding the beacon, so he'd never had a chance to get to the rest of us.

He, too, looked calm for someone in that kind of

situation, but it wasn't the same emotionless, effortless calm Roger had. If you knew Owen as well as I did, you could spot the signs of tension in his bearing. He held his shoulders like someone squaring off for a fight, and his eyes were wary, darting around to take in his surroundings.

The room grew very quiet and very still. "What are you going to do, Merlin?" Roger asked. "The moment you make a move on me, your wonder boy gets it. I know he's good, but can he really take on that many people at once?"

It would have been just like Owen to say something like, "Don't worry about me, do what you need to do." In fact, he'd said that sort of thing before. But I don't think any of us expected him to do what he did.

He knelt very slowly, so slowly, in fact, that it was hard to tell he was actually moving. When he was low enough that he could bend and touch the floor, he dropped something small and shiny—the beacon. It rolled across the floor to the other side of the room.

I was just starting to wonder why he'd done that when there was a loud cracking sound, like a very close lightning strike. I felt a surge of magic so intense that it was almost painful, and suddenly all the harpies and skeleton creatures were in a different part of the room, surrounding the beacon, and surrounded by the MSI people. I figured Owen must have somehow managed to trigger the beacons the creatures had used to home in on his beacon, sending them to its new location. He had said he'd been studying it.

"Now would you care to surrender?" Merlin asked.

"Actually, no," Roger said genially. "I'd rather fight.

You see, I figure if I manage to take you out, I still get what I want. I can take over."

He raised his hands as though to attack Merlin, but although Merlin was really, really old, his reflexes were fast, and he was already on the defensive, easily deflecting whatever Roger had aimed at him.

At the same time as Roger's attack, his creatures also turned and went after the people who surrounded them. It turned into a massive magical free-for-all.

I noticed Trish standing stunned near the doorway and made my way through the melee toward her. "This—this is insane," she said.

"Yeah, magical fights can be pretty intense, but we should be safe enough. Their magic can't affect us. We should probably stay on the lookout, in case they try something sneaky."

"Do you do this sort of thing all the time?"

"Fights like this? Once every few months, give or take. It depends on who the bad guy is at that time."

I racked my brain, trying to come up with a way I could contribute to the battle, aside from shouting the occasional warning when a skeleton creature came up behind one of our people. Then I came up with an idea, based on my brief experience from having magical powers. Magical power wasn't unlimited. People with magic had the ability to turn latent power in the atmosphere into power they could use. Some places had more natural power than others, so there was more power to draw upon. This building had extra power supplied to it, to support all the magic used within its walls. Without that, there would be less power to draw upon, and the people who had the ability to store more power or create more power with less input would have an advantage.

I knew that Owen and Merlin were among the most powerful wizards around. In fact, Owen was so powerful that he was watched very carefully in case he went bad. They'd be able to keep going long after everyone else was drained.

What I needed to do was shut off the power.

Twenty

"Come on, I have an idea," I said to Trish, then began making my way around the lobby. Even though I knew the magic wouldn't affect me, I couldn't help but flinch when a bolt of something flew toward me, and those harpies were also pretty nasty if they got your claws into you. After glancing back and forth between the battle and me, Trish hurried to catch up with me.

"What kind of idea?" she asked.

"One that should turn the power down here a lot and give us an advantage. I hope."

"Does this mean getting out of the war zone?"

"It does."

"Then I'm with you."

We were almost to the stairs, where I was pretty sure they'd put up extra wards to keep the outsider wizards and creatures out of the main part of the building, when one of the harpies noticed us. She swooped in our direction, claws out and body flat. "Run!" I told Trish.

She put on a good sprint, and I was right behind her,

but I was afraid we weren't going to make it. Magic might not have been able to hurt us, but talons would, and I'd seen what those talons could do to a person.

"Sam!" I shouted, hoping the gargoyle could hear me over the ruckus. He was probably my best bet for intercepting the harpy before she could reach us. Sure enough, he wheeled around and zoomed toward her. I put on a burst of speed and quit looking behind me, trying to narrow the gap between me and safety. But I couldn't resist a peek over my shoulder once or twice so I'd know whether I needed to hit the deck.

That was when I saw that Sam wasn't going to make it in time. I threw myself flat on the ground, making myself a harder target to hit. The harpy was now so close that I felt gusts of wind coming from her wings, and I could smell the stench that surrounded her. I curled up in a ball to protect my vital organs. I was just about to bend my head to protect my face when the harpy suddenly flew backwards.

I didn't think that was possible, but I wasn't about to complain. I looked around and saw Owen, his arm still outstretched from whatever he'd thrown at the harpy. I sat up, blew him a kiss, and got back on my feet to run the rest of the way to the stairs. I didn't know if Owen knew what I was up to, but I figured he was okay with any plan that put me on the other side of a magical barrier that kept the bad guys out.

Trish was still waiting on the landing in the middle of the grand staircase. I reached her and said, "Come on." She joined me in running the rest of the way up the stairs. The tingle of the wards as we passed through them was a welcome relief. I stopped and caught my breath, bending over to brace my hands on my knees until I stopped shaking.

"This is nuts. You know that, right?" Trish said.

"You get used to it."

"I take it the dark-haired hottie is your boyfriend, or something?"

"Actually, we're engaged."

"If there are any others like him here, are you hiring?"

"They're always hiring people like us. We'll talk after we survive all this."

In my time at MSI, I'd had a few thorough tours of the building, and I'd frequently had to run all over the place to get my job done. I'd only seen the control room once because I didn't have much business there. I thought I might be able to find it again, though it was easy to get lost in this place. It might not have had hallways that were portals to other buildings in other parts of the world (or did it?), but it was still a confusing maze.

I'd thought we'd left the danger behind once we crossed the barrier, but I'd forgotten that the Collegium had plants within MSI. Some of them appeared to be showing their loyalty by rushing to their allies' aid. I didn't think the barrier would let them through to join the fight, but we were still left to face them.

"Wait a second, is that Shrek?" Trish blurted, her face twisted with disgust.

"It's Gregor. He's not always an ogre, but he must be really agitated."

Fortunately, I still had my purse with me, and that meant I should have a canister of pepper spray somewhere in there—a concession to my mom, who was worried about me living in New York. I fumbled in my bag, not taking my eyes off the people moving toward us. My fingers closed on the canister, and I pulled it out of my bag. The Collegium plants were almost upon us. There were only a few of them, not nearly as many as my research had suggested there would be. I guessed that not all of them were willing to out themselves. Showing up like this was a big risk and a firm commitment to their cause. I wondered what they'd do if they realized that their boss was now a frog—or were these Roger's people who were personally loyal to him?

Trish dropped into a defensive position that suggested she'd had martial arts training, and I allowed myself to glance away from the approaching wizards just long enough to make sure I was pointing the pepper spray in the right direction. There weren't a lot of them, but even with us immune to magic, we wouldn't be able to fight them.

But then it occurred to me that these people probably didn't want a fight with us. They were trying to join their comrades in the bigger fight, and would probably only attack us if we tried to stop them. I grabbed Trish's arm. For a second, I thought she'd hit me, but her reflexes were good and she pulled back in the nick of time. "Let's just get out of their way," I suggested.

She glanced at the oncoming traitors, then back at me, then shrugged. "Worth a shot. And I'd rather have my back against a wall, anyway."

We moved to the far side of the passageway, clearing the way for the oncoming group. I kept my finger on the pepper spray button, and Trish kept her defensive stance, but they walked right past us. I didn't want to be there when they discovered they couldn't join the fight or when they figured out that we might be a threat to their allies, so as soon as they were past us, I whispered to Trish, "Run!" We hurried out of that passage and around the corner so that they couldn't see us.

"What is this place, anyway?" Trish asked when we'd stopped running. "It looks like some kind of castle mixed with a university, mixed with an old office building."

"It's Magic, Spells, and Illusions, Incorporated. Think of it as kind of like the Microsoft of magic. They create most of the spells magical people use. I guess you could say they're rather traditional, but that probably comes with the territory when Merlin is the boss."

"Wait, the old guy in charge is Merlin? *The* Merlin?"

"Yep. It's a long story. Now, we need to go turn the magic off."

"You can turn the magic off?"

"We can cut off the extra juice they run through this place. That should put our guys at an advantage. It has to do with how they process magical energy. Ask Owen for a lecture on it later. He'll be more than happy to oblige. Now, I think it was down this way."

This passageway seemed familiar. It was more utilitarian, less like it was trying to emulate a castle or an old European university. That was where I expected to find the utilities. In a normal business, that's where the server room and switchboard might be. Actually, those were here, too, but there was an additional utility in a magical company.

We reached a room that said "Power" on the door,

and I tried to open it. It didn't budge, and I saw that it required an access card. I normally had a card that gave me universal access in the building, but I'd left it behind when I'd pretended to quit. I supposed I could always run up to my old office to get it back, but we didn't have time for that.

Instead, I pounded on the door, shouting, "Open up! This is an emergency!" Surely a system so critical would be manned, especially when we were under attack.

A face appeared in the door's narrow window. "We're on lockdown," the man said. I couldn't tell if he had a long, skinny face or if the window distorted his shape.

"Yes, I know. There's a battle in the lobby. That's why I need you to shut down the enhanced power circuits."

"Why would I shut it down during a battle?"

"Because the bad guys are using our extra juice, too."

He whirled away from the door. I didn't know for sure whether he was turning things down or calling security to report the crazy woman who was demanding that the power be turned off.

"How will we know if it's working?" Trish asked.

"We won't notice anything, and it will take a while before it affects anyone else. We'll just have to go back and see how things are going."

"We can stay on the safe side of the barrier, though, right?"

"I think that would be a very good idea. This is definitely a case where discretion is the better part of valor."

"And it keeps them from having to worry about rescuing us."

"Exactly!" Though I had to admit that I hated watching from the sidelines.

We hurried back to the lobby, not running, but not dawdling, either. We paused on the upper landing to watch. The battle was still raging, but it had scattered. Roger and the skeleton people were still more or less surrounded, though a few creatures had managed to break past the surrounding good guys. The harpies were all over the place, engaging in aerial combat with the gargoyles and a few fairies. I noticed Trix looking like some kind of warrior Tinkerbell, flitting around and blinding harpies with sprays of sparkling dust.

The traitors were grouped at the barrier, shouting in frustration as they stood by helplessly, like football fans watching a game on TV when their team was losing. A couple of gargoyles guarded them, so apparently they'd already been rounded up. I recognized Rocky and Rollo, who weren't the brightest of Sam's gargoyle corps, but I didn't think they'd let their prisoners get away. I allowed myself the tiniest of thrills that Gregor was probably out for good after this.

I focused my attention on the lobby. All the combatants looked rather tired. They were using a lot of energy. I knew from experience that Owen would probably collapse after this, sleep a few hours, wake up and eat everything in sight, then collapse again and sleep for about twelve hours. But was the exhaustion here the regular stress of prolonged magical battle or the effects of a decreased power supply? I wasn't even sure how big an impact the power would have. New York was on a nexus of power lines, which was why there was such a huge magical population here.

But it did seem like Owen and Merlin were starting to have a bit of an upper hand. Everyone else was more or less evenly matched. A few of the harpies and skeleton creatures had been taken out of the fight and seemed to be magically immobilized. Now they just needed to deal with Roger to shut it all down for good.

Owen finished off the skeleton he was fighting and turned to see Merlin closing in on Roger. He ran to join Merlin. Roger was still utterly calm. You'd never have guessed that he was in a crisis. Only the spark of anger in his eyes, so strong that it was clear from where we were, gave away the fact that he was fighting an all-out battle.

The two MSI wizards got him backed against a wall. Roger shouted for backup, but his creatures couldn't get away from the MSI people or the former frogs they were dealing with. I noticed that the frogs fought with a rather intense ferocity, and I supposed I could hardly blame them after what they'd been through.

Philip and his brother made an especially good team, and Evelyn had joined them. It was starting to look like the fighting was winding down, that victory was in the cards. But then the creatures began moving whatever fight they were involved in toward Roger, so that soon Merlin and Owen were surrounded by lots of little battles, and every so often, the creatures were able to get in a blast of something at them.

"This looks like it could get real ugly," Trish remarked, and I had to agree.

"They probably remembered that they won't get paid if Roger goes down," I said. "But I think I have an idea."

"Does this idea involve going down there and running through all that?"

"It does. But you don't have to come with me."

"You think I'd let you leave me behind? Come on."

We headed down the steps to where Rocky and Rollo were. "Hey, Rocky!" I said.

"Katie! How's it goin'?"

"It's been better. Can you do a favor for me?"

"Sure thing. What?"

"Can you make us invisible?"

"Why'd ya wanna do that?"

"So nobody will see us."

He nodded. "Yeah, that makes sense. Sure thing. Here you go!"

"I thought magic didn't work on us," Trish said.

"An illusion like invisibility works on other people. It makes them see what you want them to see."

"I clearly have a lot to learn."

"Are you ready to go?"

"Where are we going?"

"Do you remember that pebble thing Owen rolled across the floor earlier?"

"Yeah."

"We need to get to it. Ready?"

"As I'll ever be."

We ran through the magical barrier and down the stairs. We had to dodge combatants that couldn't see us, though when Trish bellowed a battle cry, that cleared a path as people paused momentarily to wonder where that noise was coming from. I saw the beacon ahead of us, but the bulk of the fighting was in our direct path. We had to skirt the worst of it because it was too intense to weave our way through it.

Just when we were almost at the beacon, someone kicked it—accidentally, it seemed, as it had merely been something in the way, but that still meant we had to change direction to go after it. I reached it and bent to scoop it up, but it got kicked again, which sent it sliding across the room. Trish moved around to block it from going any farther. It felt like we were playing the world's tiniest soccer game.

I bent to pick it up when it bounced off her shoe. "Now what?" she asked.

"Outside," I said. We ran for the front door. She threw it open, and I hurled the beacon outside, then shouted, "Owen!" He looked around, hearing my voice but not seeing me. I didn't have time to run back to Rocky to get him to lift the spell, and I didn't think he'd hear me from this distance, so I ran toward Owen, calling out, "The beacon's outside."

Shouting like that meant that everyone could hear me. A couple of the creatures, apparently realizing the implications, ran for the door, but Owen was faster than they were. He was already saying the words of the spell. There was a loud crack, and soon all the creatures were gone, transported outside. Without a beacon inside, they wouldn't be able to get past our wards, and I had a feeling those wards would be adjusted before the end of the day.

Now it was down to all the MSI people and the former frogs against Roger. For the first time, he actually appeared to be scared. There was no way he could escape the inevitable outcome. Owen and Merlin exchanged a look, then stepped out of the way, leaving the path clear for the former victims. One big burst of magic later, and all that was left of Roger was a small frog on the floor.

Merlin bent to gently pick him up. "I'll have to get a terrarium for my office," he said. "I'm not sure that's the most humane way to treat him and Mordred, but it is perhaps the safest. They'll be well cared for and unable to cause trouble."

"Just make sure you label that terrarium with a sign saying 'Please don't kiss the frogs.'" I said.

Everyone looked around, trying to see who'd said that, and I realized that Trish and I were still invisible. Owen waved a hand, and I assumed that must have broken Rocky's spell. We moved toward each other, colliding in a huge hug.

"Thank goodness that's over," I said into his shoulder.

He kissed me on the forehead and rubbed his hand up and down my back. "No more undercover missions, okay?"

"That will depend on what my new boss has to say."

"New boss?"

"I'm going to take Sam up on his offer to join the security team. That's probably the best use of my talents. And I have a new recruit for him." I raised my voice and shouted, "Hey, Sam!"

The gargoyle flew over from where he was supervising cleanup of the creatures incapacitated either by the battle or from being the first ones sent through the barrier. "Yeah, doll, what's up?"

"Meet Trish," I said. "Trish, this is Sam. He's head of security here. You two should talk."

"He's a gargoyle," she said warily.

"Yeah, I'm absolutely amazing at surveillance," he said.

"I bet you are."

"She's immune, like me," I said, "and she helped me deal with all this."

"Does that mean you're finally comin' aboard with me?" he asked.

"Yeah, I think so. I have to admit that I have the most fun doing stuff like this. I never liked doing marketing."

"You know it's not all big fights and undercover ops, right?"

"It's also not sales meetings."

"Are you sure about this?" Owen asked me, tightening his arms around me.

"Look, I keep getting into danger and trouble no matter what job I have, so I may as well be in a job where that's the plan and I'm surrounded by people who know what they're doing."

"Whatever makes you happy." He yawned and shook his head, as though he was trying to clear cobwebs. "I am *beat*. That fight really took a lot out of me."

"You may still be suffering some from that sleeping spell. Oh, and we probably need to turn the magic back on."

"The magic?"

"I had them shut down the extra circuits. I figured that would give you and Merlin an edge."

He laughed and shook his head. "Yeah, you're suited for security. I never would have thought of that." He looked over to where Sam was perched on the guard's station, talking to Trish. "Sam! Can you get them to turn the magic circuits back on?"

"Will do, kiddo."

"I think I still could do with about twelve hours of sleep and one of your mother's chocolate cakes," Owen said to me.

"Do you want the cake before or after the sleep? Because I have her recipe."

"After would be fine, but we have some things to wrap up here."

Actually, things seemed to be going pretty well. The bad guys were all gone, and the magical healers were tending to any injuries among the combatants. Rod and his assistant, Isabel, were getting information from the former frogs to help them get situated. Some of them were only from Roger's current campaign for world domination, so they were able to go back to their homes and businesses. Those who'd been out of the way for longer needed more help.

The accounting team was already gearing up to get into whatever they could find of the Collegium's records and holdings to try to get property back to its rightful owners. Evelyn was helping clue them in on the physical locations the Collegium had used, since most of the portals linking the buildings had collapsed.

The security team rounded up the traitors for immediate dismissal and possible prosecution, depending on what they'd actually done. Magical Council enforcers had arrived somewhere along the way, and I got debriefed about Roger's activities, including his meeting with a

Council employee. It looked like this particular takedown was going to have far-reaching effects in the magical world, since the Collegium had its tentacles in just about everything.

We weren't entirely sure what to do about all the employees who may have had Collegium ties, but who hadn't done anything about the fight. It looked like there would be lots more interviews and discussions going forward, but since there wasn't an actual Collegium anymore, what could Collegium plants really do?

Then again, that had been a huge organization. Something was bound to rise from the ashes. There were too many ambitious people involved, and at least one of them was likely to get ideas.

But that was something to worry about some other time. When I finished talking to the enforcers, I looked around and found Owen working with the team that was reinforcing the building's wards. Now that the magic circuits were running again, he seemed to have more energy, but I suspected he needed a boost.

I went up to my office—soon to be former office—and found Perdita there, hard at work, and apparently entirely oblivious to the battle that had raged in the lobby just minutes ago. "Katie! You're back! I thought you quit!" she said.

"Not really. It was part of a plan."

"Oh. Okay. So you're taking your job back?" She looked a little dismayed.

"No, I'll be moving to a different department."

"So maybe it can be permanent!"

"What can?"

"I took over in the interim, supposedly until they hired someone new, but they didn't seem to be making much progress on that, so I was kind of hoping they'd consider me."

"I'll put in a good word for you." I wasn't entirely sure what good my word would do, since to most of the company, I was a traitor who'd quit and gone to work for the enemy, but I hoped my participation in the day's battle might count for something in public opinion. Telling Perdita was a good start in making sure everyone in the company knew, even before Merlin sent out a memo about my role in the Collegium takedown.

"What were you doing, anyway?" she asked.

"Have you heard of the Collegium?"

"It really exists?"

"It did. Not anymore."

Her slanted eyebrows rose. "Because of you?"

"I can't take all the credit, but I was the one on the inside, undercover."

"Wow! That must have been exciting."

"Most of the time, it was actually kind of boring. Today, though, yeah, it was really exciting. Anyway, I came up here to ask you for a favor."

"Sure. What do you need?"

"Do you still make fancy coffee drinks?"

"Yeah, what do you want?"

"I need a couple of mochas with extra whipped cream."

A second later they were in my hands. "I've been thinking of selling my spells for that," she said. "I've got them pretty much perfected."

"You'd know how to market them. Thanks a bunch."

Before I was even out of the office, she was already on the phone, spreading the news about what I'd really been doing when I quit MSI.

I found Owen still hard at work when I returned to the lobby. I approached him, handed him a cup, and said, "It's not chocolate cake, but it's sugar and caffeine, which you need, and you need to take a break."

We sat together at the bottom of the grand staircase. He took a sip of his drink, then closed his eyes for a moment and took a deep breath. "Yeah, I did need this. Thanks."

"I have a lot of catching up to do in looking after you."

"Speaking of which, you never did tell me what happened to me while I was under that sleeping spell. How did I end up in Roger's office?"

"Trust me, you really don't want to know."

He looked suspicious. "I was a frog, wasn't I?"

"I'm not sure it counts, since you were unconscious the whole time."

"But I was a frog. Please tell me you were the one to break the spell."

"Of course I was. Though I should probably confess that I broke a lot of frog spells today. But they didn't mean anything. Yours was the only kiss with emotion to it. And I kissed each one with the hope it would be you."

He laughed. "I won't hold it against you." He glanced around the room. "I'm thinking we should have the altar there, on the landing, where the staircase splits. We'd stand here on the steps, in front of it. We'd set up the chairs for the guests out here in the lobby."

It took me a second to realize he was talking about the wedding. Not that I'd forgotten about it. I just hadn't really thought much about it lately. "You mean, have the wedding here?"

"Why not? It's church-like, and we'd surely be able to book it. I was thinking we could have the official wedding here, with all the magical trappings, then have a small ceremony and reception in Texas for your family. That way we can deal with the paperwork where we live, but still have something your family can attend."

I leaned against him. "Mm hmm, sounds nice. Tell me more about this wedding."

"And I think I should start out as a frog so the first kiss will be more dramatic."

I elbowed him in the ribs, and he caught me with his arm around my shoulders, pulling me against him. "Okay, we can skip that," he said.

"I suspect the kiss will be just fine." And then I made him put his mocha down so we could practice.

About the Author

Shanna Swendson earned a journalism degree from the University of Texas and used to work in public relations but decided it was more fun to make up the people she wrote about, so now she's a full-time novelist. She also writes the steampunk fantasy Rebel Mechanics series and the contemporary fantasy Fairy Tale series. She lives in Irving, Texas, with several hardy houseplants and too many books to fit on the shelves.